If wishes were horses,
beggars would ride

Best wishes
Pan Littlewood

PAM LITTLEWOOD
BEESTHORPE BOOKS

First Published in 2008 by Beesthorpe Books, Beesthorpe Hall Farm, Caunton, Newark, Nottinghamshire NG23 6AT

ISBN 978-0-9541750-1-6

Printed by Q3 Digital/Litho Print Project Management, Loughborough, Leicestershire LE11 1LE

Acknowledgements

Cover designed by Dragons Tail Design.
Photography by Rachel Littlewood.

Dedication

*This book is dedicated to my grandson
Gabriel, who gives much joy.*

Chapter 1

NOTTINGHAMSHIRE, 1796

Resentment surged through him. Even after the long ride into Newark it was still there, simmering away, but the April air grew chill as dusk rapidly descended and Will Bristowe crossed the bridge leading into the town. He reined back his horse and tossed the penny to the tollkeeper. Beastmarket Hill was deserted, but on the open ground close by the castle ruins a number of small fires burned. Beggars and vagrants gathered over the smoky embers, crouching protectively over the scraps of offal they had either scrounged or stolen from the nearby knacker's yard. Like ragged vultures quick to defend, their quarrelsome cries echoed around the stone walls.

'Spare a penny, Sir!' Will ignored the plea. He had ridden into Newark because he was in need of diversion, an excitement of some kind. He hardly cared what form it would take, just so long as he didn't spend another night of stultifying boredom at home, enduring the disapproval of his parents, and where the sole subject of conversation was of what he should or shouldn't do with his life.

He decided to make for the Saracen's Head, enjoy a few tankards of ale, and then maybe move on to the card tables in the back room. The memory of his father's rage over his previous debts did nothing to change his plans. In fact, it tinged the prospect of a forbidden night's gambling with an even keener thrill. This time, he was sure, luck would be with him.

The shops in the market square had closed for the day and the few people about were making their way home for supper or heading towards their favourite tavern. There were plenty to choose from in Newark.

'Evening, Mr. Bristowe,' a local carter called out and, as Will turned his head to acknowledge, he recognized in the distance, even in the half-light and some way down the street, a familiar horse and rider.

'Ned!' he called out, kicking hard into his horse's flanks. The rider continued on for a few paces but then turned as Will drew level. 'It is you, Ned! Where have you been lately, you old rascal? We haven't met up for months.'

Will's low spirits soared with anticipation, as any time spent with Ned Hobbs, although never planned, always proved full of cheer and excitement. Conversation between them came easy, so the chance meeting was a great piece of luck. Even so, Will noticed Ned's hesitation.

'Oh, I've been around. In fact, I've passed through Newark quite a few times this year.' Ned's long, black hair was tied back from his strong and handsome face. A confident man of some education and decent breeding, Will had always thought, but today his long coat was spattered with fresh mud and encrusted with layers of dried dirt. His once-white shirt and stock were scruffy and worse for wear.

'I'm travelling through tonight, as you can see.' Ned said by way of explanation, and continued on up the street.

Will fell in beside him. 'To York? To your family?'

'Yes. That's right.' He glanced admiringly at Will's mount. 'New horse, I see. So you're not disinherited quite yet then?'

'This is Hector. I'm getting him ready for the start of the season. He'll be a great hunter, but he's still young.' Will slapped Hector's neck and banished the tinge of guilt concerning his father's direct order not to ride the young horse so far. 'Look Ned, I'm in dire need of good company tonight. Which alehouse is it to be? I was making for the Saracen's.'

Ned scoffed. 'Hah. For the card tables, more like. Tell me, have you paid your debts yet?'

Will inwardly winced. He knew precisely to which unfortunate night of gambling Ned was referring, it being etched so deep in his memory, and his father's constant reference to it at times of family tension only compounded the ignominy. Yet any real pangs of remorse had been conveniently nudged aside, it being much easier to deny personal responsibility, and simply focus on the bad luck of it all. Festering resentment was far preferable. He refused to be shamed. 'I was unlucky that night,' he said, waving a dismissive hand.

'And distracted, if I recall, by the charms of a certain lady.'

'Maybe I was.' Will grinned and his eyes twinkled. 'Come on. Let's go.'

But Ned was reluctant. 'No. Not the Saracen's. In fact, I'm not sure it's such a good idea. I am fairly pressed for time.'

'What? Why ever not? Where are you making for tonight?'

Ned looked briefly up and down the deserted street. 'Not far. And to tell you the truth, my throat is parched and as dry as a hare's back. Better make it quick though – and the White Hind will do us well enough.'

They turned back through Bridge Street, where old houses squashed together and the overhanging upper floors jutted out into the narrow road. Candle stubs were being lit, illuminating the tiny cottage windows, and families were settling down for the night when Will and Ned dismounted by the arched entrance to the stables on Carter's Gate. Will led Hector into the inner courtyard and tied the reins to a wall ring. Ned followed, glancing into the stalls as he heaved a weighty saddlebag from his mare and onto his shoulders. From within the tavern, the muffled sounds of conviviality filtered out to them as they hurried to the door.

With the clunk of the latch, conversation halted and all eyes turned to stare as they stooped to enter the low doorway. In the dimly lit room, Will struggled to make out the faces of their fellow drinkers as he edged his way to a table and a couple of vacant stools by the fire.

The pungent sputtering of tallow candles cast shadows against the wall, and watchful customers silently breathed clouds of swirling smoke from their clay pipes. A smouldering log in the fireplace sent tendrils of yet more smoke spiralling upwards and curling over the gnarled oak beams. Will's eyes stung and the bitter, acrid taste at the back of his throat forced him to cough.

Ned kicked the log back in the grate and the smoke began to draw up the chimney. The landlord slapped down two tankards of beer. Will felt uncomfortable, for there was a distinct lack of welcome. This was not a tavern he frequented and he didn't like the chilly atmosphere of unease and suspicion

'Your health, Will.' Ned drank deeply, seemingly unconcerned. 'So, tell me what has been happening to you. You were pretty much in disfavour with your father and uncle, I recollect. Have things improved? I can't imagine your gaming debts have helped; or did you find a way of keeping that secret?'

Will put down his tankard, wiped his mouth with the back of his hand and rolled his eyes. The muscles in his face tensed in frustration. 'My life,' he said, 'is frustrating beyond words and extremely dull. There's nothing I can do to please my father, my uncle makes every decision for the entire family, and now even the hunting season has finished. There's little wonder I need the excitement of the gaming tables.'

'Come on, Will. You lead an easy life. Perhaps you get more criticism than you want – but that's because you've yet to settle on any direction. How old are you now?'

'Twenty-one in a few weeks. But there's little chance that between now and then anything will change.' Will raised his hand and called across the room for more ale. The doorlatch clicked as someone left.

'Your trouble is that you've been raised to be a gentleman. And if gentlemen are to be self-indulgent and idle all their lives, they need to know where their money is coming from. You must have talents. You need to use them.'

Will smarted. 'You sound like my father.' The latch grated softly and he noticed a dark figure had slipped silently onto the high-backed bench by the door. Ned's head remained down over his tankard, but his eyes repeatedly darted over towards the door and back again.

This was not a good start. Will didn't like this gloomy tavern and would be glad to cross the market place and join in the laughter and brightness of the Saracen's Head. He disliked Ned's plain speaking, and drank deeply once more. 'The nature of this conversation is very familiar – and tedious. Tell me more about your life. You're really quite evasive, you know.'

Ned did not reply. His face remained watchful as he peered across the taproom. He shifted the weight of his saddlebag, which had never left his shoulder. 'You stay and enjoy your ale. I'll be going now, Will.' He spoke quietly and stood up.

'No. Wait. I'll come with you.'

Ned's hard hand restrained Will as he struggled to rise, pinning him down in the chair. 'You stay here.' His voice was almost a hiss. 'Take yourself off to the card tables and try not to lose too much. I'll see you again before long, perhaps.'

4

Will opened his mouth to argue, but in one movement, Ned had slipped through a side door of which Will had been totally unaware, and vanished. Gulping down the last dregs of ale, Will followed. The stable courtyard was lit only by the moonlight, but he could see Ned securing the saddlebag and then reaching deep into the pockets of his long coat. He heard the click of the buckle as the girth was tightened on the saddle.

'Where are you going? What did I say?' Will darted across the yard and began to untie Hector.

The reply was sharp. 'It was a mistake to come here tonight. If I stay, there'll be trouble. Best I leave now.' Ned swung into the saddle and ducked his head as his mare trotted through the low archway.

Will felt resentful at being dismissed like a child, but his curiosity was aroused. Once more he caught up, and despite Ned's obvious irritation, they trotted side by side into the market place. The night air was cold and their breath hung before them as the moonlight shone silver on the cobblestones. The Palladian columns of the grand Assembly Rooms towered over the square and Ned turned in the saddle. Will thought he was about to be dismissed again when the sound of hard-ridden horses carried across the air. Wheeling around, they were confronted with the sight of four horsemen yelling and bearing down on them, brandishing pistols. A volley of gunshots filled the market place with deafening noise. Small sheets of red flame seared the end of the barrels as lead shot whizzed through the air.

'What in hell?'

'Constables!' Ned yelled, as he dug his heels into his mare and she responded with a mighty leap. Horrified, Will reacted instantly, launching into a full gallop right behind Ned. The castle loomed dark and menacing in the moonlight as the pair clattered past and, ahead, the toll bar chain stretched out across the road. There was no sign of the keeper.

Ned checked his horse, allowing her time to see the glittering links of the heavy chain, and then gave the mare her head. She soared over. In an instant, Will was plunged into dilemma. He had no idea whether Hector could jump. He was certain he had never jumped before. The double chain hung suspended before them, blocking the way. It was like a wager, Will thought. A bet. All or nothing. He could pull up, hold up his hands and hope he wasn't shot, and then face the sorting-out of whatever it was that was happening. But the challenge was already turning to excitement. No-one could outride him. Just get this horse over the bridge and outrun them all.

The first tingle of fear crept into his chest as the vital seconds when a halt could have been called to this headlong flight passed by in a thunder of hooves, shouts and adrenalin. Too late now. Will prayed that Hector had it in him. Had he seen the chain? Heavy though it was, and glinting coldly in the moonlight, was this young horse bold enough to go for it? Hector gathered himself ready to make the leap, and with every muscle in his body Will urged him on and over. 'Go on, boy, go on. You can do it ... you must do it!' The moment seemed endless. Had he misjudged his stride? Would Hector pick up his hind legs or break them on the heavy chain? Would a shot finish them off before they even landed?

The euphoria that surged up within Will when they landed safely on the bridge exploded in a wild yell. Behind him, he could hear the commotion as the constables hauled back their horses and shouted curses upon the sleepy tollkeeper to make haste and let them through.

The bricks of the bridge resounded under the pounding hooves as Will leaned low over his horse's neck, urging him on to catch up with Ned. The ground sped past, the thick mane flicked up in his face and his coat tails flew out behind him.

Horse and rider strained hard. As the gap closed between them, Ned stuck out his left arm and yelled. 'Take the track to Kelham. We must split up.'

'No. I'm staying with you.' The horses were galloping along side by side now, and they made good speed on the low-lying flood-plains of the North Road.

'Curse you. And curse this damned moonlight. They'll pick us out plain as day.'

Will risked a look back. The constables were still trailing them, but their lead was good and their pursuers too far distant to shoot. What excitement! Exhilaration flooded through him. This was just like hunting – except he was the quarry. For the first time in his life, he was the hunted.

After a mile or so, they turned off the north road and followed a moonlit stony track. 'Let's hope we lose them now.' Ned had slowed to a steady canter to give the horses a respite before the oncoming hill and now they sat back in the saddle.

'Why are they after you?' Will called breathlessly. 'What have you done?'

'Just listen. When we get to Dark Turn follow me and do as I do.' Moments later, Ned turned to look back. 'Damnation. Will they never give up?' He whacked his mare hard on the rump and they were galloping off again.

Will tried to keep up, kicking Hector hard and slapping his neck with the reins, urging him to give all he had. The response this time was less than reassuring. He could feel the gelding's stride shortening, his neck was extended and his ears back. Will knew there was not much gallop left in him. Ned's mare was pulling away from them, and the constables were gaining ground. His earlier confidence deserted him as he faced the reality of his chances – a fugitive rider with a tired horse. The gap was definitely closing.

The crack of a pistol burst into the darkness. Will kicked harder. Would they never reach the top of this hill? 'Come on, boy. Just keep going.' The real possibility of being shot in the back washed fear right through him. This was madness, and not the sort of excitement he had been looking for at all. At last Will crested the hill, just in time to see Ned.

Dark Turn, so named because of the trees which grew up and came together in a canopy above it, was a sharp left-hand bend. Ned yanked his horse to a slithering halt and she reared and wheeled back. Setting her to the steep right-hand bank, he kicked hard into the mare's flanks. In two strides she had leapt up and disappeared into the dense vegetation.

Chapter 2

Will could hear the riders closing. A few more seconds and he would be seen. He knew he had one chance, but was it too much to ask of his exhausted horse? Cursing his own cruelty, and following Ned's example, Will cracked the whip down hard and poor Hector made the leap. The bushes closed in behind them.

Thorns pierced his coat and Will held his hand up to protect his face from the low branches. The moon's glow failed to penetrate the vegetation and he could make nothing out. His heart hammered in his chest and his lungs could only manage breathless gasps. Sweat trickled down the side of his face and the only sound was that of his horse's heaving flanks.

A hand shot out and snatched the bridle. Ned was at his side. They backed under a thick canopy of low branches and waited. Despite the noise of their winded horses, the sound of pounding hooves carried through to them. Less than twenty yards from the fugitives, the constables negotiated the turn, galloped round the bend and on down the road.

Hector was trembling violently, and the reins in Will's hands were wet with the sweat that ran over the young horse's neck. Ned jerked his head for Will to follow and they forced their way through the dense thicket and on up towards Bathley Hills. At walking pace now, avoiding the open fields, they stuck close to the hedge sides and from the cover of trees turned back to view the silvery shadows of the moonlit valley. With their eyes keenly attuned for night vision, they picked up the merest movement and watched a patrolling barn owl flap his white wings lazily along the hedgerow. They spoke barely at a whisper, aware that the still night air carried the slightest of sounds. Satisfied that they were in no immediate danger of pursuit, they slowly followed a trail, over-grown and little used, through the woods.

'Isn't this woodland supposed to be haunted?' Will whispered uneasily, ducking to avoid the low branches.

'Yes. And be grateful that others believe it, for no-one comes here to set traps. I know this land well – in fact, every trail and field in the county and beyond.'

Now that his heart rate had almost returned to normal, the questions surged up in Will's mind again. 'What have you done, Ned?'

Ned totally ignored the question.

'I think I deserve an answer!'

'Keep your voice down! It's best you know nothing.'

Ned reined back and turned in the saddle. He held up his hand and listened keenly for distant sounds. 'It's too risky for you to make your way home now. They're combing the woods to the south.'

'So, where can we go? And for God's sake tell me what you have done to bring this upon yourself.'

Ned's voice became resigned. 'Alright. Our meeting tonight was accidental, and I should have followed my instincts and kept riding – but it was good to see you Will, and I did have a powerful thirst. As for the past few months – well, let me just say my life has taken a different turn. It's unlucky for you that we were seen together. But we'll not be caught. I have a few hideaways.'

The horses, although badly sweated, had at least recovered their breath and, once through the dense woodland, they resumed their escape along the moonlit pathways at an easy trot. Only wildlife witnessed their passage as badgers scuttled off the trails and foxes slunk silently into the undergrowth. From Brunk Wood they picked up a track through the newly planted Cocked Hat plantation which brought them out well beyond the village of Caunton. They halted frequently and strained their ears for unfamiliar sounds. The lonely barking of a faraway dog was the only sound to disturb the still night. At the village of Kersall they struck out for the distant hillside and the relative safety of Hare Hills Wood.

'We'll hide here for the night.' Ned hissed. 'We can lie low until the morning.'

Will felt fairly sure that by now it was safe enough for him to part company with his dangerous friend and skirt back via the lanes and bridleways, to his home at Beesthorpe Hall. Having shaken off the pursuers, he was free to return home, an innocent man, guilty only of association – but with whom? It was this over-riding curiosity which kept him at Ned's side.

Their friendship, although sporadic, had come about through a genuine mutual regard. Will thought he had recognized a soulmate, with a common ground of understanding. But this alarming turn of events had exposed a chasm of ignorance concerning his friend, whose exploits were serious enough to warrant no less than four constables to hunt him down.

It had been a narrow escape, and as they plodded on Will's thoughts turned to his father. He did not relish the thought of being thrown into the squalid pit of Newark jail alongside the vagabonds, scoundrels and rats; but even more daunting was the prospect of facing, and offering some sort of explanation to his father. Still, he argued to himself, with the beginnings of a wry smile playing at the corners of his mouth, the evening had proved to be by far the most exciting of his, up to now, very dull life.

At the edge of Hare Hills Wood they dismounted and forced their way into the dense undergrowth amid a low tangle of boughs. The ground was uneven and the woodland covered a steep hillside, making progress difficult. Over fallen, grass-covered and half hidden branches, Will led his horse along, stumbling in the darkness as vicious brambles snatched at his legs.

Eventually, Ned led them to a narrow ledge along which they were able to walk with comparative ease. Up to the right the lower bushes thinned out and in the eerie light the trunks rose up in straight formation. Down to the left, the bank fell steeply away, and the bare earth exposed the black holes of badger setts and rabbit warrens.

The two men, leading their horses, crunched through a deep layer of last autumn's leaves and came to the fallen trunk of an enormous elm. The weight of the falling tree had partly uprooted it and the bank had given way, forming an accommodating hollow. A couple of well placed branches, over which had been secured a tapestry of woven brash, provided cover for both men and horses.

Exhausted, they settled themselves on the dry leaves. Safe for the moment, Ned relaxed and gave a short, throaty laugh. 'I think you were telling me earlier, Will, that your life lacked excitement. Perhaps tonight has added a little something.'

Will chuckled, but it was in relief rather than humour.

Ned raised his arm expansively and slapped his hand down on Will's shoulder. 'Welcome to my hideaway, Will Bristowe of Beesthorpe Hall. As you sleep sound in your feather bed, there's many a night I pound the roads. Even though I've a number of safe inns, it's often too risky to approach them, and I need to bide my time out in the woods like this.'

Feeling foolish and naive, Will knew that the limited knowledge he had of his friend's circumstances was all false. 'May I take it that your story of an inheritance is untrue?'

The moonlight shone on Ned's white teeth as he smiled broadly. 'You may. Generally speaking, I find it inadvisable to reveal the true nature of my work.'

'So you're a robber. A common highwayman.'

Ned's usually soft voice took on a hard edge. 'Not all of us are born to your advantage, Will. We have to live on our wits and see to ourselves as best we can. But I've enjoyed our friendship.' He paused and then continued thoughtfully 'Although I doubt after tonight we shall meet again. The mailcoach companies are angry. You saw how desperate they were to catch us tonight. There must be a good price on my head, so, if I'm to live a little longer, I'd better move on. Though where is another question.'

In part shock and part admiration, Will stared at his friend. 'Aren't you concerned for the consequences? You would be transported for your crimes, surely?'

'Ah. If that were so, Will, I'd almost welcome capture, except of course for the loss of honour, which would be a shame, judging by the exaggerated stories I hear about my own exploits. No. For me, it's the hangman's noose. But not if I can help it – and not while that little mare can gallop her heart out for me. Isn't she just the best, Will?'

'Yes, the best.' Will glanced nervously across at Hector, trying to assess his condition.

A silence developed, filled only by the gentle hooting of an owl overhead and the distant yapping of a fox. 'But you know you must lie low now, Will. Just for a while. Your face has been linked to mine. After tonight, suspicion will fall on you too. Stay out of Newark. Keep away from the alehouses.'

'Perhaps I should go away. Make a new life.' Will's voice flattened as the old despondency returned. He considered his prospects. The future suddenly seemed deadly dull without even the occasional meeting with his charismatic friend.

'America. I hear that's the place to head for. Long sea voyage, mind. But a new country, not under British rule now.'

'Is that your plan, Ned? America?'

'Who knows? Perhaps a couple more years on the road – God willing.' Ned gave a small sigh. 'Snatch some rest now. We'll move at daybreak.'

Will felt quite unable to prepare his mind for sleep. He knew that the town of Newark, gateway to the North over the river Trent, had long been notorious for coach hold-ups and that lately the mailcoach companies had lost their patience and embarked upon a campaign. They had declared themselves determined to eradicate the menace of robbery on the Great North Road and would not rest until all robbers of the King's highway had been strung up from the roadside gibbets and left to rot.

Generous rewards had lured informants into keeping careful vigilance and the movements of strangers had prompted watchfulness. The furtive comings and goings in the tavern all now made sense to him. Of course, the problem for the authorities was guessing where the robbers would strike next. From York to London travellers risked an unscheduled halt to their journey, leaving them much the poorer.

Will had read that some roadway thieves operated in small groups and some in pairs, but the common description of the robberies between Grantham and Bawtry was of one lone horseman, armed with a knife and a pair of pistols. Always elusive, he rode a fast chestnut mare and knew all the secret paths and bridleways, appearing out of nowhere and then melting away. And now Will knew the identity of this notorious robber. And wished he didn't.

Will recalled the snippets of gossip and news that he had heard regarding this highwayman as he scraped up the leaves to make a pillow. It was incredible that it had turned out to be Ned. His thoughts pitched to and fro and, in this state of turmoil, his eyes refused to close all night. He heard every furtive nocturnal scurrying but, at his side, Ned's breathing grew deep and regular as he slept soundly.

Eventually the pale dawn light began to filter through the trees. They emerged from the makeshift shelter to the pungence of sodden vegetation and led their mounts back to the edge of the woodland. Mist hung between the tree trunks and, as they parted the branches to make their way, heavy dew spattered off the leaves like raindrops. The grass underfoot, saturated and slimy, drenched their boots.

'Here's where we part company, Will.' Ned held out his hand and grasped that of the younger man. The early light showed the pistols that at some point he had taken from the deep pockets of his long coat and stuck into his belt. His dark eyes regarded Will affectionately, and he pulled a few twigs from the sleeves of Will's coat before relinquishing the grasp of his hand. 'Don't be angry with me for deceiving you. We've had good times. I'm just making my way the best I can. Well, God speed, my friend. One day, we may meet again, but in truth, I think not. Our circumstances are a world apart.'

Will felt a sudden pang of deep regret at the parting. Perhaps it was the damp, dawn chill that raised the goose pimples on his skin and made him shiver. 'Good luck, Ned,' was all he managed to say. He turned away but then called back. 'Doesn't it worry you that I might give you away?'

Ned laughed softly. 'And where will you find me? Besides, I haven't achieved the grand age of twenty-four without becoming a good judge of character. You have soul, Will. You won't let me down. Have a good life. And stay away from the gaming tables.' He raised his arm in salute, turned his chestnut mare and headed north-west. Will mounted his horse and made his way east.

Hector was not in good shape. His legs were stiff and his gait uneven. As a cock crowed from a farmstead across the hillside, Will urged him into a reluctant trot through the secluded, tree-lined cart tracks of Valley Farm. Beyond Kersall he linked up to the driftway that would take him on to the Beesthorpe estate. At the top of Bark Hill he rested briefly, as he usually did, beside the old oak tree. Its massive branches reached out and almost down to the ground as it stood like a sentinel, guarding the valley. Will sat in the saddle and surveyed the view. Despite his churned up emotions, he still appreciated the beauty of the gently rolling hills and woodland stretching out before him.

But life weighed even heavier than ever today. Everything seemed complicated and wrong. This farmland before him was his future. The Beesthorpe estate would one day be his, for that had always been clear and understood from an early age. And yet, lately things had changed. Hints of his 'unworthiness' to inherit had begun to sound like threats. Despondency descended.

Farmer Greaves had recently ploughed the nearby field. Harrowing had begun in Far Cross Stead in preparation for a seedbed. On the freshly turned earth, two brown shapes cavorted and played, leading each other on and then turning to box one another's ears. The hares took no notice of the tired horse and rider standing motionless on the hillside.

Will could just make out in the distance the chimneys of Beesthorpe Hall. He urged Hector on again, anxious to get back before everyone was up. And then, disaster. The horse was lame. Another thing to have to explain. Will dismounted and led him at a painfully slow pace down the track leading to the home farm. As he trudged alongside, the horse's head nodded up and down beside him and Will really began to worry about the reception he would receive. But it was still early, and with luck, no-one would be up and about yet.

The most important thing was to hide Hector away until he had recovered. He tried to invent a plausible story to present to his father, but none came to mind. He had no idea what he was going to tell him.

Entering the yard between the almost depleted winter straw stacks, Will skirted the barn. He could hear the pigs beginning to stir and grunt as he passed the sty. A small gate led him into the apple orchard at the back of the Hall, which was overlooked only by the servants' windows. His father's room faced the front of the house.

Hoping for the best, Will led the horse, heavily favouring a foreleg, through the side gate and into the stable courtyard. He carefully picked his way over the grass, so as not to announce their arrival on the stable-yard flagstones. Thankfully unobserved, he reached the sanctuary of a stall, unbuckled the saddle and heaved it off. Underneath, the horse's hair glistened with sweat and a patch was rubbed raw and bleeding. Will groaned and turned. His father stood full-square behind him.

Thomas Bristowe was in a rage. His face was red with anger as, with a trembling finger, he pointed to the horse – his horse. 'You will rub that animal down for an hour before reporting to me. By God, William, I'll have a full explanation for this.' His eyes bulged and his voice shook as he tried, and failed, to take control of his emotion. He turned and stomped out of the stable.

Will slammed the saddle on a post in the tack room, cranked the water pump and carried fresh water back into the stall. He was filled with remorse when he looked properly at Hector's condition. The horse stood dejected, trembling slightly and covered in deep scratches on his legs, neck and face, one deep wound perilously close to an eye. His coat was caked in mud and clogged with dried sweat and the saddle marks looked bad, the sort where the hair grows back white, a reminder for all time of careless ill-treatment. Will picked up a handful of straw and started to rub. His arms ached and he felt too tired to think.

What should he say to his father? Should he tell him the truth – a half-truth perhaps? He would have to try to impress upon him his innocence and the very real danger in which he had found himself? But his father was always demanding explanations and then flatly refusing to listen to them, so what was the point? A vision of Ned ascending the steps of the gallows came to his mind and Will closed his eyes and shook his head to shun the image. Nausea welled up in his throat.

Behind him, a voice came, heavy with a country accent. 'Shall I tek ovver now, Sir?' Dick, the young stable lad stood there with brushes in hand. 'I'll put salve on his cuts and bathe his fetlocks. Get that coat shinin' good and proper, you see if I don't. It'll take a while mind. He's in a right state, but the master won't be angry by the time I've finished.' He nipped past Will and started to work on the matted coat.

Happy to leave Dick to put right his careless treatment of Hector, Will mumbled his thanks. With a heavy heart and a strong feeling of foreboding, he turned. In a sudden burst of frustration, he slapped the riding whip against his leather boots and flung it down in the straw. Back at the pump once more, he primed the handle up and down until the water gushed out and he splashed it over his hands and face. The cold water helped to revive him. Eventually, squaring his shoulders, he walked resolutely towards the big house to face the wrath of his father.

Chapter 3

Thomas Bristowe stood behind his desk in the library, rage emanating from every fibre of his body. 'Do you realise that I have had little or no sleep since the constables came to the house late last evening? They were looking for a highwayman.' His hard, staring eyes bored deep into Will. 'A highwayman and an accomplice, probably hiding in woods nearby. They asked if all the household were at home and in their beds. And I lied to them – for you.' Thomas thumped the desk. 'I can't believe that my disappointment in you can have brought me so low.' He began to pace the floor. 'How can I have failed so totally to instil in you any sense of responsibility or thought for the future? You know full well what is at stake here. The consequences of your actions now could haunt you for the rest of your life.'

Will stood silently, his tired face a mixture of resignation and resentment. Fatigue began to wash over him. He had seen his father's blusterings before. Soon his fury would begin to run out of steam. As if on cue, Thomas threw up his hands in a gesture of bafflement and took a deep breath. 'Mistaken identity, you say?'

'Yes, Sir.'

'And this friend, whom you decline to name, how did you come to make his acquaintance?'

'We met in Newark from time to time – mostly by chance. Father, he has done nothing wrong. He is an intelligent, educated man.'

'Then why did you run?'

Will rolled his eyes and sighed. 'When four angry constables bore down on us with pistols, it seemed the best option. We had no idea that they would pursue us with such tenacity and for so far.' Even Will was quite impressed with his conviction.

'And the horse? Yet again, Will, your headstrong recklessness has resulted in damage to a good horse. He is not mature enough to be treated as a hunter. He's galloped too far. You were warned to have more regard and promised that you would – especially after … after Prince.' Thomas' voice trailed off a little and he turned his head away, as if to dissociate himself from the memory of his magnificent hunter, ridden hard and carelessly to his death.

Will winced too, at the memory of Prince. He well remembered how he had whooped and hollered with the excitement of the chase as the field, in full cry, pursued the fox across the countryside. No ditch had been too wide, nor fence too high – except the last one which, taken too fast, had proved his undoing. Will had been thrown clear and, in the main, was unhurt, but the hunter – his father's beloved, fearless Prince – had suffered a badly broken leg. None who had witnessed it would forget the trauma of shooting the horse where he lay, and loading the body on to a wagon to be transported to the knacker's yard. An ignominious end for such a noble and loved animal. In the library, a heavy silence developed.

'I take it that you have forgotten that your Uncle Samuel is expected at one o'clock today?'

'Oh, no.' Will groaned and put a hand to his eyes. Facing his father was one thing, but Uncle Samuel was entirely another matter.

'Your inheritance, boy!' Thomas suddenly shouted as he beat the back of a chair with his fist. 'Your inheritance depends on Uncle Samuel's approval. Already his patience with you is sorely tried. How could you be so blind as not to see what is at stake here?' Thomas tried to speak calmly. 'As the second son, my inheritance was pitiful and all my life I've been totally dependent on the generosity of my brother. But in keeping your uncle a single man with no children of his own, fortune has smiled on you, Will. You, his only nephew, could inherit all his wealth and estates. But you must show yourself to be worthy of it. You must find a way to redeem yourself in his eyes.' Thomas stopped talking when he noticed that his son was having difficulty in staying awake. He shook his head in exasperation. 'Go to your room now.' he ordered, 'but present yourself at one o'clock and be in good shape. I'll do everything I can to prevent Samuel going into the stables.'

'Thank you, father.'

With his eyes half closed, Will stumbled into his room and fell on to the bed, exhausted. He still wore his muddy boots but felt disinclined to summon the energy to remove them. Why couldn't his father see his need for a little excitement in his life? It wasn't his fault that Prince had broken his leg, or that Ned had turned out to be a highwayman. The events of the previous night surged around in his mind, and in bewildered disbelief he shook his head. Had they really galloped out of Newark with constables in close pursuit and lead shot whizzing past their ears? Or had he dreamed it? He knew it was no dream and once again, despite everything, a slight smile played in the corners of his mouth as he recalled the adventure. It had been more thrilling than any of the runs he had known on the chase.

A soft knock sounded on his door. Will made no reply and continued to lie still, his limbs heavy with inertia and his face deep in the pillow, and turned away. He heard the door open gently and the rustle of silk skirts told him that it was his mother. She came to the end of the bed and bent down to pull his muddy boots off. She crossed the room and Will heard the splashing of water poured from a pitcher into a bowl. He opened his eyes and watched her wash and dry her hands. Unhurried and calm, her grey eyes rested on him.

Eventually she spoke, and her voice was without judgement or accusation. 'You don't understand, do you Will? Why your father pushes you so hard to make the right impression?' Will stayed silent but she came closer and sat companionably on the edge of the bed. He knew she would. He also knew she wouldn't scold or lecture. She left that to her husband, preferring to offer love and warmth to her children, and thereby balancing out his strictness and distance.

With her dark hair swept neatly back and her gentle face composed for concern, Elizabeth Bristowe gazed down at her son. 'When I married your father, my parents were so disappointed. Not in him as a person, of course – but because he was the second son. Failure to inherit can make life so much harder. They knew how difficult life could be.'

'You must understand, Mother, that there is nothing that I could do that would please my father. Nothing at all.'

'He is disappointed. Not just with you. Mostly with himself.' Will turned to look directly up at his mother. 'Have you ever thought what it is like for him to live in this house only because of the kindness of his brother? To have an allowance for living expenses only because of the kindness of his brother? He so longs to be worthwhile, to be given some responsibility for the estate, to feel that he is earning his living. But no, Samuel is the master, the first son, the head of the family. He alone makes decisions and is accountable to no man. Unlike your father.'

'And when Uncle Samuel gives the order, we all dance to his tune. We live in fear that we shall offend and his displeasure will deprive us of our home at Beesthorpe. I know, Mother. I know.'

'Samuel is a good businessman and we are grateful for our position here. But whilst we have every comfort, it gives your father no satisfaction. The house and the estate are not his and never will be. But you, Will, you stand to inherit everything. Your father wants that very much. He wants you to have the security of your own property. It hurts him to see you jeopardise your position.'

'There's just one problem. Uncle Samuel despises me. He makes no show of pretence about the matter.'

Elizabeth reached down and stroked her son's forehead. 'No-one could possibly despise you, Will.' She leaned over and kissed his cheek and Will breathed in the familiar scent of lavender water.

At midday, the door opened again and this time it was not a soft knock or a gentle rustle of skirts. Like a summer storm, Jane, Will's sister, rushed into his sleep. 'Time to get out of bed now. He'll be here within the hour.' Unceremoniously, she dumped a pile of clean clothes on top of him and gave him a vigorous shaking. Will groaned. He knew he would not be allowed to retreat into a silence with Jane in the room.

The questions tumbled out un-checked. 'Where were you all last night? Papa was in a furious state. I heard the constables knocking on the door. He came up to check that you were here and then he lied to them. A bare-faced lie, Will! I listened at the door of the library this morning. I heard him ranting. Were you really with a highwayman?'

'No, no of course not. Please, Jane. There's nothing to tell. Now go away.'

At sixteen years of age, Jane showed no sign of losing her childish enthusiasm. Physically, she did resemble her mother, with her dark hair and slim waist, but as yet, the calmness of manner had eluded her. She was excitable and rushed around like an exuberant puppy. She adored her brother, and hopped between teasing and defending him for the scrapes in which he so frequently found himself. Yet Jane was an ally and Will loved her for it. For the moment, knowing that Will must on no account be late for the visitor, she retreated to the door. 'I'll find out the whole story, you know. And I've seen the horse.' With a defiant swish of petticoats, Jane flounced out of the room and the door slammed behind her.

As the carriage rolled down the road through the park towards Beesthorpe Hall, a thrill of excitement passed through Samuel Bristowe. Being a landowner and Justice of the Peace, he was accustomed to privilege and control, but Beesthorpe occupied a special place in his heart. His inherited estate at Twyford in Derbyshire meant much to him and he had administered it well and profitably, but twenty years ago an opportunity had arisen, and he had seized the chance to buy, from his cousin, this run-down and near derelict estate.

Henry Bristowe had been a feckless man. In 1722 he had inherited the Beesthorpe estate outright, and because he had married into the Burnell family, half the Winkburn estate had also come his way. Reckless spending took its toll and before long he was forced to sell out his half share of Winkburn. Gambling and drink being his main occupations, Beesthorpe began the slow decline into dereliction. The big house became shabby and run-down, and the farmhouses on the thousand acres were little short of squalid. With no re-investment or even repair work, the farmers struggled to make a living, and frequently gave up, leaving debts and misery behind them.

When the plight of the estate came to Samuel's attention, he made an offer for it, which his cousin, Henry, was glad to accept. Taking the money, he went off to drink himself to death somewhere, and Samuel became the saviour of Beesthorpe. Urgent repairs had to be carried out to the Hall to halt further decay, and he had installed his brother, Thomas, and his family to supervise the modernisation. For the first few years, investment had been concentrated on the farms. Decent brick barns, stables and dairies were built and farmhouses restored, thereby attracting viable tenants. Samuel never over-stretched himself. He always made sure the money was secure before it was spent.

The carriage slowed to enter the gates and Samuel poked his head out to give full scrutiny to the house. He was satisfied that the new window frames and the columned porch had given it an air of dignity and importance. Soon it would be time to make further improvements, but the purpose of today's visit was to check on the progress of the farms.

Thomas was waiting. 'Samuel, my dear brother. Welcome. Welcome.'

'How are you, Thomas?' The gravel crunched under Samuel's heavy steps as he strode to the door. His jowls wobbled beneath his chin as he surveyed his property, but he gave scant regard to his relatives, lined up to greet him. In the hallway, he shrugged off his black coat, mopped his brow and adjusted his wig. His long waistcoat struggled to hold his bursting stomach in check and, as he walked through to the dining room, his breathing was laboured. He grunted his satisfaction as he lowered himself into his chair at the head of the table, and then proceeded to study the rest of the family as they took their places.

'So, what is happening at Beesthorpe?' His voice had a gruff hoarseness, his expression was formidable and his manner blunt, as always. Thomas and Elizabeth launched into light conversation about springtime and daffodils, and Will and Jane did their best to answer the blunt questions fired at them.

'Still bent on foxhunting next season?' Uncle Samuel directed his steely eyes on Will. 'Harriers not good enough for you? Too slow you say? I say foxhunting is too dangerous, when you and your like ride recklessly and expensive horses must be shot where they lie. What do you say to that? Speak up, boy!'

Will caught a warning look from his father. The palms of his hands began to sweat. 'The harriers I like well enough, Sir. Hunting the hare has always been a country pastime, but since reading of the excitement experienced by the Quorn hunt in the pursuit of the fox, I only wish to do likewise and help rid the countryside of the loathsome vermin.' Uncle Samuel's face remained inscrutable. Will ploughed on. 'But the loss of the hunter this year was a terrible blow and I feel I shall not return to the chase.'

With a low grunt, Uncle Samuel proceeded to fork his game pie into his mouth. The family remained unable to gauge whether the reply had been satisfactory and the luncheon continued. When he had finished, without noticing whether everyone else had done the same, Uncle Samuel abruptly stood up. 'We shall start the inspection now, Thomas. The Hall Farm first.'

Thomas meekly followed his brother through the back garden and into a small plantation. They passed through a wicket gate and entered the muddy farmyard of John Greaves. Samuel's ungainly body waddled uncomfortably from side to side as he picked his way through the mud, but he was undeterred. He regarded the red-brick barns, built adjacent to the farmhouse, with satisfaction. High up at the granary door, a figure carrying a sack over his shoulder appeared and started to descend the stone steps. Samuel hailed the man with his stick and changed his course, oblivious to the mud splattering his white stockings. 'Good day to you, John Greaves.'

The farmer reached the ground before looking up and twisting off the sack from his back. Carefully, he propped it against the wall. His rough smock and leggings were dirty but his smile was that of a contented man and he pulled his cap in respect to his landlord. 'Good afternoon to you, Squire.'

'Did your sow farrow well, John?'

'She did that, Squire, and only one lost.'

'And the cows?'

'Three dry at present. Should be calving afore long, though. Heifer due any day. Two calved last month and milking a treat. Butter for the market now.'

Samuel nodded, approvingly. He liked John Greaves. When John had taken the tenancy, the farm was in such a state that Samuel had given him six months rent-free. It was an opportunity that an energetic young man could not resist, and was the beginning of a strong bond between tenant and landlord. Now turned forty, John Greaves was still as strong as an ox, and his face and hands, leathery and lined, gave testament to his hard work. 'Where are the horses working today, John?'

'Far Cross Stead. Top o' the hill. Harrowing down a nice seedbed for sowing oats tomorrow.' He indicated the hessian sack of seed. 'If the rain holds off. Been a wet spring. Just need a few more dry days.' John looked up to study the sky and Samuel and Thomas did the same.

Samuel lowered his voice. 'Now, John. Tell me the truth, what is happening on the old Beesthorpe Common? If Savile is still instructing his men to graze it as common land, then, by God, I swear I'll take him to court this time.'

22

'Well, Sir, no. We've had no trouble from that quarter this spring and the word in the alehouses is that he's backed off. Accepts that it's yours since the enclosure. I don't think he'll be sneaking a free day's keep there again.'

Samuel stiffened in a righteous attitude and gave a nod of satisfaction. 'Good. Savile gained more land than most in the enclosure deal – but I had to serve a writ on him to stop him claiming grazing rights on my land. Hah! So he's backed off at last.' Samuel turned to go, but hesitated and cast his eye once more over the barn and cowsheds. Pointing with his stick he said proudly 'Good barn, John. Never regretted the investment.' Tenant and landlord nodded to each other to indicate the termination of the conversation and Samuel and Thomas picked their way back across the mud.

'Good man, John Greaves.' Samuel said. It's worth a lot to have a good tenant. Always pays his rent on time. Every Lady Day, every Michaelmas.'

Back at the house, Thomas steered Samuel to the door. 'I'll send for the carriage to take you up to Willoughby and the farms over there.'

I'll see the stables while I'm here, Thomas, if you don't mind.'

Thomas sighed to himself in frustration behind his brother's back. He should have known that the one thing he could never do was impose his will. Samuel would not be side-tracked. In the stables, the stalls were neat and clean and sweet smelling. 'What is the matter with this one?' Samuel's eyes had gone straight to the young horse.

From nowhere, and before Thomas could even open his mouth to speak, Dick, the stable-lad appeared. 'Had to put the blanket on him this morning, Sir. I think he's got a bit of a chill.'

Samuel continued to stare at the horse, grunted and moved on.

'Thank you, Dick.' said Thomas quietly.

Samuel set off on his tour of the other farms to indulge in another half-dozen conversations of a similar nature about the price of wheat. At each place he made a mental note of the state of the buildings, animals and fields. He knew who was making a go of their farm and who was not. Nothing escaped his attention.

That evening, the family once again sat down to a formal meal. The servants had scurried about all day, making sure that everything was as it should be. They, too, knew from experience that nothing could be hidden from Samuel Bristowe. As a consequence, the silver gleamed, the crystal sparkled and the tureens were filled with plain, wholesome food, served just the way he liked it.

On these occasions, even Jane's ebullient character became subdued. Tension and unease hung almost visibly over them. Elizabeth was her usual gentle self but, being a bachelor, Uncle Samuel merely regarded her femininity as weakness. Thomas did his best, but the real pressure was all on Will. As usual, the conversation was steered towards his future.

'Now, tell me, young man, what have you done with yourself since we last met?' The sound of silver on china halted as everyone held their breath. 'You are shortly to come of age, are you not?'

'Yes, Sir. At the end of this month.'

'And what is it, when you are of age, that you propose to do with yourself? You say you have no desire to go into the Church. The Law holds no interest for you and you have no stomach for a soldier's life. I think, dear boy, that there is but one option. You must find yourself a rich wife. Or is it that you intend to live off my allowance and do nothing but chase foxes across the countryside?'

Will coloured slightly at the jibe. 'No, Sir. That is not my intention. But I do have a plan of action to discuss with you, and which I hope will meet with your approval.'

The words came from nowhere and Will felt slightly dizzy at the sudden rush of blood. If only he'd given it a little forethought, a few moments to weigh up the consequences, to change his mind and come up with another plan. But it was too late. Uncle Samuel was waiting. As Will sat there, he became acutely aware of his mother's look of concern, his father's worried expression, and Jane's look of wide-eyed wonder at what this revelation could possibly be.

Will cleared his throat. His heart hammered in his chest and he so wished he had been able to discuss this newly formed option with his parents first, before being forced to blurt it out to the whole family. Everyone had put down their knives and forks and waited for him to continue. 'I should like, Sir, with your approval of course, to … to sail for … America.'

No-one spoke a word. Will felt the pressure of disapproval bearing down on him and floundered on. 'I hear there are opportunities. That ... that, since the war, educated men are welcomed to indulge in business and commerce.' He risked a glance across the table at his parents, and then at his uncle. Even Jane had the sense to remain quiet until he had spoken.

'I see. America.' Uncle Samuel wiped his mouth with his napkin and clasped his hands in front of him, regarding Will solemnly. 'Well,' he growled 'I think America sounds a fine place for a young man to seek his fortune.' He nodded slowly, mulling over the situation. 'Indeed – a good plan, young man. Well done.'

Will swallowed and he and his father exchanged a look of relief. At last something he had done had met with Uncle Samuel's approval. Jane sat stock still, her face registering disbelief that her brother could be sailing halfway across the world. Elizabeth's face drained of all colour and her hands trembled, her efforts to compose her expression and hide her shock being utterly futile. Was her fear, so visible in her eyes, for her son or for herself?

In a most unusual display of good humour, Uncle Samuel raised his glass. 'I give a toast to you, young man. To your new life and to your new fortune.'

Will felt the pressure evaporate from his shoulders as the atmosphere in the dining room became more relaxed. No-one could ever have imagined that the evening would turn out so well.

Chapter 4

It was a heartbreaking morning to leave. The whole valley had conspired to deck itself in its finest glory, and the May morning was like a parting gift. Unable to sleep, Will had risen early. He stood in the wet grass of Lockabeck Meadow and watched the delicate wisps of morning mist clinging to the fields before him. The hawthorn branches lining the banks of the stream bowed low and graceful under the profusion of creamy blossoms, whilst from beneath, heads of hemlock and cow-parsley burst upwards in a shower of silky white. The beauty quite took his breath away. He couldn't remember it ever having been lovelier.

Lockabeck, Will felt, was his meadow. He had always had an affinity with the rolling field with its abundance of wild flowers and the beck meandering through the middle. It had been at the very centre of his childhood days – a place to play, to dream and now, unexpectedly, to leave.

Will gazed back up at the house as the colour of the red bricks slowly emerged under the light from the brightening eastern sky. A wet nose nuzzled into his hand and he looked down at his faithful dog. Chaff had caught his master's melancholy mood and looked up at him with accusing and sorrowful eyes. 'It's alright, boy. I shan't be away long.' Playfully, he cuffed Chaff's head and pulled his ears, but the dog whined softly. Will stroked the wiry coat for a while and then made an effort to lighten his voice. 'Come on, Chaff. Let's go and find rabbits.'

They set off along the cow-trail snaking down the length of the field. John Greaves' cows began to heave themselves to their feet, leaving the lush grass flattened where they had lain. A few began to tear at the grass, but gradually they ambled towards the gate, knowing that soon they would be called for milking.

Will cut back up through the farm and back to the house. The servants were about and Robert, the young butler, rushed up to him. The excitement of Will's adventure to cross the ocean and seek his fortune had infected them all. 'Is the travelling box ready to be brought down, yet, Mister William?'

'Yes. Almost.'

Jane clattered down the stairs. 'Shall you be ready on time, for once, Will?'

'Yes.' he sighed. 'I'm ready. Now don't fuss.' He didn't remark on the anxious face and the dark circles under his sister's eyes.

Thomas entered the dining room in a sprightly manner. 'Aha. There you are. All set, Will?'

'Yes, Father.'

Thomas helped himself to kidneys. 'The big day, at last. Eat up, my boy. Always travel on a full stomach.' His heartiness had a hollow ring.

Elizabeth stood outside the mahogany door for a full minute to compose herself before entering. She had been dreading this moment, this separation from her son. From the moment he had informed the family, so unexpectedly, of his plans, she had battled with these feelings of dread. She doubted the suitability of Will's personality and character to launch out by himself. It was a harsh world and she was unsure how well equipped he was to deal with it. At just twenty-one, he had been sheltered, cosseted by the family against the realities of life. Despite his impatience and exuberance, he was a gentle character, painfully lacking in intuition and experience. He was altogether too trusting, and too naive. An easy target for scoundrels.

Elizabeth entered the room with a smile and crossed over to kiss her son's cheek. 'I hope you have packed the diary.' she said. Will pulled out of his pocket a small red leather notebook. The elaborate, gold filigree work on it stood out, bright and shining. 'It will never leave me. I shall record everything and then write it all in letters to you. I promise.'

The breakfast was awkward, with everyone speaking words which in no way reflected what was in their hearts – hopeful, optimistic, positive words to hide the dread of their future without Will.

Dick brought the trap around to the front of the house to take him on the short journey to the coaching inn. Thomas felt a sudden pang of envy. This is what I should have done, he thought. Made my own way, taken my own decisions. Instead, I followed the easy route and now my life holds no satisfaction. It is sterile and pointless. He grasped his son in a rough embrace and slapped his back. His voice was hoarse with emotion. 'Take care, Will. God speed you.'

An unaccustomed silence had descended on Jane as she stood, scrunching the gravel with her foot and watching her brother gather up his belongings. Will hugged and then released her, equally silently.

Elizabeth held up with all the bravery she could muster. She did not want Will to see her tears but a lump formed in her throat and her chest felt heavy. 'I shall live for your letters. Don't forget that. My darling Will. God bless you.'

As the trap set off down the drive, Will turned to wave to his family. They waved back and stood, huddled together, watching until he had disappeared out of sight. Chaff whined and Jane sulked off. Elizabeth rested her head on her husband's shoulder. Her words struck him cold. 'I understand his need to go, but I can't help but feel, deep within me, that I shall never see my son again.'

At Caunton Common, Will stood waiting outside the inn. The ostler led from the stable four fresh horses and tied them to their appointed ring on the wall. 'Mailcoach will be along any minute now.' he said confidently.

The sound of the post horn announcing the impending arrival of the coach carried along the valley. Stable lads scurried about as the coach and four crested the hill and bore down the roadway at a canter. At the last moment, the coachman eased back and pulled up and within seconds the lads were unbuckling the horses from the traces and trotting them into the stables. The fresh horses were backed up and their harness secured as Will's travelling box was stowed in the rear boot. The guard offered a hand as Will climbed up on the scarlet painted wheels. In less than four minutes all told, the coachman was cracking the whip and they were off at a fast trot.

Perched on the top of the coach with the other passengers and mailbags piled high, Will's eyes never left the Beesthorpe direction until they were well past the estate. When at last he turned his attention to his fellow travellers he noticed that they were in the company of an armed guard. 'Highwaymen.' the red-coated man said by way of an explanation, patting his ancient blunderbuss. Will nodded and looked away.

The day grew hot and the coach swayed rhythmically as the horses kept up their pace. An elderly gentleman seated alongside

Will began to doze. The guard reached forward to shake him. 'Sir, try to stay awake. We don't want you dropping off.'

Asleep or not, Will thought there was every possibility of someone dropping off when the roads became pitted with potholes and rutted by the narrow coach wheels. The coachman cursed when they were forced to curb their pace, and became even more determined to make good time on the next stretch. As the post horn sounded a warning, all vehicles cleared the way and toll-keepers dashed out to open the gates. The tolls having been paid in advance, the coach careered through, leaving the tollkeeper and a group of curious children spluttering in a cloud of dust.

The countryside rolled by at a great speed. Sometimes it was an open road but on other stretches trees lined the route. When the coachman's shout went up, everyone ducked as leafy boughs brushed low over the coach and swept all before them. Each stage took roughly an hour to complete when, with fresh horses, they hurtled on yet again. Will paid threepence per mile for the privilege of riding the flying coach and by the time they reached Chesterfield late that night, he was thirsty, hungry and exhausted. As usual, it was the Red Lion they pulled into and Will climbed down at last, stiff and dusty.

The next day, Will booked onto a stagecoach travelling west to Buxton. The scenery began to change and also the weather. In the main, his fellow travellers were a congenial group and, to pass the time, they enquired of each a little of their lives and the purpose of their journey.

At one time the conversation turned to highway robbers and Will's thoughts turned once more to Ned. He still found it hard to grasp the reality of Ned's life. How had he found it possible to make his hold-ups, escape from the crime scenes, organize his hide-aways and lead a life that had, at least for a time, appeared to Will to be fairly normal? He had to slip up sooner or later. Will couldn't bear the thought of Ned being caught – and hanged. Even so, he was glad of their shared adventure, for who else would have advised him to travel to America? Now, his future was mapped out. He would sail across the Atlantic Ocean, make his fortune, and return home with the whole family's blessing – to claim his inheritance.

As the mist rolled in and the rain began to beat onto their faces, the guard passed Will a spare cape and he gratefully wrapped it close around himself. Exposed as they were on top of the coach, they had no escape from the elements. In Buxton they transferred to a coach and six heavy horses, for the next stage would not be a fast one. The coachman began to mutter darkly and the horses bent their heads low against the rain. As they began the steep climb out of the little town, the landscape onto which Will gazed was bleak moorland. The stony road they followed went up higher and higher and looked sound enough, but once they were out on top the mist began to swirl and visibility decreased alarmingly. The passengers huddled and endured in miserable silence as the freezing rain lashed across their faces. The only sounds came from the rattling bar chains of the traces and the massive hoofs pounding into the roadway as the horses bent to their task.

Before long the coachman called back to the guard. 'You better get yourself down, Jake. I can barely see the lead horses let alone the road. If we so much as touch one of them peat bogs, we've had it.' After lighting a lamp, Jake duly clambered down and took up his position walking ahead of the horses. In great discomfort and at an agonisingly slow pace, the passengers finally crossed the most southerly end of the Pennine range and, with the brakes protesting loudly, negotiated the steep slope down into Macclesfield.

On the third day they arrived at the port of Liverpool and Will's travelling companions shook his hand and wished him well. Excitement flooded through him as he heaved his travelling box on his shoulder and made his way down to the quayside. Never, in all his life, had he witnessed such a vibrant scene of activity. Endless numbers of ships were moored up alongside the enormous length of the quay. Tall masts, draped with rigging, reached high up to the sky. From the gaping windows of the warehouses, ropes and pulleys deposited crates of cargo and sacks of provisions on to the decks to be taken down to the hold. Men swarmed over both the ships and the cobbled quayside. Sailors, Captains and ware-housemen vied for attention, shouting orders and 'Aye, ayes', all contributing to the general cacophony. Will marvelled that this unholy din could represent any semblance of order, but everyone seemed to know what they were doing, either barking an instruction or striving to carry one out.

'Out of the way, mate.' A sailor, struggling with a huge coil of thick rope, tried to push past and caught Will's box, spinning him around.

'Wait. Can you tell me where to go to purchase a berth to America?'

The sailor adjusted the coil and indicated a small building at the end of the warehouse. 'Over yonder.'

Will could hardly believe his luck when he was informed that the Lady Henrietta was sailing for America in a few hours' time and there was a cabin still to spare. The fare was ten pounds but he happily paid an extra two pounds to ensure that he would have a cabin of single occupancy. When the ticket had been purchased he looked down at the guinea in the palm of his hand – all he had left. At least he hadn't had to pay for lodgings in Liverpool whilst waiting for a berth.

Handing Will a chitty, the clerk indicated the far side of the quay. 'Go to the King's Dock and take this to Captain Forshaw straight away. If you've purchases to make, there's little time, so make all haste.'

Dodging through the ropes, handcarts and crates, Will found the Lady Henrietta, and introduced himself to the Captain. 'Very good, Mr. Bristowe. The first mate here will show you to your quarters. Glad to have you aboard and to make your acquaintance. We sail just before midnight, on the tide.' Captain Forshaw's manner was brusque and authoritative, and he gave every indication of ability. Will hoped that his impression was correct.

Below deck, the companionway was narrow and the travelling box awkwardly bumped the sides. When the door to his cabin opened, Will saw the very small space in which he was to live for the next three or four weeks. There were two small bunks with a narrow standing area between and he was relieved that he had paid extra to occupy the cabin alone. A small porthole above a tiny table completed the cabin – adequate but claustrophobic.

Will dumped his box and decided to go off to explore the ship and the wharf. The sights and sounds, not to mention the smells, were unfamiliar and exciting and he wandered around, absorbing every detail so that he could write and tell the family. The whole range of humanity seemed to be here, from elegant ladies in fine dresses and plumed hats to coarse, unwashed women attempting to lure the sailors. Will watched them all with equal fascination.

Using his last few pennies, he bought a pie and found a vantage point from where he could look out over the vast river mouth. The realisation that this would be his last meal on English soil brought on mixed emotions, but when the setting sun suddenly lit up the western sky and sent fingers of flame over the water before dipping out of sight, he decided to take it as a good omen. Nothing that beautiful, he thought, could be the prediction of something bad.

The scurrying activity seemed to have mostly died down so Will, aware of the onset of darkness and the need to be aboard in good time, picked his way down to the Lady Henrietta. He opened his cabin door and found himself facing a young man.

'Ah, so you must be my sailing companion. Seamus Branagan's me name. At your service.' The stranger thrust forward his grubby hand and pumped Will's with enthusiasm.

Will stared. Was he in the right cabin? 'I … I think there must have been a mistake.' he said. 'I have paid to occupy this cabin alone.' He looked over the man's shoulder to see a small canvas bag deposited on the bunk next to his.

'No. No mistake. I checked with the mate, and this is definitely where I'm to be. I checked twice.'

The strong Irish accent forced extra concentration for Will to follow, but he stuck to his protestations. 'I think you will find, Sir, that there has most definitely been a confusion, because I have paid extra so as to share with no-one.' The stalemate continued and each eyed the other up and down. Will saw a young man of short stature and similar age to himself. He had lank, black hair and piercing blue eyes and his expression was frank, even bordering on the insolent. His clothes were rough and not too clean, his boots well worn, and his hands were that of a labourer.

'I'll go and sort this out.' Will left the cabin to find the mate. On deck, activity had begun but the sailor he was looking for was nowhere to be seen. Captain Forshaw, noticing the passenger hindering the duties of his crew, called to him and Will came over to where he stood. 'Sir, I paid an extra levy for my passage to include the luxury of a private cabin and now I find that another man has been allocated to it.'

'Is that so, Mr. Bristowe.' The captain's concentration was solely on his ship. 'Prepare to slip moorings. Come on now, lads.' He continued to issue orders and his eyes never left his crew and their scurryings to and fro. 'Well, unless you want to jump ship in the very next minute, Sir, I'm afraid if company has been allocated to you for the voyage, then company you shall have. Now please be so good as to allow me to concentrate on the job of negotiating the departure of this ship.'

Will had been dismissed and was at a loss to do anything further. Indignation flooded over him at the thought of an Irish ruffian occupying his cabin for the whole of the voyage. There was barely enough room for the two of them to stand at the same time. Trying not to get in the sailors' way, he retreated to below deck, where he found the man lounging on a bunk, totally unconcerned. Will stared at him.

'Like I said, me name's Seamus Branagan. I think we should try to be civil to each other.'

Will shot him a look of contempt. 'I've been cheated. Not a yard off England's shores, and I've been deceived.' He raised his fist and banged the cabin door in frustration. 'How can we live in such a space?'

'Sure, this is a pretty space for two people to share. In my home, there were so many of us that to find any space in the bed at all of a night was a pure luxury.'

'Well, that sort of Irish squalor is not what I'm used to. I didn't part with almost all my money to be incarcerated with a peasant.' Will felt his face flush with anger.

'And didn't I leave my homeland to escape the tyranny of the English? Not to sleep alongside them?' The man squared himself up and his eyes flashed. Will decided to back off and stormed off above deck again.

The Irishman leaned back, clasped his hands behind his head and sighed. 'A bloody Englishman. Tis goin' to be a long voyage, for sure.'

As darkness fell and the tide eased the ship slowly down the Mersey towards the mouth of the estuary, Will stood on deck and watched the lights of the port slipping further away. It was a warm night and the balmy air carried the sounds of other ships leaving their moorings to head for the open sea. There being only a light breeze, sails did not fill, but with the help of the tide the little fleet made gentle progress. With their dark hulks merging with the black water, the seemingly disembodied watch lanterns appeared to glide alone, with only an eerie hint of white sail visible to Will's peering eyes. For the first time in his life, he could smell the salt in the air and, as they neared the open water, the ship began to bob up and down as the current took them.

On the threshold of a great adventure, the magic of the moment soothed Will's feelings and he felt a pang of regret at his outburst of rudeness to the Irishman. It wasn't his fault that the shipping agent had cheated him. He had nothing against the Irish, though clearly this one was of the lower class. Still, he resolved to at least be polite to him, although he had strong reservations regarding the probability of his personal habits.

Will returned to his cabin, prepared to introduce himself and engage his enforced companion in conversation, but he was not there. He must have slipped on deck, unnoticed by Will. He decided to take advantage of the space to prepare for sleep and do his best to stow his box. It stuck out from under the table, a danger to shins. The curses which followed his companion's later arrival in the cabin were of such ferocity that Will decided it was better to feign sleep and not enrage the man further.

The creaking of the timbers and the gentle movement of the ship were comforting and gradually he was rocked into a deep slumber, only to find, after a distressingly short time, his rest disturbed by the most almighty snores he had ever heard. The nasal grumblings reverberated around the tiny cabin, depriving him of peace and sleep. Will pulled the blanket over his head and hoped that the morning would soon come.

Chapter 5

On waking, Will once again had the cabin to himself and so hastily set about dressing. The ship rolled and creaked and he felt remarkably hungry as he entered the dining salon to meet the other passengers for the first time. As they were only a dozen in total, introductions were soon made. The Irishman sat at the table, helping himself to bread, and watched Will suspiciously from under his dark eyebrows.

Up on deck, Will viewed the sea with wonder. With only a light wind, the waves were low and a gentle swell rocked the ship from side to side in a languid motion. He leaned over the rail and gazed into the deep ocean. In fascination he followed the white spray as the bows displaced the water and sent it surging up and away. The blue sky met the sea in a mist of indistinguishable horizon and Will was over-awed by the vastness.

Apart from polite observations from his fellow passengers, the morning passed quietly. Gulls wheeled overhead in a display of acrobatics and their cries followed the little ship on its Atlantic course.

By mid-afternoon, the sky had changed and the wind picked up. Now Will could feel the boat surging ahead as the sails filled. The wake snaked out behind them in a silvery ribbon as they made good progress through the white-topped waves. The wind whipped against his cheeks and he could taste the salty spray on his lips. Revelling in the wonder of this new experience, Will stayed on deck until it was time for the evening meal, when he made his way to the dining salon.

The captain, whilst displaying little charm, was polite enough to his passengers. 'Had the wind continued to evade us in the manner of this morning's, I'm afraid our passage would be very long indeed.' he informed them.

Will had selected a place at the table some distance from his cabin companion, who spent a considerable amount of time engaging a family in conversation. The greasy stew and potatoes eaten, Will went up on deck to enjoy a last breath of air before enduring once more the claustrophobia of the cabin and the closeness of a complete stranger.

The evening light quickly faded and with it the first drops of rain spattered against the sails. On the opposite deck, the figure of the Irishman stood, bracing himself against the pitching of the ship, and Will decided to go below and take advantage of the privacy of his cabin.

He found himself taking more care to keep his balance and frequently staggered and knocked his shoulders in his progress down the companionway. By the light of a lamp swinging from a hook, he prepared for bed and realised as he lay down his head that he felt decidedly unwell. Every heave of the boat was followed by a dip, and Will's stomach was doing its best to keep up. The Irishman did not appear for a long time but finally the door burst open and he lurched in, cursing under his breath. With horror, Will realised that the sickness in the pit of his stomach was rising and that soon he would have to vomit. The Irishman blocked the doorway.

'I am sick. I must go up on deck.' Will tried to find a way past but was pushed back on his bunk.

'I've been heaving over the rail for the past hour gone. It seemed a good idea to bring a pail down. Here.' Seamus shoved the wooden bucket at Will and groaned as he slumped down on his bed. With the bucket between them and the seasickness taking a good hold, the night was long and miserable.

A knock on the cabin door roused them from a fitful doze and a sailor appeared. Will recognized the weather-hardened face and the grey beard of the cook's mate. 'Not feeling so chirpy this morning then, Sirs?' He slapped down a pitcher of water and two pewter mugs on the table. 'I'll take this.' he said picking up the odious bucket and grinning as the two men groaned. 'With luck, you'll be feeling better by tomorrow, lads.'

The inside of Will's mouth felt as though it was lined with fur and his teeth stuck to his lips. His stomach was lodged somewhere in his throat and every pitch and roll of the boat increased the profound nausea. He glanced across at the Irishman, who was chalk white and had his eyes tightly closed. With a masterly effort of concentration, Will raised himself and reached across to the pitcher of water. His hands trembled and he spilled a little, but as the cool water trickled down his throat, he truly believed that nothing he had ever tasted in his life had been sweeter.

He leaned across and shook his companion. 'Lift your head. You need to drink.' His voice was low and husky but already the water had revived his spirits. He held the mug to Seamus' lips and tipped the liquid down. The Irishman let his head fall back on the pillow but his blue eyes fixed a level stare on Will and he nodded his thanks.

Will opened his box and rummaged through. He tipped water into a bowl, soaked a cloth in it and handed it to Seamus, who softened his crusted lips and wiped his forehead before handing it back. They both sank gratefully back on their bunks, exhausted by the effort.

After some time, the soft Irish voice penetrated Will's semi-sleep. 'So, your name's Will Bristowe and you're an Englishman. Is that it? Or is there anything else about yourself that you would like to share, given that conversation is the only diversion we're likely to have today.'

'I come from Nottinghamshire, in the middle of England. Have you heard of the legend of Robin Hood? Well, Sherwood Forest is close to my estate.'

Your estate? Is it a bloody English landowner you are?'

'Well, it's not mine yet. My uncle owns it but I am his only heir, so one day the whole estate, a thousand acres or so, will be left to me.'

'A thousand acres!' Seamus whistled low under his breath. 'Sweet Mary, what does a man do with such an amount of land? And why would you be making your way to America when you've all that in England. Is it more you're wanting?'

The last thing Will wanted to do was explain his circumstances, especially to a stranger, but he suspected that in the end he'd have no choice. 'As I said, my uncle owns the estate, not my father, but we have lived on it for all my life. It has a beauty, not dramatic like moorland, nor flat like some farmland, but rolling with pretty valleys and woodland, streams and meadows.' Will's voice trailed off. For some reason his eyes began to prickle.

'I know what you mean.' Seamus' voice was wistful. My home is nothing, just a little mud house on a hillside in County Clare with the little stony fields below spreading right down to the sea. But it's a place where you leave your heart.' A long silence developed. 'So, why did you leave?' Seamus suddenly demanded.

Will sighed. 'My uncle doesn't like me. He doesn't approve of anything I do. He resents me hunting and I was expected to earn my living somehow. Really, I suppose I wanted the adventure, to see what would happen, but mostly I hope to make my fortune so that my uncle will see that I am worthy to inherit.'

'Hah. Inherit another fortune! Where is the justice in the world?'

Will felt too tired to explain further and drifted off into a fitful sleep. On waking, he decided to quiz Seamus. 'So, why did you leave?'

Seamus gave an exaggerated sigh. 'Do you not know anything about Ireland? Leaving is about all we can do. Sure, we had a sound little house and we rented the land – owned by an English landlord, of course. But there were too many of us. Ten acres is all it is. One pig, some chickens and a few sheep to run on the mountainside, and a couple of strips to grow the potatoes. You know I spent all my life digging up stones from those strips, enough to build a wall around the whole of Ireland. We put potatoes in, but it's stones that come up – every year a new crop of stones.'

'How could you afford the passage?'

'Two years ago, my father's brother, Daniel and his wife, Kathleen, sailed for America with their son, Joseph. We've had word from them that it's a great country. No class system holding you down, keeping you in your place. Just hard work. And that is something I know all about.' Seamus turned his resentful eyes on Will. 'My mother had saved a little, God only knows how, and somehow she scrimped and squirrelled away the pennies to send me over. I shall send money back, of course, and then my brother will follow.'

Will thought of his own mother and wondered if the feelings of Irish mothers were the same, struggling to bring up sons, only to send them all away, halfway around the world.

"Do you know about life in Ireland – for us Catholics?' Will shook his head. 'Well, we're the lucky ones. It's lucky we are to pay the high rent to the Protestant landlord and then pay the tithes to the Protestant church. We've no education to speak of since our lands were taken from us a hundred years ago, though we're grateful not to have to follow the Penal footpaths to take Mass in far-off places now. Oh and we're barred from purchasing land or owning a horse worth more than five pounds.' Seamus' laugh was bitter. 'Not that it's a problem to us, you understand.'

Will mulled over all this information. The day dragged on with sporadic bursts of conversation the only means of taking their minds off their miserable sickness.

In the evening, the cook's mate came back once more and this time put down two hard, flat cakes on a plate. 'Ship's biscuit. Captain says you've to eat it and you'll be right as ninepence by the morning. Lines the stomach, see.' Once more, he removed the offending bucket.

Seamus picked up a biscuit and gingerly took a bite. 'I hope he's right. I've had enough of the sickness to last me a lifetime.'

Will thought the biscuit bland and unappetizing, but munched steadily through it and then waited for the vomiting to start again.

By morning, although weak, Will felt considerably better and so staggered up to the deck to escape the foetid smell of the cabin. Seamus followed. 'Did I tell you I walked the whole breadth of Ireland, from Galway to Dublin? And what a city Dublin is! Grand houses and a massive Custom House right on the quay. By just going up the Liffey a way, I got a job herding cattle aboard a ship bound for England. That way I came over for free.'

Will took a few deep breaths and listened patiently to the garrulous Irishman as he continued with his tale. 'I hung around the docks for a while and worked here and there, mostly the dirty jobs, 'til they agreed to give me a ticket for half price.'

'Half price?' Seamus suddenly had Will's attention.

'When you fell for the single occupancy deal, I pitched in a fiver and here we are – both on our way to a land of freedom and adventure.' Seamus' eyes twinkled merrily and his smile was broad as he studied Will's reaction.

Indignation flooded through Will as he realised how he had been used by the impertinent Irishman. He glared at him, struggling to find the right words of retort, but none came. Instead, the intense blue eyes locked on to his and before he could help himself he had given in to a wry smile.

The fresh wind filled the sails and revived their senses and, in sudden appreciation of their new-found health, they turned to each other and smiled. Their adversity had forced them to endure each other's company and conversation at close quarters, and their weakness had engendered a patience of one another's circumstances.

A bond, of sorts, had been forged between them. They had grudgingly discovered depths in each other that ordinarily would never have come to light. Their defences had come down and now, though they remained poles apart in their social standing, they had achieved an understanding that bode well for a friendship. Though neither would admit it, to have a friend at your side when embarking on a new and unknown adventure was far preferable to going it alone.

The days passed by. Will thought he would never tire of watching the ocean, feeling the wind on his face and straining his eyes for the distant horizon. He constantly admired the agile sailors skimming up the rigging, barefoot and dangling precariously, to alter the set of a sail. It was a hard life, but they had the skill and alacrity expected of them by Captain Forshaw, who continued to treat his paying passengers as a necessary but unwanted nuisance.

The ship's table provided food that was bland and monotonous. The cook rarely roused himself further than to prepare potatoes with some kind of fat-laden stew, but conversation was the main diversion when they came together in the panelled dining salon. Every passenger had high expectations of the bounty of this new country they were about to discover. The disappointments, losses and betrayals they had suffered at home were briefly aired and then put behind them. The future was the main focus and optimism the only way forward. All of the passengers could be described as distressed gentle folk, that is educated but with little money, with the exception of Seamus. Some had trades and ideas of employment, whilst all understood the need for hard work.

Seamus' lack of social standing did not hold him back at all. It was as though, on leaving Ireland where his position in the scheme of things was one step up from the gutter, he had wiped the slate. He was equal and he would not be ignored or put down. He was a good looking young man and quick to smile, and gradually achieved his acceptance. In the first few suspicious days when he feared the worst of his English fellow passengers, he had been wary, but gradually everyone realised that whatever their previous background, they all faced the same challenges, and secretly harboured the same fears. It was their unwritten future, as well as the ship, that bound them together.

Seamus decided to embark on his education, starting with social matters. His mother had taught him to write his name but beyond knowing that he must doff his cap to the English land agent to show a respect that he did not feel, he knew little else. If a subject or conversation came up about which he knew nothing, he asked. When he noticed that he did not hold his knife and fork in the same manner as Will, he changed. Always, he kept his eyes and ears receptive to new information, and because he was accepted and liked by the others, his natural confidence grew.

Will's clothing was, of course, of good quality and cut. His long brown jacket and green waistcoat and breeches stood out as the attire of a gentleman. When he opened his travelling box and sorted through for something, Seamus peered inside and saw fresh linen and luxuries entirely unknown to him. He compared his own battered boots with Will's new leather ones, and knew that his rough homespun jacket, patched and mended so many times, spoke only of poverty.

Resentment could surface in an instant, especially knowing that Will had never laboured for one day in his entire life. What he needed was to get himself on to Will's level and to do that he had to know things – all manner of things – but first of all, to read and write. Seamus had ambition.

After fourteen days of fresh winds and good progress, they awoke to the quiet of a calm and level sea. Gone were the white horses dancing above the waves, the bow spray and the taste of salt in the air.

'We're becalmed.' whispered Will, as he and Seamus stepped out on to the deck. From a cloudless sky, hazy in the distance, the sun bore down on the little ship. What sails were rigged drooped low without so much as the occasional flap, and the boat sat motionless in the dull, flat sea. The silence was profound.

'Indeed we are becalmed, Mr. Bristowe.' Captain Forshaw said in a resigned voice. 'We could wallow here for days, weeks even. The only thing we can do is pray that a wind comes to fill our sails sooner rather than later. And by that I mean before our supplies run out entirely.'

The atmosphere of the ship changed. Sailors sat about, knotting ropes and stitching canvas. Passengers alternated between walking the deck and lolling on their bunks. All sense of purpose disappeared, for there was nothing to do but wait. As midday neared, the heat haze thickened and the temperature rose. Mercilessly, the sun beat down, causing immense discomfort to everyone. They sought shade, but the cloying airlessness of the cabins drove the passengers on deck. A canvas canopy was rigged up and they sheltered under it, staring out on to the vast glassy ocean.

That night Will and Seamus slept out on deck under the stars. The cool night air soothed Will's skin and he lay on his back watching for shooting stars. Still Seamus probed for information. 'How is it that you intend to make your living in America? I bet you've a load of money just waiting for some nice little business to break into.'

'How I wish that was true. The fact is, I have just one guinea to my name. But with my education I'm sure I could find a job – as a clerk, perhaps. Anything.'

'Hah. You don't mean anything, Will. You wouldn't last a day as a labourer.' Seamus scoffed at the idea but was impressed with the guinea. 'Why that's a fortune in itself to some – well, to me, for certain.'

'Do you have any money at all, Seamus?'

'Not a single penny. But I have something worth more than money.'

Will laughed. 'What could you have worth more than money?'

'An address. That's what. Where there'll be a welcome, a place to rest my head and a share of whatever food is on the table.' Seamus gave a satisfied sigh. 'My Uncle Daniel and Aunt Kathleen. You must come with me, Will. Sure, when they take one look at you and your fancy clothes, they'll think I've lost my senses, taking up with the English gentry and all – but so long as you don't come the high and haughty they'll be alright.'

Will thought for a moment. He couldn't agree to the offer, for the Irish family were bound to be rough and probably not half as agreeable as Seamus had turned out to be, but he knew that the suggestion was well meant, and anyway, he had no ready alternative. 'Thanks. We'll see.' Whatever would his father and Uncle Samuel make of this curious and unlikely friendship?' Will thought to himself. He had the comforting feeling that his mother would probably approve.

Seamus lay back and gazed up at the twinkling sky. He smiled to think what Uncle Daniel's reaction to Will might be. He just hoped that their arrival would not coincide with too heavy a drinking session.

The following day took exactly the same form, and the day after that. Enduring the intense, sultry heat with the ship languishing in a flat sea sapped all their energy and patience. Will felt as though they had been abandoned, forgotten by the world and condemned to exist in a void forever.

Even so, it was a blow when Captain Forshaw made his speech to the assembled passengers. 'We have no way of knowing for how long we shall remain becalmed. It could be days or even, God forbid, weeks. From now on, food will be rationed, but that is not my main concern. Water is another matter. Since leaving Liverpool, we have not had any great amount of rainfall to replenish our barrels. We must now observe the strictest of rationing. Anyone found wasting water or taking more than their share will be punished. Observation of this rule will be the difference between life and death. If you value your lives, take heed of my words.'

The passengers exchanged fearful looks. They had set out knowing the possible danger of storms and shipwreck. In the middle of a vast ocean they were being told that they may die from the simple want of water.

For three more days they endured the suspension of time, drenched in their own sweat with their throats parched and their lips cracking. Tempers frayed and the crew bickered and quarrelled. The passengers remained introspective and most of the time in a soporific inertia, stirring themselves to see to basic necessities only at night or in the early morning. Captain Forshaw stood on deck studying the sky and straining his eyes for the merest hint of a cloud. None came.

On the seventh day, Will lay under the makeshift canopy on deck, staring sightlessly out towards the horizon. A light rustling suddenly filled the silence. He craned his neck around towards the direction of the sound. Instantly, there was the sound of footsteps on the deck and then a shout went up. The sail flapped again. Everyone scrambled to their feet and stood watching as the canvas rippled with the breeze. In the distance, in stately formation, white clouds were definitely coming their way.

A flurry of activity and anticipation suddenly overcame the ship. With evident relief the Captain issued his orders, and with eagerness the crew carried them out. The passengers, whose faces had been weary with the tedium, now smiled at one another in a new rush of hope. At last, they were on their way again.

In a shorter time than they could have imagined, the sky changed, the wind filled the sails and the ship was riding the waves just as before. From high up in the rigging, a sailor hollered and pointed out to sea. When they focused on the direction, a massive black shape loomed out of the water and dived down, exposing an enormous forked tail. 'A whale!' shouted Seamus. 'As big as a bloody house!'

All anxiety now gone, Will and Seamus looked at each other and laughed. When the rain came, they held their faces up to the sky, the water barrels filled and everyone slaked their thirst and washed themselves and their clothes. The supper that evening had the air of a celebration and when they slept it was to the familiar creaking of the ship as she laboured through the waves, taking them on to America.

Chapter 6

The sea breeze billowed out the cloak that the woman had wrapped around herself. She stood, a lone and desolate figure on the New York quayside, looking out to sea. The sailor knew she had been standing there, motionless, for over an hour, because he had been observing her from the deck of his ship as he stood his watch.

Eliza was oblivious to the wind. The chill came from within her – like a block of ice, she felt brittle and lifeless. What would the future hold now? Now that the only true love in her life had gone.

She had always known that Eduardo's greatest passion in his life had been the sea. It was in his blood, and she knew too that he loved his ship as much as her. But the sea had made the final claim and stolen him forever. She looked down into the dark, deep water and then up to the distant horizon. Her eyes turned to the south. Somewhere, down there in the Caribbean Sea, just off the island of Jamaica, lay The Betsy in her watery grave. Had he thought of her as the water closed over him? Had he called her name?

Eduardo, with his dark, curly hair and laughing eyes, had fallen in love with her and in the resulting heady delirium of desire, she had defied her aunt and uncle. They had been her guardians, had given her all they had in their modest Connecticut lives, but with Eduardo she was mesmerised and alive for the first time. She had been visiting a cousin in New York and after a chance meeting with the handsome Captain, had decided that her future lay with him. Eliza never returned to Connecticut. She married her love and set up a home in New York for him to return to whenever he could. She had been content to share him with the sea, knowing that it was the only way to have even a part of him. It had been an intense yet short-lived bliss.

The letter came from the shipping company in the morning. She had opened it with an innocence, a lightness of heart, that she would now give anything to retrieve. Eduardo's return was not overdue. There was no cause for concern. And then she read the words which darkened her sight and her soul. 'The Betsy has gone down in a storm off the coast of Jamaica with the loss of all hands.' Such simple, short words.

And what of the cargo? Nothing was mentioned of that, but an unbidden picture came into her mind. Black bodies, chained, terrified and helpless, drowning where they lay as the hold filled with water.

Eliza shook her head and closed her eyes. As the teardrops formed under her lashes and rolled down her face, a voice came from behind her. 'Are you alright, Miss?' She turned. The sailor saw a pretty face crumpled by despair and grief. The overwhelming sadness in the woman's eyes told him everything. She was unable to reply so he nodded acknowledgement and walked away.

The dark water looked inviting. It lapped almost playfully against the jetty, sending spumes of lighter green shooting upwards. She played with the notion that if she just stepped into it, the wretchedness would be over and Eduardo would be there to welcome her. She could join her husband and the sea would enfold them both. But as if to remind her of its existence, the unborn baby moved and kicked, and broke her morbid thoughts. A child, Eduardo's child, to love and care for. She could watch it grow and every day be reminded of his love. The pain in Eliza's heart was unbearable, but perhaps the child would help to ease the grief. In time perhaps. To end her own life would be so easy, but not the life of Eduardo's child. She decided she would live for her baby. Eliza bade a final goodbye and turned away. Relieved, the sailor watched her go.

Chapter 7

The first glimpse of land was a cherished moment. Will had, like everyone, risked an ocean in search of a new life with new opportunities. At times it had seemed that they were destined to sail on forever, that no new country awaited them, that they would never feel the solid comfort of dry land beneath their feet. The first shout of sighting was a moment of reality, and Will's heart leapt.

He stared long and hard at the coastline of America as the ship negotiated the Hudson estuary and came in on the East River. The port and township seemed to be teeming with activity, and vessels of all kinds cluttered the river mouth. Unperturbed, Captain Forshaw stood on deck, issuing the orders that would bring them safely into the sheltered harbour. Eventually, they berthed with ease alongside the piers on the dockside of New York.

Will and Seamus bid their fellow passengers farewell and everyone wished each other luck. As they leaped off the gangplank, their legs felt wobbly from the thirty-eight days at sea, and they began to weave their way through the throng. It was a busy and vibrant scene and the wharves were bustling with activity.

Hawkers calling out their wares and handcarts containing every commodity packed the causeway. Gangs of men rolled barrels to and from the ships and heavy horses pulling enormous carts cleared a path. Seamus weaved and dodged but Will became distracted at every turn, earning collisions and cursings in equal measure. He stared at the colourful confusion all around them, and the black men – the first he had seen in his life. There seemed to be so many of them, pulling carts, carrying sacks and scurrying in and out of the warehouses. 'They must be the black African slaves.' Will whispered.

'We've to make for the Lower East Side. Come on.' Seamus urged.

They turned into a street off the dockside and headed in a generally eastern direction. The roads were baked hard but uncobbled and the wooden houses were built close together. Seamus asked the way a couple of times and received curt replies and hard stares. At other times they were accosted outright by prostitutes and pimps. At one time gunshots rang out and a woman screamed. In the narrow streets and alleys the atmosphere was one of threat and suspicion.

With his travelling box on his shoulder, and his expensive clothes, Will stood out as easy pickings. Seamus looked more like the residents, so he did all the talking. 'Would you be knowing where Daniel Branagan might live? Daniel and Kathleen Branagan?'

The pointed directions they received took them into a more and more crowded area – a jumble of alleyways and wooden houses, bursting with families speaking a variety of languages. The overpowering stench of humanity and decay lodged itself at the back of Will's throat as they threaded their way through the maze of rubbish-strewn slums, stepping over the stinking open drains and channels in the narrow roadways. Mangy dogs roamed and pigs squealed as they foraged amongst the filth and debris.

Eventually, they stopped at a rough, wooden house and Seamus knocked on the door. Will glanced uneasily around. This district was worse than anything he could ever have imagined. He'd been a fool to come.

'Does Daniel Branagan live here?' Seamus asked of the woman who stood staring suspiciously at them.

'And who wants to know?' The accent was strong and Irish.

'His nephew, Seamus Branagan. Come from Ireland.'

The woman's face broke into a wide smile and she raised up her arms and called 'Kathleen! He's here at last. The boy is here. Come quick!'

Aunt Kathleen peered from behind the woman and exclaimed in delight as she recognized Seamus. 'I am so pleased you're here with us and safe at last.' She reached up and taking his face in her hands, kissed his cheek. 'We began to wonder if you had met with ill-luck. Come in, Seamus. Come in.'

Seamus held back. 'I'd like you to meet my friend, Will Bristowe. We sailed over together. Will has nowhere to go and, since we met on the voyage, I wondered if he might stay with me for tonight.'

Aunt Kathleen stared at Will. He raised his hat to her and smiled. 'Pleased to make your acquaintance, Ma'am.'

'Well, I'm sure I don't know what to say. We have very little here, Sir. No comforts to speak of.' She hesitated for a moment, clearly taken aback by Will's smart appearance. 'But you're welcome, Mr. Bristowe. Come in both of you.'

They entered the Branagan home. The other woman was introduced as Mrs. O'Grady from next door. She helped Aunt Kathleen prepare tea and breadcakes, and fortunately for Will, the women's natural distrust of him was pushed aside in view of their delight at the arrival of Seamus.

'Delicious.' Seamus declared with a happy grin. 'Just like my mother's, at home.'

Before long, the door opened and Uncle Daniel stood on the threshold. Seamus went forward and was met by a roar and a hug. Will rose from his stool and stood nervously waiting to be introduced.

'Uncle Daniel, this is my friend, Will Bristowe. We sailed over together.'

'Good day to you, Sir. Thank you for having me in your home.' Will extended his hand.

'An Englishman?'

'An Englisman of no account.' Will said quickly. 'Like Seamus, I need to find work immediately. We hope to be of help to one another.'

The burly Irishman, with his wiry grey hair and bulging muscles, quietly scrutinized Will. 'Well now, you'll be knowing that the English are no friends of mine – but, I suppose that if Seamus knows you well enough, I'll take his word.'

Will smiled his relief. 'Thank you, Sir.'

Uncle Daniel, remembering the figure lurking behind, turned and pushed a boy forward. 'This is Joseph, my son.' Joseph came nearer and Will could see a dark haired youth dressed in dirty, working clothes and with a resentful expression. Will extended his hand and reluctantly Joseph offered his, blackened and grimy as it was from his day's labour.

'We need to talk about work.' Seamus said, eager to begin.

'It's the docks is the first place to ask around,' Uncle Daniel said. 'But first we'll have your welcome supper and perhaps a tankard of ale for the occasion.'

That night Will and Seamus slept on the floor of the little house. Though swept and clean enough, the wooden boards were warped and broken and insects freely came and went. Cockroaches scraped along the floor and mosquitoes whined around Will's head, but it was the intimate and personal sounds of humanity in such close proximity that he found most disturbing. Indeed he was depressingly aware of every cough, snort, snore and breaking of wind, not to mention noisy coupling, in the entire lane. At last the first light broke. Heading back to the dockyard in the early morning, Will carefully made mental notes of landmarks, so as to find his way back. He could make little sense of the higgledy-piggledy arrangement of lanes, alleys and crude wooden houses.

'Are you going to try the shipping office, while I go down to the warehouses?' Seamus asked. Will nodded. 'Good luck.'

It was the first of July and the sun sparkled over the harbour. Hundreds of ships lay alongside and dozens were either heading out to sea or creeping gently in to berth. So much coming and going. It seemed to Will to be the centre of commerce to the whole world. He knew it had to be regulated and recorded in some way, and true enough there were many trading boards displaying company names and indicating offices within.

One stood out sufficiently to catch his attention: J. BONHAM & CO. TRADING COMPANY, printed in large letters over the side of the building. He decided to try his luck. Inside, away from the cries of the quayside, it was quiet, subdued even. He could see a clerk at a desk, his head bent over a ledger and a quill in his hand.

'I am looking for work,' Will explained when the man came to see what he wanted. He peered up at Will for a moment and said, 'I'll fetch Mr. Bonham.'

Mr. Bonham, when he finally arrived, was an elderly man. Smartly dressed and wigged, he nevertheless had an air of frailty about him, though his voice was firm and authoritative. He looked Will up and down and listened to his story. 'We always need good clerks here. You're sure you will cope with the writing and arithmetic? Accuracy is paramount, you know. When the manager brings you the bill of lading, it must be recorded in the correct ship's ledger.'

Will assured Mr. Bonham that he was up to the task and so was conducted to the ledger room, given a quill and ink, and a huge pile of bills to be recorded. It was late afternoon before he emerged, blinking, into the sunshine. He had been warm in the airless office, but outside the heat was blistering. He pumped himself some water and then returned. Mr. Bonham was scrutinizing the ledger, reading every entry. 'Very good, Mr. Bristowe. The columns are neat and clearly legible. You may come back in the morning. Today is Tuesday. I shall pay you at the completion of every Saturday.'

Will's spirits lifted, although his stomach growled for food. He stood for a while just watching the scene before him. Dockhands scurried to and fro, and a crew rhythmically hauled on thick ropes to secure a ship to a berthing post. Labourers off-loaded sacks of grain on to barges, destined to manoeuvre through the network of canals deep within the city. Outside a tavern where sailors caroused and whores lounged provocatively, a preacher stood on a box urging the crowd to resist evil. No-one took any notice.

By some miracle, Will eventually found his way safely back to the Branagans' house. There was no sign of Seamus. It was long after the return of Uncle Daniel and Joseph that the door burst open and an exhausted but triumphant Seamus entered. His face was smeared with dirt, and his shirt clung to him, plastered with grease and sweat, but his blue eyes blazed with pride as he held high the payment for his day's labour. The silver dollar shone bright in his work-soiled hand and everyone cheered him.

'Sacks of maize. The whole day, I've shouldered sacks of maize into the warehouse. Never have I known it so hot in my life! But here it is. A real piece of eight.'

Will felt self- conscious when he recounted his day's work, seated in the cool of an office, but Seamus was impressed. 'So, the first day's work of your life, Will.' he whispered so the others couldn't hear. 'You're in the world of the working man now.'

Despite the wildlife on the floor beside them, Will slept well that night.

Feeling guilty about eating the Branagans' food, Will assured Aunt Kathleen that on receipt of his first wages, he would repay it and more. He was reluctant to break into the guinea, for whilst it was in his pocket, he felt secure. It was an insurance; there only for a dire emergency.

He felt a degree of reluctant acceptance by the household, with the exception of Joseph. The youth was resentful and sullen. Will often looked up to find Joseph's glowering stare sending a silent message of hatred across the room. Mercifully, their time spent together was short.

By the end of the week, it was Will's turn to proudly display his wages and give half to Aunt Kathleen. It was a celebration meal that night, accompanied by a pint of ale and much laughter. Will watched the family with fascination. He had never been so involved with a working-class family before. Even his dealings with the tenant farmers had never allowed him a real glimpse of their intimate family life. Uncle Daniel sang the old Irish songs and, as he did so, Will saw the shadow of homesickness pass across their faces. He knew how they felt. Joseph slipped out to join his friends.

By the Sunday, even Seamus' amazing energy had flagged and he needed to rest. He spent a stifling day in the airless house, exhausted by the week's arduous toil. Will ventured out to explore the city. He set off north, more confident now of his bearings, and used to the sights and sounds of the working-class area. There were all kinds of nationalities here, from the Dutch to Russian Jews to the French fleeing from the aftermath of their revolution. They had all come in the hope of finding their own particular kind of freedom.

As Will walked on, the districts gradually became more salubrious and genteel. Brick houses of the English style, with columns and porticos, were set back on wide cobbled streets. Building was being carried out on a fairly grand scale, with mansions of style and solidity. This was the area for the rich, their houses being as far away as possible from the stinking, disease-ridden and rat-infested slums of the working class. There was plenty of money here.

Slaves were decently dressed and walked the streets, Will presumed on errands for their masters and mistresses. He found himself watching them closely as they passed by, and tried to weigh up their demeanour. The issue of slavery troubled him. At home, in England, he had read a few publications on the subject, but had taken little real interest. Now, however, he was observing these black slaves at first hand. He often saw the same withdrawn expression, eyes hard to read, head held high. It was, he decided, almost a secret superiority. But then these were the lucky ones, employed by a household with easy domestic duties, not whipped into cowering fear, toiling under an endless sun.

It was the morality of slavery that sat uneasily with him. How must it feel to be owned by a master; for someone to have total control over you, even to life or death? He knew there was a growing movement for abolition but he remembered his father's observation that while white men continued to make money out of slave labour, the practice would continue. He walked on.

Expensive carriages with matched horses conveyed well-dressed occupants through the tree-lined avenues. It was obviously to the north of the city that he needed to go. The overcrowded shambles of the Branagans' house was a world away. Just a short time, he told himself, to save some money and then rent a room in a less squalid area.

Mr. Bonham had grown to trust Will's work and given him other tasks. Ships came and went all the time, and the clerical tasks piled up daily. Despite the tedious nature of the work, his sore eyes and the cramps in his permanently ink-stained fingers, Will asked to work on Sundays. He needed the money and had no desire to spend one night more than necessary in his present accommodation.

The Branagans were good people and laboured hard for a meagre life. They told themselves that theirs was a life of opportunity, and indeed it was better than the existence they had endured in Ireland, where there was little or no hope of a better future. In America there were jobs. If you could work, you could eat.

Will wrote his first letter home. He imagined the excitement it would bring to the household and so wrote in glowing terms regarding his prospects. He told them of the voyage and Seamus, but omitted most of the colourful details of the circumstances of the family. He gave them a return address as care of Bonham & Co. Trading Company and made sure the letter went on a fast clipper bound for England.

He could, of course, never divulge the true details of his uncomfortable nights spent on the rough-hewn floorboards of the little wooden house amongst the open sewers. He could never tell them of the rats squeaking beneath his appointed space, or the cockroaches endlessly scraping alongside him, or the way every evening the narrow streets filled with clouds of mosquitoes. He spared them the embarrassing facts of life that were constantly imposed upon him by the lack of privacy in the flimsy houses. He could never describe to them the shouting and bickering, and the crying babies. And it would be too much for them to understand that it was only exhaustion, brought on by a long day's work, that ever allowed him to sleep at all. And how could he tell them that although any draught of air, however malodorous, was welcome in the summer heat, it was certain that the gaps between the warped wooden planks would make the winter intolerably cold and miserable?

Towards the end of the second week, Will trudged his way home through the alleys. Tiredness and familiarity had lessened his awareness, although he knew he was in constant danger of being robbed or set upon. From further up the street, stones were suddenly hurled and a pack of scavenging dogs ran yelping past him. He watched them disappear around the corner but as he turned back he found his path blocked by a gang of ruffians. They stared at him, sizing him up with their hard faces and cruel eyes, jeering him with a confidence that told him he was their victim. Unkempt and ragged, they jostled together, gaunt faces taking on an eagerness to be done with this easy prey before them. The majority of the boys, for most of them were little more than that, were thin and under-developed, but in possession of an attitude more fearsome than Will had ever encountered before. Knowledge of the territory, and ability to survive by the rules of the pack, gave the gang its power. That and the heavily spiked cudgels they brandished.

Will turned to run, only to find that the group had divided and cut him off. He was completely surrounded by thugs. They moved in closer. Will could see nothing beyond the sea of dirty, menacing faces. A knife flashed.

'I've nothing to give.' he said quickly. 'No money. Nothing.'

The leader's face was criss-crossed with scars, old and new. Enjoying every minute of the easy sport, he leered at Will, revealing broken teeth and a blast of foul breath, and moved in closer. Will circled, but rough fists in his back prevented any retreat. There was no avenue of escape and his persecutors knew it. He cast about desperately looking for help but could not see beyond the gang and there were far too many of them for him to ever escape. The situation was grim and Will felt real fear.

'Well, we'll just have to take your fancy clothes then, won't we?' the leader grinned in anticipation. 'I'm sure we'll find something of value on such a well dressed young man. And you won't be wanting any clothes when we've finished.' He slowly brought up the knife towards Will's throat, and although Will struggled, many hands held him rigid. His eyes were transfixed by the knife as it came ever closer, and he became mesmerised by the glinting steel dancing just inches from his face.

Shouts of encouragement from those anxious to see blood, rang around the lane – 'Go on, cut him!' Get on with it! Let's see him twist under the blade. See how he likes it!'

Suddenly, a shout came from down the street and a group of youths charged full pelt into Will's assailants with fists flying. The knife went clattering over the street and heavy punches sent bodies spinning and sprawling over one another. Will watched in astonishment as noses were smashed and heads beaten. The efficiency of the fighters was impressive and in no time the gang was routed. Limping, bleeding and nursing their wounds, they scattered into the alleys.

Breathing hard from the fight, Joseph came towards Will. In an instant the surly youth had changed into a hero, a saviour, causing Will to feel weak and heady with relief and gratitude, and no small degree of astonishment. But Joseph was angry and his eyes blazed. 'You're not wanted around here. You with your fancy clothes an' all. I don't know how you've lasted this long.'

Will knew that he had been unimaginably close to losing his life. The fight had been quick but vicious, and this gang of Joseph's had displayed an impressively efficient method of despatching the thugs. Yet despite having done nothing other than scramble clear of the melee, and watch in astonishment, Will was breathing heavily and his heart was hammering. 'Joseph, thank you.' He offered a shaky hand. 'I don't know what would have happened if you hadn't come along. I think you saved my life.'

Joseph wiped away a trickle of blood from his nose and knocked aside the offered hand with a sneer. 'Oh, you'd have been dead alright. But save your thanks. I didn't do it for you. You've no business here. I did it for Seamus. He likes you, but God knows why. Next time, we won't be around to save your rotten English hide, so just understand that and go.'

Will hadn't thought Joseph capable of making such a long speech, but his words penetrated and he knew they were right. Still reeling from the shock of the attack and of Joseph turning out to be his reluctant protector, Will knew that he had already outstayed his welcome, that it was indeed time to go. That night he squared his rent with Mrs. Branagan and told the family that he would be leaving in the morning. When he recounted the details of the incident in glowing terms of Joseph's bravery, Seamus slapped Will's back and laughed. 'Surely you know you have provided him and his pals with the best entertainment they could have had. They love nothing on this earth more than a good fight, Will!'

But Seamus also knew that it was dangerous for him to stay and the time was right for him to go. This wasn't Will's place. That night as they settled themselves down on the floor and lay waiting for sleep Seamus said 'There's something I have to ask you. When you find a place, and on Sundays, if you're not working, could you maybe teach me to write? I need to write, Will. I don't intend to stay a labourer all my life.'

Will shifted over on the hard floor and spoke into the darkness. 'Of course I'll teach you. You'll pick it up in no time. I'll send word to you and you know where to find me at Bonhams.'

Early in the morning, before sunrise, Will heaved his trunk on his shoulder and quietly slipped out of the house. He was anxious to be away from the vicinity before anyone was up and about. Even so, as a light mist hovered between the ramshackle houses, and he picked his way down the rubbish-strewn street, it was to the sound of a hacking cough and a crying baby, some of the sounds he would always associate with his time in the slum district of New York.

Chapter 8

Outside the warehouse, Will sat on his trunk and waited. When Mr. Bonham arrived, he explained that he needed the morning off to go and find lodgings. The day promised to be just as hot as ever. He made his way towards an acceptable district, where the houses were brick and the streets wide enough for two carts to pass, and people could walk safely without risking limbs in collision with handcarts.

There were small shops of all kinds, and the streets were lively with people purposefully going about their business. Trade carts plied up and down, delivering stock and street traders called out their wares. Tantalising aromas of pies and delicacies wafted the air. Will enjoyed the colourful scene and busy atmosphere.

Eventually, he found a room on the second floor of a substantial building. The air inside was relatively cool, the window afforded a view and the fire-grate was large enough for heating the room in the winter. He was left with little money after paying for a week's rent, so deposited the box and hurried back to the warehouse to work.

That evening he rushed back to his street and bought a small pie for supper.

Sparsely furnished, with one chair and a lumpy bed, his new home was not the height of luxury, but it afforded privacy and was better than sleeping on the floor of a crowded slum in a smelly lane. In fact, Will felt quite proud of it. He wrote another letter home.

Although he sent word to Seamus, two weeks went by before he made contact. As Will left the office one evening, he was waiting. Will noticed the fatigue on Seamus' face. His eyes looked red-rimmed and sore and despite the sunburn, his face was haggard.

'You look exhausted.' Will said.

'Fourteen hour shifts. And the heat really builds up in the holds. Now are you going to show me your new home?'

They walked along the streets to the modest lodging. Comparing the district with the run-down wooden houses in the dockland area, Seamus was impressed. 'Can you afford to eat after you've paid for this?'

'Yes, I can. Just. In fact I can afford to buy you a pint of ale,' Will said impulsively. He was pleased to see his friend. They walked to the end of the street and entered the tavern.

'So you've worked every single day?'

'When the ships are in and the work is there, you take it. The loading foremen know I'm a good worker. I'm one of the first to be picked now.'

'Your health will suffer if you don't take a rest soon. I take Sundays off. Why don't you come over here?'

'To start the writing lessons?'

'Of course.'

'Then Sunday it is.'

The leaves began to turn to deep gold, fiery red and burnished bronze, and the autumn air became noticeably cooler. Will felt confident that he was making progress at Bonhams and had received a welcome pay rise. Week by week, his meagre existence allowed him to add to his small but significant savings. He had been told that the winter could be severe, and he knew he would need to buy coal.

Seamus proved an able pupil and was quick to learn. Will looked forward to their Sundays together. The lesson was always followed by a decent meal and a tankard of ale.

Seamus laboured over his alphabet, head down and forehead crinkled in concentration. Will put down his letter to his parents and hoped that they wouldn't have too much difficulty in deciphering his cramped scrawl. Paper was not cheap or easy to find. He picked up and re-read for the twentieth time the letter from his mother. What a great day that was. A letter from home. He had torn open the seal and read it immediately, even though he had been halfway through a ledger entry at the time. It had remained in his pocket, like a talisman. Just knowing that it was there was his link to home, reinforcing the belief that kept him going; that this was just a temporary life, an endurance from which he would learn and become strong. He never expected to enjoy it.

He pictured the Beesthorpe woods in their autumn colours, the blackberry hedges and the horses straining to pull the plough over Bark Hill. Without realising, he sighed wistfully.

'Ah, your inheritance, Will. Is all well with your estate, then? Is your uncle caring for it properly, while you wait for him to die?'

Seamus teased constantly about his privilege. Will ignored him and went to stand by the window. The view across the road was of more buildings all the same, but a short way down a side street stood a cluster of mature maple trees and various bushes. It was a sanctuary amidst the bustle and constant activity of the new city, and Will watched as the branches swayed in the blustery wind. Crisp leaves, a mixture of shades, still clung to the boughs, but each gust sent a flurry of colour whirling into the sky, then gathering in heaps on the ground.

Through the leaves a woman slowly walked. She carried a baby against her chest and turned her face close to her child in maternal protection. She gazed up at the colourful boughs and beyond to the clouds chasing across the sky. Will watched her intently. The hood of her long cloak was turned up, but strands of hair had escaped and flicked up and down the side of her cheek. Will struggled to gauge the colour but the woman turned and walked away.

The very next Sunday, she was there again. Will had been reluctant to tear himself away from the window to attend to his teaching duties and was rewarded with the sight of her walking across the street. This time, the day being mild, the hood was down and revealed her hair in its full glory. Rich and full, the curls fell to her shoulders in chestnut waves. She held her child close and sauntered on down the street. Where was her husband? Why was she always alone? Will became intrigued and watched out for her every week.

The pleasant autumn days turned colder and as December arrived, so did the harsh frosts. Will spent his days huddled over his account books, scratching out the bills of lading with half-frozen fingers The port stayed open and, although reduced in numbers, shipping continued to bring in trade. Wealthy men bought up whole consignments and then sold to merchants for distribution. The wheels of commerce continued to turn. Even the prostitutes still earned their living.

One commodity, however, continued to fill Will with unease and distaste; the regular arrival of slave ships. They tied up on the pier, herded the occupants of the filthy holds on deck and, after cleaning them up, led them, manacled, to the slave market. Shivering in the poor clothing that had been distributed to them, they shuffled down the quayside, bewildered and dejected, to await their fate.

Every time Will witnessed the pitiful procession, he was filled with shame.

He attended church on Sunday mornings and was relieved to find that there was a spirited movement for reform. He gladly added his name to petitions, but had little faith that the practice would ever be stopped. Despite being regularly denounced from the pulpit, it was big business. Most of the wealthy households owned slaves, and many businessmen bought and then sold the black human cargo for work in the mills or on the farms in the north. The slave market flourished.

Will was thankful that slaves were not a commodity with which Bonhams dealt. His conscience would have been sorely tested. Undoubtedly, trade was what drove New York on. Businessmen made fortunes and the effect worked its way down to even the lowly. The money circulated, and jobs were available.

Will became more and more concerned for Seamus. Occasionally, he would catch sight of him on the docks. Usually, he was bent low under a weighty sack, working in all weathers. The exertion made him sweat, and then the freezing wintry winds made him shiver. He developed a hacking cough and often fell asleep in Will's chair on his one day of rest. Yet despite the relentless toil, Seamus never missed a Sunday and made good progress with his reading and writing. Will knew it was the daily physical drudgery which drove him on and forced him to persevere all the more. The only way out of doing that for the rest of his life was to learn to write.

'I'm not staying a labouring dock-hand forever, you know. There's money to be made in this city and I can do it as well as the next man.' Seamus focused himself on his future, even during that first long and painful winter.

Will wrote a letter home to Ireland for him, but he couldn't help asking. 'Will your family be able to read these letters, Seamus?'

'No. But my mother will take them to the priest and he'll read them to her. Believe me, her chest will be fit to burst with pride. And look,' Seamus dug into his pocket and brought out five dollars, 'I shall send this home for my brother, Patrick. He'll be coming to America as soon as he can – maybe even by this time next year ...' Will looked down at the money and knew how hard Seamus had driven himself to earn it.

January brought the snow and the city lay muffled under a thick white cover. Will trudged through the icy streets to the warehouse but the activity on the quayside was muted. Only the bare necessities were completed. As he warmed his cramped hands by the warehouse office fire, for once, all ledgers up to date, he took advantage of the lull to speak to Mr. Bonham about Seamus. 'I have a friend, who is a labourer and works very hard. He is honest and reliable and can read and write. If a position of foreman becomes available, in the spring when the ships come back, would you consider him?'

Mr. Bonham leaned back in his chair and scrutinized his young clerk. 'You say he can read and write – and know his figures?'

'Yes, Sir. I know it for a fact because I have taught him myself. Every Sunday for months now. He has a good grasp of his letters and has learned very quickly.'

'And you sailed over together from England? Did you know one another before you sailed?'

'No, Sir. We met on the voyage.'

Mr. Bonham continued to regard Will silently. Eventually, he spoke his thoughts. 'I know you were penniless on your arrival, but you are well educated and obviously from a good family, and yet you have gone out of your way to help and look out for an Irish labourer.'

'Mr. Branagan's family were very kind to me on my arrival in New York. And yes, he is a good friend. I want to see him do well for himself.'

'Very well. I'll see what I can do. In the meantime, Mr. Bristowe, it is your prospects that we must address. Although I did wonder at first how long you would last, you have acquitted yourself well here. Would you consider taking the post of head clerk? You could take some responsibilities off my shoulders. Keep the accounts in order. I need someone I can trust. Naturally, your wages will be increased considerably.'

Will stammered and stuttered his acceptance and Mr. Bonham's wrinkled old face broke into a rare smile. 'Good.'

The pride with which Will wrote to his mother and informed her of his promotion was evident with every line. He felt confident and independent, and sure that even his father and Uncle Samuel would approve of his modest success. He bought an extra bag of coal for his fire and celebrated with Seamus that Sunday.

As always, although he couldn't have explained why, he kept a look-out for the woman. Briefly, he thought he saw her, but it was unlikely she would venture out in the snow with her baby.

Will hardly knew anyone living in his building, being only on nodding terms with a few familiar faces as they passed on the stairs or entered the hallway together. Everyone's rest was precious and the working day came around all too soon. But the street tradesmen and inn-keepers were another matter. Will knew most of them by name. He enjoyed their jovial banter, conducted in a variety of languages, and always returned their greetings.

One day, purchasing a pie from the corner shop, he hesitated, looking for a reason to spend a few more moments in the comforting warmth next to the baking oven. 'I wondered, Mrs. Brown, do you know of a lady in this street, with chestnut hair and a baby?'

The enquiry sounded foolish but Mrs. Brown immediately gave it her full attention. 'Well, now. Unless I'm very much mistaken, that sounds like Mrs. Garcia. Such a nice lady.'

'Ah,. yes, of course. Thank you, Mrs. Bailey. Goodbye.' Will raised his hat and fled from the shop. Of course she would be married. She had a child, after all. He didn't know why he needed to know her name anyway.

The ships from England were fewer, and Will had to wait for the letter which would tell him how pleased everyone was with his news. The chilling damp penetrated his clothes. There were, it seemed to him, two types of snow. Either it was frosted with bitter cold temperatures which froze the lungs, or wet and melting, when the damp chilled him to his very bones. But his life was much easier than that of his friend.

Seamus' cough grew worse but he never eased up. With fewer ships to unload, the foremen still chose him for work, knowing they would get their value. Every Sunday he dragged himself to Will's lodgings, dozed in front of the fire and ate the food that Will brought up from the corner shop. His lips were cracked and bleeding, and his cheeks red and raw with the cold. The rags he had wrapped around his hands did little to protect them, but even with swollen fingers he still struggled to hold a quill and form his letters.

Seamus' determination earned him Will's deep respect. 'They said the winters could be harsh, but this just seems to go on and on. How much more can you take?'

'Don't you worry your English head about me. I'm glad of the work. Plenty of them laid off until the ships start coming regular. And me? Why, by then I'll be writing like a scholar, won't I?'

'Yes, Seamus. You will.'

'And by the springtime, this cough will be gone.'

Will nodded. He rubbed his hands to help the circulation, and huddled nearer to the meagre embers in the fire-grate. He quite forgot what it felt like to be warm. He really thought that springtime would never come.

It was late February when Will caught sight of the woman. From his window, he gazed down on the colourless street in the fading light of the Sunday afternoon. He recognized her cloak and the form of the child, clutched to her chest. Snow still lay on the ground and the street was icy. She leaned into the wind and stumbled forward as she struggled to keep her balance. Without thinking, Will turned and raced down the stairs. Out on the street, the cold wind blasted him as it funnelled between the buildings.

'May I help you? I saw you stumble.' Will drew level with the woman and she turned towards him. They stared at each other for a moment. Will couldn't remember having seen green eyes before. The cold had pinched her cheeks and her lips were blue and cracked, but all he saw were her eyes.

'I live only a few buildings away, up the street.' Her voice was soft and she seemed genuinely surprised at the offer of help. 'But thank you, anyway.'

The child squirmed and a mop of black hair escaped from the blanket. The woman quickly covered the baby up again.

'I'd like to help you, if I may. Perhaps I could carry something for you?' She smiled and shook her head.

'Then take my arm on this icy part of the road.' Without waiting for a reply, Will grasped her elbow and together they negotiated the ice and made their way up the street. Will discovered that she lived on the ground floor of a building barely one hundred yards from his own. He stood awkwardly in the doorway as she crossed the room to place the child in a cot. From under her cloak, she brought out a bag and laid out the provisions she had ventured out to buy, on the table. 'You are very kind.'

Will hesitated on the threshold. 'My friend will be wondering where I am.' He cast his eyes around the room, looking for some sign of a husband, but there was none. 'Do you live alone?' he asked.

'Yes.'

'Oh.'

Glancing at the baby in the cot, she offered an explanation. 'My husband died. Last June. His ship went down.'

'I am so sorry. My name is Will Bristowe.'

The woman walked towards him and extended her hand. 'Eliza Garcia. Thank you for your help.'

'You are most welcome.' Will managed a small smile, trying to hide the rush of emotion that he so inexplicably felt, and finally turned with reluctance towards the street. He raced as fast as the slippery roadway would allow, back to his room. Seamus blinked sleepily from the chair by the fire. 'Where did you go? And in such a hurry?'

'Oh, just to help someone over the ice.' Will tried to sound casual.

'Someone? Who?'

'Well ... actually, a lady.' Will stopped trying to hide the excitement. 'I've seen her all winter, in the street from time to time. She has a child and she's very beautiful. And now I've discovered that she's a widow.'

'So, you've taken a fancy to her, have you?'

'No. No. I know nothing about her. I don't know how old she is, or anything.' Will pretended to read one of his letters and Seamus grinned.

The winter wore on and finally the snow disappeared for good. Will threw himself wholeheartedly into the responsibilities of his new job, returning to his room late every evening. The port was soon operating again at full capacity. Once more, the coopers' yards turned out hundreds of barrels to order and the quayside chandlers did a constant trade. The preacher resumed his position on a packing crate. Armed with his bible and a passionate desire to rid the world of sin, his rich voice boomed out over the wharf as he did his best to persuade the fallen to renounce their evil ways and turn to the Lord for their salvation.

Also mingling with the sinful and the lost was the quiet figure of an Irish priest, Father Kennedy, lately of County Cork. He considered no-one, however lowly, undeserving of his time and attention. Will had frequently noticed Seamus in conversation with him.

Mr. Bonham, true to his word, put forward Seamus for the job as foreman with a neighbouring warehouse, and he was given a week's trial. At the end of the week, the boss declared himself satisfied that Seamus had grasped the task of labelling and signing the loading bills, and marking off the correct weights. At last he was using his head instead of his muscles.

Will was just as delighted as Seamus with the promotion. The hard work and the winter had taken a worrying toll of Seamus' health, but now it was time to celebrate the upturn of his fortunes. At the local tavern they drank a toast to each other. 'I broke the news to Aunt Kathleen and Uncle Daniel today.' Seamus said. 'I'll not be lodging with them now I've enough money to have a room of my own.'

'I'm glad. It'll be better than the floor with all those draughts round your backside.'

'Ah, when you've done a hard day's work, you'll sleep anywhere. But it's time to move on. The first step to success. I've some money saved, you know, as well as sending some home to Ireland. I'll be looking for smart lodgings like yours now, Will.'

'Perhaps some new clothes, too?'

'Ah. Maybe. Nothing fancy, mind. I don't want to be taken for a bloody Englishman!'

The search for lodgings proved fruitful. Just a couple of streets away from Will, Seamus secured a room with a bed and a fireplace – and privacy. 'Can you believe it? A whole room to myself?' This upturn in circumstances renewed Seamus' vigour and before long he was back to his old self.

When the mood took him he called on Father Kennedy to attend confession or Mass, and later indulge in nostalgic dreams of home, but still Sundays were spent with his friend.

'Have you seen your pretty widow again lately?' Seamus asked.
'No. I haven't.'

'Why don't you call on her? You know where she lives.'

'I've been hoping to see her in the street, but there has been no sign. Perhaps she's gone away.'

'If you don't call on her, you won't find out. At least you know her name.'

At the corner shop, Will asked Mrs.Brown if she had seen Mrs. Garcia lately.

'Gone to Connecticut. To her relatives.'

'Is she coming back, do you know?'

'I'm sure I've no idea. She pays her bills is all I know.'

The April sunshine bathed the trees opposite Will's window and played on the fresh green leaves gradually unfurling in the warmth. His world of constant work was becoming tedious. He wanted to escape, to go out into the country and explore the area – the dock-yards he knew well enough. He had thrown himself wholeheart-edly into his new job and was beginning to get a sound grasp of business, but he wanted more. He looked back fondly at the pampered life of comfort that had been his upbringing. But it didn't do to dwell on it too much. Generally, looking back on the old life brought on dissatisfaction and melancholy; not a frame of mind he cared to battle with all week, waiting for Sunday when he'd see Seamus, and perhaps Mrs. Garcia.

True, this new-found independence brought its own satisfac-tions, but it had been a hard six months. Both Seamus and he were doing well, paying their bills and managing to save a little money – yet even so, the life was not as he had imagined. Despite the fact that they had annoyed and irritated him, he really missed his family. Josiah Bonham was a good man, as were his other acquain-tances, but Will had not exactly fitted into a society. Were it not for Seamus, he would be feeling very isolated in this growing city.

Will longed to hire a horse, head out into the open countryside and enjoy again a sense of freedom. He felt confined in the streets, there was no diversion and his life seemed intolerably small. What he wouldn't give for a day's hunting! He thought of the spring-greened hedgerows at Beesthorpe and imagined himself thundering down the valley, his heartbeat quickening at the sound of the horn and the baying hounds. Spurred on with the excitement of the gallop, ever faster and ever more daring, he would clear the hedges and be up with the hounds for the kill. The dream faded but the pangs of homesickness stayed deep within him.

Will wandered outside to sit under the trees, listening to the whispering boughs and smelling the freshness of the small park. From up the street he noticed a woman walking towards him and his heart lurched as chestnut hair billowed about her in the breeze. The child she had hoisted on her hip was bigger but he knew the woman was Eliza. She had recognized him too, and when she came closer she smiled.

'I thought you had gone away for good.' Will finally managed to say.

'No. Just for a few weeks to stay with my family in Connecticut. They wanted to see Mary Ann and I needed some care myself.' She looked a little embarrassed. 'It was a hard winter.'

'Yes, it was.' Will knew she didn't just mean the weather.

'So this is Mary Ann.' Will looked closely at the child who clung so tightly and bore little resemblance to her mother. Out of the baby face, solemn eyes regarded him and dark curls framed the serious expression. She turned her head away, not wanting the attention of the stranger.

Will's spirits lifted considerably after his encounter with Eliza. They began to meet by the trees on Sunday afternoons and gradually formed a bond of friendship. Long and easy conversations revealed to each other their personal lives. Eliza heard all about England, the farms and his family. Talking about them made the memories more real for Will, and his enthusiasm to relate anecdotes and descriptions led him to chatter on for a long time.

Fortunately, Eliza was a good listener. In turn, when she felt confident enough to embark on it, she related the story of her romance and love for her husband, and how bleak her future had looked when he died. All the while, little Mary Ann lay on the grass beneath the trees, content with the close attention of her mother. For the first time since leaving England, Will felt happy and lived the whole week in anticipation of Sunday afternoons.

'Isn't it time for you to go and meet your lady friend?'

Will had held back, not wanting to run out on Seamus, but the sunshine beckoned, as well as the prospect of some precious time with Eliza. 'I shan't be long.' he said. 'Do you mind?'

'Mind? You great fool! That lady brings a smile to your face that no-one else can. If you want my opinion, it's a lucky man you are.'

Chapter 9

Will realised quite soon that the affection he had for Eliza was beginning to turn into love, but he couldn't decide whether the whole business of being in love was worth all the anguish of being apart. When they were together, he studied carefully every aspect of her features and curve of her body. On Sundays, as they strolled the streets and explored the city together, he listened attentively and carried the tone of her voice in his head so that he could daydream of her and replay their conversations later in the week.

Sometimes he would carry Mary Ann, enabling Eliza to walk with her parasol. It was green, the shade of fresh grass, and matched her dress, which in turn brought out the vivid colour of her eyes. Her chestnut hair was fastened high on her head and ringlets curled down to the curve of her neck, where she wore a silver locket.

Will had to force himself to turn his head away from her occasionally. He wanted to gaze and gaze, just drinking in her loveliness, but he feared his unrelenting stares made her uncomfortable. Before long, just the simple anticipation of their meeting set him dancing with a lightness of spirit. As the appointed hour drew close, the whirling and spinning sensation in his head virtually catapulted him into a state of nervous incoherence. By the time they actually met, he felt almost sick with delight. And then her nearness imposed even more exquisite torture. The lightest brush of her arm or touch of her hand sent excitement searing through his veins. How odd, he reflected when alone in his room, that such a wonderful feeling could evoke such agonies. For the first time in his life, Will was in love.

Along with this surge of passion and happiness, the springtime gave way once more to the full heat of summer.

The tasks facing Will at the warehouse office continued to mount. Import and export tariffs levied on the company's consignments were carefully monitored and recorded. The clerks battled daily with the mounting paperwork, their ink-stained fingertips gripping the quill pens as they scratched the numbers into the appropriate columns. Ledgers, bills, forms and customers dominated the working day, but more than once Will blessed the fact that he was earning his living in the cool of the warehouse rather than the merciless heat of the dockyard.

Every day, as he left the office and the cavernous building in the late evening, he encountered the prostitutes sauntering along the roads leading to the quayside. Will had come to know them all by sight, easy as it was to single them out by their gaudy attire and colourful shawls. Night after night, they walked the streets, hopeful of earning enough money to pay a few debts and eat a decent meal. The ships constantly entering and leaving port brought a plentiful supply of customers, both to the whores and the taverns. The sailors had barely to stagger a few yards off the ships to find themselves all the drink and women they could want. Fights were commonplace but Will knew which alleyways to avoid and had become well acquainted with all the signs of possible dangers.

He looked back at the innocent young man he had been just a year ago and smiled at his own naivety. He had been so ill at ease and ill prepared for survival in this bustling city, but now he felt quite at home amongst the crime, the immorality and the danger.

Seamus' new job as foreman took him a significant step up the labourer's ladder. Thankful to be no longer heaving great sacks around from one place of storage to the next, sweating and parched under the relentless sun, he now dashed from site to site, checking consignments. The first time he had signed his name on a loading bill had been a precious moment to savour. He had stood and stared at it for quite a while, and nodded seriously in a kind of homage, before resuming orders to the men.

Seamus had had little time for leisure since arriving in New York, yet nothing had escaped his notice. He had witnessed the luxurious lives of the rich, as compared with the daily struggle for existence of the poor, and constantly kept his eyes open for an opening, a way of doing some small business that would in turn help him achieve an advancement in his circumstances. Seamus Branagan was ambitious and had set his sights on a lavish lifestyle. Whilst he was prepared to work hard for his pay, he also expected the small daily deals he made to provide the beginnings of the extra security he craved.

Slowly, the year moved on for Will and Seamus. Each week the pitiful savings, made by paring down the basic living expenses to the very minimum, grew steadily. For Seamus, it was an improvement to his lifestyle that he once could only have dreamed. For Will, it seemed a meagre life consisting only of toil and drudgery – except for the one person for whom he now lived, who was responsible for an extraordinary explosion of happiness, and who made him long for every day to be Sunday.

One suffocatingly hot Sunday afternoon, Will and Eliza fanned themselves in the shade of the trees, and Mary Ann crawled around them on the grass. Although the thought had been with him day and night for weeks, it was on a sudden impulse that Will summoned all his courage and took Eliza's slim hand gently in his own. He looked deep into her eyes. 'You have come to mean so much to me. I can't imagine life without you. I know I have nothing to offer at the moment. But in the future ...' Will trailed off and took a deep breath. He searched her face for a sign of encouragement though none was visible to him, and all the tender words he had rehearsed seemed to just slide out of his head. 'Well, you know that I stand to inherit the estate in England. I love you so much, Eliza, and more than anything in the world, I want you to be my wife. Please say you will marry me.' In the end the words cascaded out as if by their own will, anxious to be said, regardless of the little hope with which they were accompanied.

'Oh, Will.' Eliza sighed as her hand remained clasped tightly in his, but a wistful look came into her eyes and her expression became one of regret. He waited for her reply but moments passed by and he could hear only the pounding of his heart. She wrinkled her brow in an effort to find the right words to say but her silence told him everything. Leaden with disappointment, Will withdrew his hand.

'I'm sorry. I had no right to presume.' He started to get up.

'No. Wait.' Eliza retrieved Will's hand. She squeezed it gently and her thumb caressed his knuckles as she struggled to express her feelings.

'Will, I care for you very much. You have come to mean a great deal to me too, but marriage is a big step to take.' She lowered her eyes as she spoke and Will felt the sharp stab of rejection. 'Perhaps it is just too soon. I need to think it through. Please ask me again in a month's time and I promise I will give you my answer then.'

'I would care for you and provide well for you and Mary Ann.' Will tried to hide his desperation beneath the solemn words, but he was hurt at her failure to declare her love for him in return. He knew deep in his heart that he needed her. For weeks he had dreamed constantly of their future together and, if she refused him, his life and hopes would be shattered. How could he carry on? For now he had no choice but to accept her prevarication. Perhaps, after consideration, she would begin to love him. At least there was hope.

Somehow, Will had to believe that Eliza would accept his proposal, and he needed to save enough money to enable them to be married. The thought helped him as he worked ceaselessly, day after endless day, living only for the Sundays when he could stroll the streets with her and then sit talking under the trees until the child became restless and brought to an end their precious time together. He confided his torment to Seamus.

'If it's what you want, then it is what will happen, sooner or later'. Seamus assured him. 'Though, since you're asking my advice, it's a big commitment for a young man with his fortune still to make – taking on a wife and another man's child.'

'It is what I want. Believe me. There's nothing else that matters.'

'Then have you considered sending for money from England. The prospect of marriage to a man of means rather than a penniless clerk might tilt the balance. Just talking of your prospects obviously isn't enough.'

'It has to be enough. I can't do that. Asking for money wouldn't be right. I'll find a way of supporting us without begging from the family.'

'So you love her more than anything? More than your precious estate?'

'Yes. More than anything. Even the estate.'

Letters from home arrived at sporadic intervals, and succeeded in fuelling a melancholy loneliness in Will that grew daily. His mother's loving words and anecdotes of the estate and family life were a precious lifeline, yet often served to unsettle his fragile emotions. Mostly, she included a message or remark, sometimes even an instruction, from his father. Will read the letters over and over. Even with an ocean between them and living a totally independent life, still his father thought he knew best. He, who had made nothing of his life, and now lived in bitterness and regret.

Jane wrote letters too. Hers were sometimes pitiful, self-indulgent and full of complaint about her life and limited prospects. '*And, what is more, Mama has insisted on inviting to the house this Sunday the new vicar for Muskham, a certain Reverend Marcus Wilby I understand that he is single and has caused quite a flutter of hearts in the area, but believe me, I am determined to not show myself in an acceptable manner, so I expect it will be unlikely that he will become a regular visitor.*' Will smiled. He knew just how unacceptable his sister could be.

She went on, '*Now, Will, I do not wish to upset you, but there is something you should know regarding your friend, the highwayman. I did listen at the door that day, and I know that's what he was. It has been reported that the robber responsible for thefts on the Great North Road has been caught. And what is more, he has, as you would expect, been hanged at York. It happened last week and everyone is jubilant that the highway threat is now over, at least for the time being. Though I am sure someone else will probably take his place and set about relieving the rich of their valuables. I am sorry if this is sad news for you, but if he is guilty, then justice has been done. Write soon and tell me more about the city and what happens there. I must say, from your letters so far, you do seem to lead a deadly dull life. Your loving sister, Jane.*'

Will had sat on a vacant berthing post on the quayside to read the letter. The hot September sun beat down and he squinted as he looked up. As ever, white sails dotted the Hudson River and the sun sparkled off the tiny waves as each ship navigated its course to an unknown destination. Will gazed unseeingly over the scene. It wasn't just that Ned had been fearless and ready for adventure. There had been a quality about him. Will hesitated to call it honesty, for how could he when Ned had, by his own admission, clearly been a common robber? Yet even so, Will felt that in his heart he had been a good man, and he was saddened by the news of his fate. He made an effort to put the unwanted image of Ned swinging on the scaffold out of his mind. Folding the letter carefully, he walked back to the warehouse.

Eliza stirred the broth simmering in the pot over the fire and then lifted the spoon to taste the brown liquid. She nodded her satisfaction and ladled a portion into a bowl, squashing down the chunks of vegetables to a pulp. Leaving it on the table to cool, she crossed the room to where Mary Ann was seated on her cot, happily playing with a bone ring and carved toys.

It was a pleasant room, filled with sunshine from the tall windows and facing the maple trees which reminded her so much of her home in Connecticut. Eliza felt sure that the building campaign taking place in the city spelled a death sentence for her trees. They could be cut down any day now, so she often stood just looking at them, watching closely as the boughs of vibrant colour swayed gracefully in the breeze. She stooped to pick up the child, talking all the while. 'Here we are, Mary Ann, it's time for your dinner.'

Plump arms and legs waved excitedly and squeaks of anticipation escaped Mary Ann's full baby lips, yet it was still a solemn expression she wore on her round face. Despite her mother's loving attention and endless attempts to amuse her, she had never been a baby given to frequent smiling, and showed no sign of ever doing so, even though she was now beginning to take her first faltering steps. Some thought she was reluctant to show happiness because she had, in some unspoken way, absorbed her mother's sadness, but in fact she was a perfectly contented child, happy to amuse herself and quietly watch her mother perform the daily chores. Her expression was not lively and her face not pretty, but she had a charm and, almost daily, her dark hair became curlier. Mary Ann had taken the colouring and likeness of her father and, being of Mexican descent, she had inherited his black eyes and dark complexion.

Eliza fed her daughter, making the usual motherly sounds of encouragement and praise as the broth was solemnly accepted. Studying the child so closely, she thought for the hundredth time of what the future might hold for them both. In an attempt to come to the right decision concerning the marriage proposal, she made a list in her mind of all the factors to take into consideration.

First, the positive side. Will was a good man. He seemed genuinely to care not only for her, but also for Mary Ann. She enjoyed his company and knew that he was industrious, honest and hard-working. He was prepared to spend his wages in keeping them both, though not in luxury, but who knew what would happen in the future and didn't he always talk about his estate in England? In all possibility she may even become a rich English lady.

Eliza scraped the bottom of the bowl for the last few drops of broth. She couldn't stay living here much longer. Modest though the lodging was, Eduardo's money was running out. The shipping company had paid her a small sum but it wouldn't last forever and she had to think of Mary Ann's future. Of course she could always go back to Connecticut where her welcome was guaranteed, but her aunt and uncle were becoming quite old now and the small area they farmed could barely make enough money to keep themselves, let alone two more. The alternative was to find a job, but what could she do and who would care for Mary Ann?

All this reasoning pointed towards an acceptance of the proposal, and yet she was reluctant. So what were the negative thoughts leaping up in her mind, spoiling everything? She guided a little tin cup towards Mary Ann's mouth and held it steady while her daughter attempted to drink the milk offered. She was trying to wean her and now only offered her the comfort of her breast before she went to sleep. Mary Ann dutifully drank and Eliza mopped up the spilt milk from her chin. Both regarded each other silently.

Eliza's attention wandered and she gazed back towards the window. Only with extreme effort did she manage to marshal her thoughts back to the problem. She mulled over her argument. So why should she refuse him? Reluctantly, she faced the issue and it was a very small voice inside her head which finally articulated the words: 'Because I don't love him.'

If she had never met Eduardo. If she had never known that dizzy spin of excitement as she saw him in the distance, or the hot rush of passion and desire when he held her, she might have regarded the pleasant passing of time with Will as love. But it wasn't. Perhaps it would come later. Perhaps the ease of her loneliness and having someone to rely on and care for her would bring about love. Eliza thought not. In her heart she knew that true love came only once in a lifetime. She removed the silver locket from around her neck and snapped open the clasp. With her fingertip she touched the lock of black hair tightly curled inside; Eduardo's hair.

As her eyes began to prickle she turned her attention once more to Eduardo's child and made her decision.

Will forced open his sleep-filled eyes and focused on the room about him. It was Sunday. It was also the day he would once more ask Eliza to marry him. What would he do if she refused? It would be so hard to carry on in this dreary and lonely state. The dusty little room had been his home for over a year now but it was nothing more than a sanctuary, a place to rest before resuming work.

In a state of self-pity, his thoughts turned to Beesthorpe. Would the brambles with their plump blackberries still be clinging on in the hedgerows, entwined with bryony and rosehips? Would the majestic Bark Hill oak leaves have turned a crisp brown and be fluttering to the earth below? How much longer would it be before Uncle Samuel died? Had he decided on his successor and named Will as his heir?

Although he would have given anything to jump on the next ship bound for England and return to his old life, he knew that the longer he remained independent, the more he would rise in his uncle's estimation. And he needed Eliza. His stomach began to churn as the prospect of a second rejection loomed before him. He groaned and pulled the bedcovers over his head.

The sparsely furnished room and his now shabby and well worn clothes depressed him. He made no haste. Extreme anxiety robbed him of all anticipation to hear the words that would seal his fate. Perhaps he could go home in a year or so. He held on to the thought and somehow found himself walking, with the measured gait and the trembling legs of a condemned man, the short distance up the street. It was with resignation that he finally knocked on Eliza's door that afternoon.

Eliza's smile was warm as she invited Will into her room. She indicated for him to sit in the armchair but he declined and went to stand by the window. Detached and distancing himself from her, he felt certain in his mind that within moments he would receive a second refusal. His earlier resolve to be warm and passionate failed him entirely and he stood stiffly and stared across the room at the object of his love. 'Eliza, I have come to ask you one more time and I need your answer now. Will you marry me?'

Desperation, he knew, was written on his face. He could hear it in his voice. There were no sweet words of undying devotion now; only a proposal of business-like formality. He waited in miserable silence as she turned her face from him and her fingers played with the silver locket at her neck. When she turned back her smile was wide and loving and her green eyes locked on to his. 'Yes, Will. I should like very much to be your wife.'

Will stared in disbelief for a few moments before her words penetrated the fog that was his mind. He had prepared himself so well for rejection that Eliza's words of acceptance failed to register. But she was laughing and holding out her arms to him – and still he stood there like a fool, rooted to the floor.

At last he took in what had happened. Eliza had agreed to marry him. She had actually said yes. His face lit up with joy and he bounded across the room to her. His happiness was so confusing that he could not settle on one action of movement, one minute sweeping Eliza up in his arms and spinning her round, and then stopping suddenly to draw her closer, tender and protective.

'It may not be much at the moment, but I promise I shall give you everything. Today, I am the happiest man alive. All because of you, my very own Eliza.' They kissed and held each other close and suddenly the future looked warm and hopeful. 'We'll plan very carefully' Eliza said. 'I'm good at housekeeping and I know we'll do well together. You'll see.'

Mary Ann was completely forgotten, until she began to cry. Will went to her and picked her up. 'Perhaps I should tell you all about England now – as it will be your home, one day. Shall I tell you about the scent of the bluebells when they turn the woodland to a vibrant blue, or the May blossom clinging to the boughs and bending them low like a snowfall?'

Eliza laughed 'Will, what sentimental foolishness.'

'Can't I be sentimental and foolish on this most wonderful of days?' Mary Ann stared seriously at the face of her soon-to-be stepfather, unaware of any understanding of his words or the effect they would have on her life.

The marriage took place two weeks later, in the little church at the end of their street. Kathleen and Daniel Branagan attended, beaming and heaping all their good wishes on the couple. Even Mr.

Bonham, having heard the news only the day before, arrived in his carriage, courteously greeting everyone. Seamus teased Will and slapped his back numerous times, but secretly his thoughts were taking a different line. Surely this was a step which could only hold a young man back. As far as he could see, the overwhelming certainty after a marriage was children. Lots of them. Lots of little mouths to feed and little bodies to clothe.

Seamus watched the ceremony with mixed emotions. It made him think of his own life and what it held. So far, good fortune had smiled on him, but there was a long way to go yet and, try as he might to glimpse the future, he was pretty sure there would be no wife for him. At least not until he had his big house and estate, by which time of course, a pretty young wife might fit in very nicely. 'Hah!' he thought wryly to himself. 'Even as I watch my best friend make his vows, it's still my own ambitions that occupy my mind. But if I don't hold fast to them, they'll disappear from view, they will. Just like Uncle Daniel and Aunt Kathleen, exchanging one life of drudgery for another. Yes, Will, you'll have the pleasure of a warm bed, but look at the responsibilities. Now, I won't be making that mistake. When an opportunity presents itself, I'll be free to follow it, unencumbered.'

Shaking all these misgivings from his mind, Seamus approached Will and Eliza with a broad smile, kissed Eliza's cheek and pumped Will's hand up and down. 'You have my heartiest congratulations! Never have I seen a more delightful bride and groom. May good fortune smile on you all your long and happy lives together!'

They decided that Eliza's room would be their home for the winter. Stringent economies needed to be made if they were to set aside enough money to find a decent house to rent in the spring. Will rushed home eagerly every evening. The warmth and welcome of organized domesticity, companionship and love quickened his step and lightened his heart. He felt great optimism for the future of his little family.

The nights grew cold, and as soon as their evening meal was over, Will and Eliza made love in the bed by the fireside. They lay in each others arms, content with their simple life, watching the embers of the coals until they died down.

In agreeing to marry him, Eliza had transformed Will's life and he wrote gushing letters, brimming with optimism, to his family in

England. He tried to convey to them his happiness and his letters, now somewhat flamboyant and rambling, ran the risk of becoming a list of the many virtues of his wonderful wife. He was determined that on the day of their triumphant return home, his parents and sister, and even Uncle Samuel, would be pre-disposed to a favourable impression. He was sure that they would love her just as much as he.

So it was with every optimism that they welcomed the new year, but by February Mr. Bonham was talking about closing the business and Eliza began to suspect she might be pregnant.

Chapter 10

'Come in, Will. I need to talk to you.' Josiah Bonham's face, Will noticed, had begun to show some strain. His health had deteriorated lately, but since he had confided his plan to sell the company, his spirit and vigour had evaporated away. Will perched himself on a chair in the cramped little office, surrounded as always by ledgers and documents. For some reason he felt profoundly sad as he faced the shrunken form of his employer.

'I have had an offer for the big warehouse.' Mr. Bonham's voice was quavery and thin. 'They want it for cotton and corn – the bulky trade. You need a big space for those consignments. I hadn't intended to split them up but an idea has occurred to me. I need to discuss it with you.' He raised himself out of his chair and went to stand by the grimy window. He rubbed at the glass with his hand and peered out on the cobbled yard below. Will waited.

'You have done well here. You have a grasp of the finances, I think. Would you like to buy the smaller warehouse and take over that side of the business? Furs don't take up so much space. A valuable commodity. Plenty of profit if you get your turnover going. And molasses and brandy. Even coal if you time it right. What do you say?'

Will stared. 'Mr. Bonham. I have no finances. You may remember that I recently married and now I have the responsibility of a wife and child. It would be quite out of the question. My savings are pitiful.'

'Yes, yes. I took that to be the case. But you are a diligent, educated man and you know the business well now. And I had not forgotten your matrimonial responsibilities. Indeed, with that in mind, I urge you to consider.'

'But, Mr. Bonham …' A raised hand silenced Will.

'Listen to me for a moment. I have built my company up over a lifetime. It means everything to me, now that my family have gone. My health is not what it was, I'm afraid. Really, I have no option but to sell.'

Will twisted on his chair. All this he already knew. But it didn't alter his own circumstances.

Mr. Bonham seemed to read his thoughts. 'But I'll tell you something perhaps you didn't know. When I started, modest though my

79

business was, I had help, a benefactor, someone who was prepared to underwrite my losses. As it happened, I was fortunate, and rarely called on his generosity. But it was there, and it enabled me to operate my dealings to my advantage. It served me well.'

Will sat perfectly still. Mr. Bonham carried on. 'What would you say if I deferred payment for five years? Would you be able to find enough for the day to day expenses? Run the trading company and build up gradually?'

The idea of owning his own company and warehouse rendered Will speechless and his pulse began to race. Finally, despite the fact that he had not one idea in his head how this could be done, he managed to nod cautiously. 'Perhaps. But I would have to work out what was involved.'

'Naturally. You could take a partner. That might help. I could introduce you to someone if you wished.'

'I need a little time to think. But thank you. You are a very kind and generous man to even think of me. Thank you.'

Will's mind was a whirl but Mr. Bonham waved a dismissive hand. 'The money I shall make on the big warehouse will keep me for the rest of my life. I've no children and my wife died some years ago. I live in a big house with servants to see to my needs.' The explanation for his magnanimity ended abruptly. 'I'm giving you a chance, Will. Find a way. Take it.'

Will left the office in a daze and searched frantically along the quayside until he found Seamus. 'Come to see us this evening. There's something I want to discuss with you.'

'What is it?'

'I can't explain now. Just come.'

'Why are you out of breath? Tell me now. It'll be nearly dark before I leave tonight.'

'I can't stop now. But …' Will couldn't help the grin that spread across his face. 'Well, we just might – just might, mind you, have a chance to start a business.'

'What?' Seamus' eyebrows shot up. 'Tell me more!' But his shouts were to Will's back as he was already running back up the causeway.

If a mistake was ever to be made in Will's ledgers, he knew it would be that afternoon. It was so hard to concentrate. All those thoughts flying about in his head, and no feasible solution in sight.

By the time he reached home he had convinced himself that despite the fortuitous offer, he did not have the means to capitalise on it.

He noticed how pale and tired Eliza seemed, and decided not to raise her hopes by discussing it before Seamus arrived.

The two men perched on the bed and Eliza sat in the chair as Will made his announcement. 'The question is – have we between us, enough money to pay our way until we start to show some trading profit?'

Seamus leapt to his feet. 'This is our chance! We've both worked hard and if we pool our resources now, we can be proper businessmen, making good money.'

Eliza caught the mood, too, and before long they were working out the arithmetic and adding together their meagre savings. Even the precious guinea, still hiding in the lining of Will's coat, was taken into account. There was not enough. A silence fell.

Desperate not to see the prospect of good fortune slipping away, Seamus turned to Will. 'Well now, with you having a rich family back in England, couldn't you be asking for a loan to help us through the first few months?'

'No.' Will's response was immediate. He had been thinking along those lines all afternoon. The risk was too great. If the business failed and his uncle's money was lost, then the Beesthorpe estate would never be his.

Seamus tried again. 'Could we give up our lodgings to save on the rent?'

'And where would we live?'

'At the warehouse. You're not telling me we can't fix something decent up and live there – just for a few months.'

Will looked across at Eliza. 'I can't ask my wife to live at the dockside with drunken sailors and painted whores for company!'

Eliza spoke up. 'We must think about this very carefully, Will. If it will make the difference that is needed, then surely we can do it. The springtime isn't far away, and we can keep ourselves private. It could work and I'm willing to try.'

'We can't let this chance pass us by.' Seamus pressed. 'Your Mr. Bonham is a good man to be making this offer. Even if we don't make it work, at least we will have tried. Isn't that what we all want?'

Glad that she had so far kept the news of her pregnancy from Will, Eliza realised that to tell him now would jeopardize everything. She would keep it to herself a little longer.

In early March, a handcart delivered their belongings to the side door of the three-storey warehouse. Eliza picked her way past the prostrate form of a sailor, sleeping off the effects of brandy, and pretended not to notice the painted women furtively loitering in the doorways. Will carried Mary Ann and ushered his wife through the rough door and into her new home.

Wooden steps, devoid of any handrail, led up to the second floor where one corner had been screened off. Daylight struggled to shine through the grime-smeared window panes, but in the gloom Eliza was able to make out a bed and a table. The pervading smell was of dust and mould with a hint of sweetness, which she presumed was from the consignments of molasses. She tried hard not to show how dispiriting she found it, but was unable to hold back a scream as a large rat scuttled across the floor in front of them. 'We've set traps,' was all Will could say.

Eliza looked around, shivered and pulled her shawl close about her. She would do her utmost to make the best of it but knew that it would be a challenge to stay cheerful. She went back outside to fill a bucket of water from the pump, put on her apron, rolled up her sleeves, and then proceeded to scrub everything in sight. She made up the bed and lay down on it, cuddling Mary Ann close. She would endure this; she would cope somehow, but she shuddered at the prospect of having her baby here.

Will and Seamus worked in a high state of anxiety. The staff had been dismissed, to be re-appointed when the port returned to full trading capacity. They were awaiting a shipment of furs from high up on the Hudson River. Mr. Bonham's final gesture had been to provide the money to cover one cargo load, and it was due any day.

'Come out here, Eliza! Come and see!' Seamus' excited voice carried up the steps to Eliza. She scooped up Mary Ann and followed him out through the door. Will was just stepping down off the bottom rung of a ladder, clutching a hammer. He grinned as he looked back up at the wall. All three of them stood side by side on the waterfront, gazing up at the new sign high over the main doors. BRISTOWE & BRANAGAN TRADING COMPANY

'Would you ever have believed it?' Seamus stood between Will and Eliza and put his arms around both of them. The three of them smiled broadly, savouring the moment and trying hard to banish the tinges of worry which crept unbidden into their minds.

If Seamus could have lived on fresh air, he would have. He had no regard for his own needs, happily making his bed in a distant corner of the warehouse, and eating only when Eliza brought him something she had prepared. In the numbing cold of the thawing snows, they settled themselves in and waited to see how their destiny lay.

The day the ship carrying the furs from the north tied up on the pier was one of frantic activity from morning until night. Seamus' natural ability and experience of making street deals carried him through and soon a bargain was struck. Unloading began and one floor of the warehouse soon filled up with bales of cured pelts, destined to decorate and clothe the elite of New York society. Will attended to the paperwork and contacted the merchants. Within a week, a healthy return had been made and the ship had returned up-river for a further consignment, duly promised to Bristowe & Branagan. They were in business.

At last, Eliza broke the news to Will that he was to become a father. He was overjoyed, yet the prospect of a baby made him even more unhappy about their living conditions. 'If the baby is due in September, then we must have found a house by August.' he said. He rushed back to the office to pore over the ledgers once more, trying to predict what returns they might have made, and how they would stand financially by then.

Every week, Josiah Bonham paid a visit to his old warehouse and its new owners. He tried not to interfere, only offering the benefit of his experience with sound advice. He understood the need for them to live on the premises but it caused him concern. 'The health of your wife and child must come above all else, Will.' he said. 'Believe me, I know.'

The warm weather eventually arrived and the nearby streets became heavy with pungent odours, causing further nausea to Eliza. Beer-swilling sailors cavorted raucously late into the night and thieves and pickpockets reaped their harvest. Will and Eliza never ventured out at night. If they needed to feel the night air on their skin, they would sit by the gaping windows of the warehouse watching the gently swaying lamps of the ships enter into competition with the star-studded sky above.

At busy times, Eliza helped Will with the ledgers, copying out and filling in the columns. Despite the difficulties, it was a happy summer, full of satisfaction at their growth of turnover, and ceaseless wonder that such unexpected good fortune had come their way. Eliza's pregnancy quietly continued.

'Will Bristowe is a very fortunate young man to have found himself such a wife.' Josiah Bonham said to Eliza on one of his visits. He had entered the office behind her and raised his hat as he approached. She put down the quill and smiled up at him.

'You can't stay here much longer, my dear. You know that. Before the baby is due, you must find a suitable house.'

'We will.' she assured him. He nodded and smiled, raised his hat again, and left.

With one month to go, Will began the search for accommodation, but the late arrival of an expensive shipment of furs set the business back. Buyers, awaiting the stock, were forced to purchase from elsewhere. Will worried that they had lost the market. He was unable to commit himself to renting a property without incurring debts, something they had all agreed to try not to do.

It was on an airless September night that Eliza went into labour in her partitioned section of the warehouse. A midwife was called and Will spiralled into a great state of agitation as he heard the agonised moans of childbirth through the thin partition. Eventually, when Mary Ann awoke, he scooped her up in his arms and went to sit by the window. Seamus joined him and from his pocket produced a bottle of rum. They took turns to swig back the rich liquor as they watched the harbour lights twinkling against the inky night sky.

With the sleeping Mary Ann in his arms, and the warming comfort of the rum taking its effect, Will found it easy to confide in his friend. 'I love Eliza more than ever. She has such faith in me and I know I don't deserve it. I feel the most terrible guilt that I have brought her to give birth in a warehouse.'

'Eliza's a strong woman. And you're a lucky man. Now stop your worrying.' Seamus handed the bottle back to Will.

When the lusty cry echoed through the building Seamus slapped Will's back and took Mary Ann from him. 'Give me the little one.

You go to your wife and child.' he said.

Will's heart was pounding as he approached the bed. Eliza's hair was matted and stuck to her sweat-drenched face, but her eyes were full of pride as she reached out her hand to him. 'We have a son; a beautiful baby boy.'

The midwife wrapped a blanket around the baby, still loudly announcing his arrival, and passed him to Will. Standing under the light of the lamp, he gazed down and felt his chest tighten with pride.

'So what is his name to be?' Eliza whispered.

'I should like it to be Samuel Ellis Bristowe.'

Eliza nodded and smiled before the sleep of exhaustion claimed her. Placing his son safe in the crib beside his mother, Will hurried back to share the news.

'Samuel Ellis Bristowe.' he declared proudly to Seamus.

'Ah, yes. Your uncle will be pleased with that.'

Will went to his office and wrote, by candlelight, and in a high state of emotion, the letter to his mother. It was an immediate connection to his home, his family and to Beesthorpe, and he dreamed of the great day he would take his wife and child back to England, to their inheritance.

The following day, Josiah Bonham arrived on the quayside. 'My warmest congratulations to you.' he said to Will on hearing the news. 'Now please allow me to help. I should like to make the offer for your wife and children to stay with me until you have found a suitable house.' Will began to protest but Mr. Bonham held up his hand. 'I cannot bear to think of Eliza lying-in here, in the gloom of this warehouse. And think of the risk – the baby could catch disease from the vermin. Besides, it would give me great pleasure to have a baby in the house after all these years.' He looked directly at Will and, with more emotion than Will had thought him capable, said 'Don't be too proud to allow an old man the privilege of being of service.'

Within hours, a carriage arrived to transport Eliza and the baby, along with Mary Ann, to Josiah Bonham's grand house. With servants fussing over them, they received every attention they could wish, and mother and child thrived. The crisp sheets and elegant rooms were a world away from the dingy, rat-infested warehouse. Josiah Bonham came daily to Eliza to engage her in conversation. They spoke lightly of fashion and food, and earnestly of slavery and politics, and whenever she tried to thank him for his kindness, he dismissed her words with a wave of his hand. She realised that he was a very lonely man.

After a few weeks, Will found a house to rent and the family left the cosseted life provided by their benefactor and moved into their own home. It was small and cramped but in a decent area where at least Eliza would be able to walk the streets with her children without fear of molestation. A servant girl was employed to help, Will firmly resisting the suggestion from Seamus that they buy a slave.

Letters from home seemed to describe a different world. Immersed as he was in his business and family, Will was less easily able to transport himself back to the land of his birth. The news that Uncle Samuel was to become High Sheriff of Nottingham and would therefore be spending more time at Beesthorpe, made him smile. How distressing the whole household would find that situation. He could well imagine his father's annoyance, his mother's stoicism and his sister's fury at the extended intrusion into their home life. Even the servants would be hurled into a flurry of confusion. Needless to say, Uncle Samuel would do as he wished and be oblivious to it all.

Seamus had not mentioned his own family for quite a while and one day Will asked after them. 'When is your brother coming to New York? You've made no mention of him for some time.'

'He won't be coming now.'

'Why not? You've been sending money, I know.'

Seamus turned away. 'Patrick decided to stay and fight for the cause. He joined the United Irishmen. They had some success with minor skirmishes against the British forces. Then he joined a group called the Wexford Rebels.' Seamus' voice became tight and hard and he looked across at Will. 'You won't want to be hearing this, any more than I want to be telling it.'

'Just tell me what happened.'

'It was at a place called Vinegar Hill last June. By all accounts the rebels fought like demons, but the British troops encircled them. Patrick died on the battlefield. As did they all.'

'I'm sorry.' Will could think of little more to say. 'You should have told me before.'

'We're partners, not politicians. We can't change the way things are. But your English soldiers are building up a hatred so deep and dark ...' Seamus didn't finish his words. He just walked away. Will stayed sitting on the bale of furs for quite a while. Through their conversations, he felt he knew quite a lot about the lives of the Irish Catholics, and couldn't always support the harsh actions of English troops, but this news of Patrick's death was a blow. It could come between Seamus and himself.

Will concentrated on his own family and their needs. Mindful that the years would soon slip by and their debt to Mr. Bonham would have to be paid, they watched their expenses closely and often struggled to pay their bills. Before long, Eliza was once more pregnant. In due course, a daughter, Susan, was born. Auburn-haired and bonny, she added to the family joy.

Months went by in a haze of domesticity, sometimes chaotic but always happy. Will and Eliza felt blessed. Mary Ann took on a maternal role and played with her brother and sister the whole day long, but just before the baby's first birthday, it became clear that Susan was unwell. At first the decline was gradual and the doctor seemed unsure of the nature of the illness. Anxious days turned into fearful weeks. Eliza was distraught, constantly watching over her child, willing her to show some sign of improvement, but little Susan never did. Each day her condition weakened, and then the doctor informed them that although he could put no name to the illness, he feared the worst. Eliza refused to accept it and spent hours gently wiping the hot forehead of the inert child.

Mary Ann and Samuel were subdued and watchful, the household hushed and sombre. Time seemed suspended, awaiting the inevitable, and yet while Susan still took her short, rasping breaths, hope still lingered. When at last the shallow breaths ceased altogether and the baby's suffering ended, Eliza continued to hold her close in an embrace of anguish. Will couldn't bear to watch his wife rocking back and forth with their dead child in her arms. The tears ran down her cheeks and Will stood helplessly by her side. Eventually, she allowed him to take the baby and put her back in the cot. Little Samuel and Mary Ann stared in bewilderment.

Will insisted that they make the journey to Newark, New Jersey to lay the baby to rest in the cemetery there. In his grief for his child, he felt it was the nearest thing he could do to taking her to Newark in Nottinghamshire.

The following year, another daughter was born and Will and Eliza sought to console themselves by giving her the same name. She was duly christened Susan Fosbrooke Bristowe, as Will felt that using his mother's maiden name would bring good luck. It didn't, for within a week or so it became apparent that the child was not thriving. She grew weaker by the day. Will and Eliza watched in horror as their second daughter began to slip away from them. How cruel of fate to subject them to another vigil of death, to watch another daughter be taken. Was it God's will? Why could He not show some mercy? Once more in a state of numbness, they made the journey. The minister walked ahead and Will carried the tiny casket in his arms as Eliza, too distraught to alight, remained in the coach with the children. The gravedigger had withdrawn to a discreet distance, but as the prayers concluded, moved forward to complete his task. Another Bristowe child had been laid to rest in the cemetery at Newark, New Jersey.

The following year, in March 1803, Eliza once more gave birth, this time to another healthy boy. Mary Ann was now seven years old and a great help to her mother, and Samuel was almost five. He was an engaging child, mischievous and happy, and devoted to Mary Ann. The new baby, named Simon, completed their family happiness, helping to put the great sadness of the loss of the two little girls behind them.

It was April when the letter arrived.

Dearest Will,

It is my fervent hope that by now, your dear wife will have been delivered of a healthy baby. How sorely we grieve for the loss of your sweet daughters and send you our fondest love. It was my hope not to add to your burden at the present time, but circumstances have dictated otherwise. My dear brother, I must tell you that our mother is quite overcome with illness. The doctor says it is her heart and indeed she is extremely weak, unable even to leave her bed.

Her one wish is to see you, Will – you and your son, little Samuel, before she is taken. Please say that you will come as soon as ever possible. Our father is most distraught and asks me to beg you to take the next ship to cross the ocean and return to us in time for our poor, dear Mama to see you and her beloved grandchild.

God speed your journey, Will. Your loving sister, Jane.

As Will read the letter out aloud, Eliza's head was bent over her breast where the feeding baby clung, and he was unable to gauge her reaction. 'You know I must go.' Eliza made no reply. 'I can't bear to leave you, my love, but I must.'

By the time Eliza raised her head, she had composed herself and managed to look directly at her husband as she confidently said 'Of course you must go. Your mother needs you.' Will nodded his relief at her ready agreement to the request.

'But not with Samuel.'

'I can't return without him. Jane was quite specific.'

'He is too young to undertake such a long voyage. He should stay here with me. Please don't take him, Will.'

Will's voice was gentle, yet firm. 'You know I shall take the best of care of our son. Whilst he is with me, no harm shall come to him. I promise you that.' He stood up and made for the door. 'I shall book our passage today. There's no time to waste.'

Eliza's eyes rested on the downy head of the baby now sleeping at her breast. She raised him slightly and bent her head to rest his soft skin against her cheek. Nothing more was said. Will had already left for the shipping office.

Little Samuel padded across the room and stood by his mother's side. She raised her free arm to invite him into her embrace and he leaned his head onto her lap and clung to her leg. From the doorway, Mary Ann watched silently. Eliza's maternal smile hid her fears but she knew that if anything happened to another child of hers, her heart would truly break.

Chapter 11

Will looked down at Samuel's brown curls as father and son stood on the deck waving goodbye to Eliza, Mary Ann and baby Simon. Samuel's outfit, complete with frills at cuffs and neck, had been made out of an old green velvet dress of Eliza's, and his black shoes and stockings newly acquired. Eliza had filled her mind with the task of kitting out her son as well as possible for his presentation to Will's family.

As the wind filled the sails and took the ship further out into the harbour, the figures on the quayside became smaller, and finally they stopped waving. Will felt suddenly lonely. He put a high value on his little family, which had provided him with such love and security, and now not only was he leaving them, but also tearing his young son away from his mother. It could be months before they were able to return. Will felt cold inside.

'What is England, Papa?' The voice of the small child piped up to Will and he felt his sleeve tugged impatiently. With little notion of the timescale involved in the separation from his mother, Samuel had been very brave, but now was full of questions about their destination. His big round eyes seemed to fill his little face as he looked up at his father, waiting for his reply.

'England is very green and very beautiful,' Will found himself saying somewhat wistfully. 'Let's find our cabin and then I'll tell you all about Nottinghamshire. We shall see the great forest of Sherwood. Come now.'

The voyage passed easily enough. The other passengers found Samuel to be an enchanting child and happily took a turn in helping to keep him entertained. He was so free with his shy smiles and childish giggles that all the ladies took him to their hearts. Father and son never wanted for company. Only once did Will know a few hours of fear. The wind had increased steadily all day and when at last the full force of a storm was unleashed on the ship, the tossing to and fro in a violent motion caused him to fear for their safety. All Will could think was how much Eliza would despise his memory, for taking her son away from her. Fortunately, the storm was short-lived and before the morning the motion of the ship had returned to normal.

Will's pulse raced and his skin tingled at the sight of English soil as the ship negotiated the estuary and moored alongside the Liverpool dock. Seven years had passed since his departure. He smiled as he thought of the gauche young man that he had been, so put out at having to share his cabin, so ill-equipped for life on the dangerous streets of New York. And now he was returning, this time as a businessman, a husband and a father.

As the stagecoach rattled along the roads, he found himself watching out for the milestones, telling him the distance they had to go before he would be home again. Samuel sat quietly beside him, his legs sticking out on the seat and his head resting against his father. Now they were so close, worry began to gnaw its way through him. How would he find his mother? Try as he might, he could not imagine her in any way other than dependable and strong. A sickly image just didn't seem to come into his head. Nevertheless, there was no guessing as to what awaited him.

At last the sweating horses pulled up at the coaching inn on Beesthorpe Common. The old innkeeper called his son and instructed him to take Will and little Samuel in the cart for the last couple of miles of their journey. The horse was slow, and Will's anxiety grew by the minute as the cart rumbled unhurriedly down the long road to Beesthorpe.

As the tall chimneys came into view and they approached the iron gates, Will became aware of an empty space over to the right of the garden. With a jolt he realised that the old chapel and schoolroom had gone. They had been pulled down and nothing but a pile of stone and brick remained. Those decrepit old buildings, smelling so dank and fusty, had been central to his childhood. A legacy from the time when Beesthorpe had been owned by the Cistercians of Rufford and the lay brothers had maintained a close community, the buildings had long since fallen into disuse. Will recalled the creaking of the hinges whenever the solid oak door of the chapel had been opened, and the fluttering and cooing in the rafters of the schoolroom as the grey doves made their home there. He looked up at the windows of the big house. What other changes, he wondered, would he find?

As they came to a halt Will lowered Samuel to the ground and reached back for his trunk. The cart lumbered away and the front door opened. Robert, the butler, stood for a moment and then hastened forward in recognition. Will had the feeling that he had arrived at an appointed hour and day, rather than having been at the vagaries of a sea voyage and an unpredictable coaching system. Robert reached down to pick up the trunk. 'Good to see you, Mr. William. Your father is in the drawing room. I'll tell Miss Jane that you're here.'

Elizabeth Bristowe lay in the great oak four-poster of her spacious bedroom and closed her eyes. Bright sunlight burst through the tall windows and lightened the shade of the red drapes hanging about the bed to a vibrant pink. Even the new mahogany panelling had temporarily turned a lighter shade under the intense sunshine flooding the room. But it was unable to work any miracles for Elizabeth. At the age of fifty three, she looked twenty years older. Her black hair had turned grey and the contours of her face had changed cruelly under the burden of wrinkles and sagging folds of skin. She felt utterly exhausted. The effort to hold a cup to her lips was more than she could manage. She knew she was dying, and although it did not suit her to leave the world whilst her family still needed her, her time was nevertheless running out. Silently, she mulled over the effect of her death on her loved ones.

Elizabeth's deep feelings for her family dominated her thoughts. She was so relieved that Jane's future was now assured since her betrothal to Reverend Wilby. At first her daughter had put up a spirited resistance to the attentions of poor Marcus, which was how Elizabeth had come to think of him, but eventually, his persistence had won her over, much to the dismay of many local mothers who had nurtured silent hopes for their own daughters. But Elizabeth was painfully aware that her headstrong daughter would initially find it hard to assume the role of dutiful wife to a clergyman. In her stronger moments, she tried to offer advice on the life that lay ahead of Jane; all the duties and compromises, the responsibilities and expectations of a wife in her position. She just hoped that Marcus would be blessed with the strength to both curb and guide the girl he loved and had waited for so patiently.

Elizabeth opened her eyes briefly and caught a glimpse of the hillside across the valley. Poor Thomas, she thought. How cross he is that life has been so unfair to him. How will he cope without me to soothe him and explain to him how little it all matters?

And Will. Her darling Will. How strange that she knew, all those years ago, as he left on that beautiful May morning, that she would never see him again. She could picture him now – so excited to be off, yet clearly anxious for what the future would hold for him. His letters, so longed for, had brought her joy and pain in equal measure. She breathed deeply and could almost smell the heavy scent of May blossom as she pictured him leaving, turning back to them and waving until he had finally disappeared out of sight.

A gentle hand on her arm roused her from her reverie. She opened her eyes to see her daughter. 'Jane, dear. I was just thinking about Will. Do you remember the day he left?' Jane leaned close to catch the whisper that Elizabeth's voice had become.

'Yes, Mama. I remember the day well. And I have come to prepare you for some wonderful news.' Jane's voice, full of emotion, trembled slightly. 'He is here. Will has arrived and has brought your grandson to see you.' She held her mother's gaze and nodded in confirmation until she was sure that her words had been understood. 'Yes, really, he is here. Now let's tidy things up before he comes.' Jane straightened the sheets and combed back the long grey hair. She eased her mother into a more upright position and plumped the pillows.

'Here?' Elizabeth whispered. 'My son is here?' Jane nodded and crossed the room to open the door. On the threshold stood the man her son had become during the seven years he had been away. By his side, the little boy clutched his father's hand tightly.

Will advanced slowly into the room towards his mother's bed. Elizabeth took in every detail. His face had become fuller and his stature more robust, but still his eyes had the same trusting innocence. He wore good clothes, a well tailored coat and breeches, and his hair had been cropped in a shorter style. Elizabeth's eyes welled with tears and the vision of her son became blurred. She raised her hand to wipe her eyes and Will dropped to his knees, beside the bed.

For a few moments, neither spoke. Elizabeth felt her throat constrict and her chest rise and fall as she breathed deeply. As Will bent towards her, she reached out and touched his hair and cheek. Gently, he took the frail hand in his and kissed it.

'I thought I should never see you again.' she whispered. 'But how I prayed to God that I would. My precious son.'

'I have brought someone very special to see you, Mama.'

The little boy had stood, uncertainly, in the centre of the room, and Jane had taken up her position with him, resting her hands on his shoulders to reassure him. Will beckoned him forward and Jane pushed him gently. 'This is Samuel Ellis Bristowe, Mama. Your grandson.'

'My grandson.' Elizabeth breathed. She held out her quivering hand and rested it against the little boy's arm whilst she scrutinized him carefully. His big round eyes were darker than Will's but his hair was the same shade of brown. He still wore his baby curls and they framed his little round face. He looked at the old lady solemnly and, following a prod from his father, took her hand and kissed it.

'I am very pleased to meet you, Grandmama.' Elizabeth's face shone with joy at the sound of the formal words delivered in the trill little voice.

'What an angel!' Looking up at Will, she said 'Your dear wife must be a wonderful lady and I'm so grateful to her. Please be sure to tell her.'

Jane came forward. 'I think you should rest now, Mama. Will shall come in again to see you later.' They left the room and with a beatific smile of thankfulness upon her face, Elizabeth closed her eyes and slept.

Down in the drawing room, Will made an effort to control the trembling that he felt deep within. 'I know you tried to warn me, Jane. But nothing could have prepared me for the shock of seeing her like that. She has changed so much, barely the same person.'

'I know it seems that way, but she is the same, deep inside. It's just that her health has been deteriorating for so long now.' Jane poured the tea and handed the cup and saucer to her brother. Little Samuel had been despatched to the kitchen to be given cakes, allowing the family to talk freely.

In the corner, Will's father, Thomas, slumped in his armchair. He seemed so much smaller and far less dominant, Will thought. His power over the household seemed to have diminished with his stature, for Will had noticed that it was Jane who was making the decisions and issuing the orders. Of course Thomas had greeted

Will's arrival with joy, as well as relief. He explained how they had been watching for him for days, hoping and praying that he would arrive in time. But Will could see immediately how changed he was, both in manner and appearance. Even so, the biggest shock had come to Will when he had entered his mother's room.

'It is so hard to accept. In these few years, the mother I knew has changed so much. She is so … frail, so weak. I would barely have recognized her, Jane. Only her eyes – still calm and accepting. She must have been ill for a long time but her letters told me nothing.'

'Don't be cross with us, Will.' Jane came and knelt beside him. 'For years she refused to allow us to tell you of her deterioration in health. Eventually, we took the decision to go against her wishes. And now you are here. And her leaving will be easier for her to face for having seen you and Samuel.'

Will studied his sister as she spoke. She had obviously taken on the mantle of housekeeper and with it a maturity. But there was something more, he felt. 'And what about you, Jane? What does life hold for you?'

'Well, now you mention it, I have had a proposal of marriage, and I have accepted. I am to be married.' She smiled self-consciously.

'What? Who? Do I know him?' Will was full of questions as he tried desperately to recall Jane's letters for some hint of who this suitor might be. 'Not the Reverend from Muskham … Marcus Wilby, was it? But you were so disparaging of him, and then later barely mentioned him at all!'

'I know, I know, but after all this time, it just seemed to be the right thing. He has been very patient and is quite devoted to me.'

'But do you love him?'

'Yes, I really do. It was strange how slowly I came to understand my feelings for him, but they are real and he means everything to me. I can hardly believe it myself.' Jane smiled happily and, for a little while, as they discussed the merits of a loving marriage, the sadness of their dying mother left them.

For the rest of the day, Will paced the house and peered around, noting all the changes made in his absence. As well as Robert, most of the staff were still there. Dick had been a young stable lad when he left, but now had grown into a man with bulging muscles and strong arms. Will remembered well the night he had spent in Hare

Hills Wood and the morning he had arrived home with the exhausted horse. He peered into the stables. Most of the stalls were empty but the horse, Hector, was still there. He slapped his neck and pulled his mane with affection.

'Hello, boy. It was quite a gallop that night, wasn't it. You were a sorry sight.' Will turned as Dick emerged from a stall, pitchfork in hand. 'No lasting harm came to him then?'

'No, Sir. If you were to hunt him, I doubt you'd be at the head of the field, but he can canter for miles. It seemed to suit your father. Not that he rides much these days.'

A whine came from the far end of the stables. 'Chaff? Of course! I'd almost forgotten about you, boy.' Will strode down to the bottom stall. The hound had got to his feet but seemed unsure of which direction to go. As Will caressed him, he wagged his wiry tail and licked his old master, whining his pleasure. But when he lifted his head, his eyes were milky and opaque and Will knew that he was blind.

'Poor old boy.'

'He's well cared for, Sir. I see to that.' Dick came up and protectively led Chaff back to his bed in the hay. Will turned hastily away. A homecoming could be very hard.

Over the following few days, numerous visitors called at the house. Will met his future brother-in-law, Marcus, and liked him. He was caring and attentive towards Jane, and it was comforting to know that they would be living just five miles away. The vicar and the doctor did their duty and relatives and friends gathered. Will was on hand to sit by his mother's bedside and, at times of wakefulness and lucidity, tell her the story of his life in America – all that had happened and all that he hoped to achieve. Sometimes she closed her eyes but he knew she was still listening when a smile played around her mouth or she nodded in agreement with his words. It was a painful yet special time, and Will knew he would look back in years to come and be grateful that he had been there for her.

Exactly one week after Will's arrival at Beesthorpe, Elizabeth Bristowe died peacefully in her sleep. The line of black-clad mourners followed the coffin into St. Andrew's Church at Caunton, where a slab had been removed from the floor of the Lady Chapel, and the coffin was interred in the vault beneath.

The carriages bringing the family back to the Hall made a formal procession down the driveway. Will glanced down the valley beyond. As usual, John Greaves' cows grazed in Lockabeck Meadow and on the far hillside, black against the skyline, the silhouette of the herd from neighbouring Readyfield Farm stood out, just as always.

As they entered the gates, Will missed the familiar shape of the old chapel. Uncle Samuel had apparently decided that the maintenance of the old stone buildings was no longer worth the while. When a winter storm had removed most of the roof slates, he had given the order for the buildings to be dismantled. Now there was just an empty space, like the one his mother had left.

Uncle Samuel had arrived only that very morning, just in time for the funeral service. Now, as he stepped awkwardly from the coach, he summoned Will to him. 'So how is business in New York? Money to be made, I'll be bound.'

'Yes, Sir, money to be made but it takes time for a business to grow. When we have made the repayment for the warehouse, then we'll start to expand and increase our prospects.'

Uncle Samuel raised his stick and poked Will roughly in the chest. 'Take your chances when you can, young man. Caution at the right time but in business you must be bold.'

'Leave the boy alone, Samuel!' Thomas called across from the doorway to the house. The roughness of the reprimand took them all by surprise, 'For God's sake, can you not stop your bullying for one day?'

A hush descended on the mourners. Slowly, Uncle Samuel turned his head towards his brother and narrowed his eyes. His jaw thrust forward and he brought his stick down hard on the gravel. Taking deliberate, heavy strides, he lumbered towards Thomas. Everyone's eyes were upon him.

Thomas stood his ground. 'It is the day of his mother's funeral,' he spat. 'Perhaps he doesn't want your advice, for once. Perhaps we've all had enough of it.'

'How dare you call me a bully?' Samuel thundered.

'Because a bully is what you are. My son had to cross an ocean to escape you.' Emotion suddenly overcame Thomas but he struggled to continue. 'Because of you, my only son has gone from me. He has made a new life in a foreign country – and I miss him.' He turned and left Samuel standing, fuming at the rebuke. Embarrassed by the scene, one by one, the relatives meekly shuffled past him, eyes cast down. No-one ever spoke that way to Samuel Bristowe. As Will passed his stunned uncle, he felt obliged to speak. 'You must forgive my father. He is grief-stricken.' But secretly he was glad at his father's outburst. He had stood up to his brother in defence of Will, and Will could never remember a time before when that had happened. Even on this sad day, it gave him a warm glow of satisfaction. Then he, too, entered the house.

The afternoon of the funeral passed awkwardly, with mourners leaving as soon as decently possible. Thomas excused himself and retired to his room. Will took the opportunity to get to know Marcus. Any notion some years earlier that Jane would marry a man of the cloth would have been unthinkable, but somehow she had managed to become a lady, and Marcus did appear to be a most affable and charming man. Later he confided to Jane that he wholeheartedly approved of her choice. The change in his sister was astonishing. She was quite a beauty now and had at last achieved some of her mother's poise. Dressed in black mourning clothes, relieved only by a cameo brooch at her neck, her complexion was pale and translucent. She played the part of hostess with grace and ease.

When Uncle Samuel had eaten and drunk his fill, he bore down on Will to continue the interrogation. Will had no choice but to answer the questions fired at him regarding commerce and opportunity, but then his uncle suddenly said. 'And when shall I be introduced to my namesake? I am given to understand you brought your son over with you. I should like to meet him.'

'Yes, of course, Uncle. I'll bring him down.' Will climbed the stairs to the nursery, the room in which he had spent much of his early childhood. His old wooden toys were still there, scattered around little Samuel as he sat on the floor happily playing.

'Can we go fishing now, Papa? Down at the lake as you promised?' The child's eager face suddenly reminded Will strongly of Eliza and he felt a pang of longing for her. His own loving mother had now gone forever and he yearned to be held and comforted. But his wife was on the other side of the ocean.

'We shall go fishing presently. But for now, I must introduce you to some people in the drawing room. Be sure to remember your manners.' Will took Samuel by the hand and led him down the stairs and into the flagstoned hallway.

From across the room, Will saw Uncle Samuel watching intently as he led his son into the room. He had placed himself in a high-backed chair and seemed to be spilling out of it on both sides. His bulging, white-stockinged legs stuck out in front of him and his black cane rested at the side of the chair. His heavy-set, square jaw jutted out and his eyes seemed almost lost in the fleshiness of his sagging face. Will silently prayed that little Samuel would not be repelled by him and articulate a rude or personal remark.

'How do you do, Sir?'

'I am very pleased to meet you, Samuel Bristowe. Do you know that my name also is Samuel Bristowe? I am your great-uncle.' The harsh tone of the gravelly voice made no allowances in speaking to a young child but little Samuel was not intimidated. He stepped forward with a childish boldness.

Will watched from a distance as his uncle barked questions at his son and received clear responses in return. The child was clearly unabashed and voluntarily moved closer to converse quite happily with his elderly relative.

'Would you like to ride in my carriage tomorrow, Samuel? I should like to show you my farms. Would you like that?'

'Yes, Sir, I would.'

'Very well. William, see to it that the boy is ready to accompany me by nine o'clock in the morning. I shall take him out with me.'

'Yes, Sir.' Without thinking about it, Will found that he had agreed to the proposal. 'Come on, Samuel. We'll go down to the lake now.'

The little boy took his father's hand, but as they left the room, he turned and smiled shyly at his great-uncle. A feeling of puzzlement passed over Will. How odd that the child seemed drawn to his great-uncle. He would have expected him to have recoiled from his overbearing and gruff manner.

The day was warm and Will took off his formal jacket before heading down to the lake. Yellow irises grew at the edge of the water and they sat on the tufted grass to watch the moorhens and mallards. Samuel removed his shoes and stockings and paddled on the edge, laughing in delight as the mud oozed between his toes.

Will looked across at Lockabeck Meadow. It was so peaceful here, just the same as always. Even on the day of his mother's funeral, he could find contentment in its tranquillity. Watching his son playing happily, he looked forward to the great day when he would bring Eliza and all his children home to Beesthorpe. Jane would soon be married, leaving his father alone in the big house. Perhaps just another year or so and then he could return. With some money in his pocket, he would have earned the respect of his family, particularly Uncle Samuel. And anyway, it couldn't be that long before the estate was his.

The next morning, Will made sure that Samuel was ready for nine o'clock. The carriage pulled by two matched greys waited in front of the house and Uncle Samuel heaved himself into it. 'Come along, boy,' he ordered impatiently, and Will lifted his son up. Little Samuel waved gaily as the horses picked up pace down the drive.

A high brick wall enclosed the garden, protecting it from the east wind, and rambling pink roses climbed and tumbled over it in untamed profusion. Will wandered over to smell the scent. How Eliza would love this place. Everywhere he looked he could picture her; walking in the garden or presiding in the dining room – this house was waiting for her. He stooped to pick up some fallen petals, feeling their velvety softness and breathing in their perfume.

'Your mother's favourite, that rose.' Will turned at the sound of the subdued voice of his father behind him. Why, he's less than half the man he used to be, Will thought. His clothes hung in folds on him, robbing him of the stature he used to command. Without his wig, his grey hair stood up in thin wisps and his wrinkled eyes were very sad.

"It's good to have you home, Will. I've missed you. We still have all your letters. You've done well and it can't have been easy.'

'No. There have been hard times. But now, God willing, I have the chance to make something – a good business. Trade is the thing, you see. Everything hangs on trade.'

'And now you have a wife and family. Your son is a credit to you, though I feel for the loss of your two daughters.'

The morning sun picked up strength as the two men stood by Elizabeth's favourite roses. As Thomas' stooped figure returned to the house, Will felt the urge to mount up and gallop away. He headed for the stables 'Saddle up, Dick! I need to ride out.'

In Upper Hades Field the turnips were up and John Greaves and a couple of farm workers were bent over their hoes, weeding them out. Will hailed them as he flashed by, and they acknowledged him briefly before returning to their task. 'Always rode at the gallop, that one.' said John Greaves dourly. 'Never spared his poor father's horses.'

As the horse pounded the track beneath him, Will felt a surge of exhilaration. How he had missed the joy of a good horse and open countryside. In the distance, the Bark Hill Oak sat as if patiently awaiting his return. He kicked on in a last burst of speed, scattering a flock of sheep in his path, and came to rest beneath its boughs. From this viewpoint he scrutinized the valley whilst the horse snorted and stamped. Had it always been this green in June? The vibrancy of the different shades struck him as if for the first time in his life. Perhaps, he thought, you have to leave something before you can see it in its entirety, before you really understand.

An image of the busy streets of New York, crammed with horses and carriages, alternately dusty or muddy, and thronging with all levels of humanity and its waste, sprang into his mind. The noise of the city was another consideration, and the smells, yet here he could only hear the bleatings of a few sheep and a late cuckoo's call echoing down the valley. It was little wonder that when he indulged in daydreams, it was here that his mind's eye always came, and where he breathed in the perfume of the dog-roses or the richness of sap-filled leaves. But he had forgotten how very, very green it was.

Uncle Samuel's carriage had not returned and luncheon was taken without them. 'Probably invited himself to the vicarage. You know what he's like. Thinks nothing of turning up on someone's doorstep and expecting hospitality.' Thomas was unconcerned but Will was on constant alert for the sound of the carriage. By late afternoon he was decidedly edgy and had Dick saddle up again.

'I'll just go down to Caunton and on to Willoughby. See if there's any sign. The child will be getting tired.'

At every farm and likely house the answer was the same. Uncle Samuel had not been seen that day. Will's frustration and annoyance mounted. How could the old man be so insensitive, both to the needs of the child and those caring for him? Dusk began to fall and still there was no sign.

Eventually, just before nightfall, the clinking of harness and rattle of an approaching carriage could be heard. Thomas and Will rushed to greet it, relief and anger surging up in both of them in equal measures.

'Wherever have you been, Samuel? That child must be exhausted!' Thomas' voice was accusing as he opened the carriage door and peered in. The sleeping boy was curled up on the seat opposite his great-uncle.

'Don't fuss so.' growled Uncle Samuel. 'The child is fine.'

Will reached in to gather up his son. 'Where did you go? I've been looking for you all afternoon.'

'Newark. I took the boy to Newark. Needed to see my solicitor.'

'You might have said that you would be away for the whole day. Didn't you think that we might be worried?' Will was challenging his uncle directly, something he had never done before.

'And what possible harm could come to the boy whilst he is with me?' Uncle Samuel's voice grew thunderous. 'I'll have no more of this nonsense.'

Will carried his son in his arms up to his bedroom. Little Samuel barely woke as he was undressed and put to bed. Darkness had suddenly fallen and Will felt disinclined to go downstairs and repeat the argument with his uncle. He went straight to his own room and sat by the open window, drinking in the night-scented air and watching for the first of the stars to appear.

Chapter 12

Birdsong, drifting in through the open window, woke Will from his sleep. The joyous heralding of the new morning seemed all the more poignant following the sorrow of the previous days. No-one had told the birds to mourn, to be hushed and respectful. The chorus of notes, trilled from all points of the garden, drifted into the room on warm, sunlit air, their delicacy and purity competing in a joyous cascade.

Clattering came from the stables, and doors from within the house were opened and closed. The servants were up and about. Will lay in his bed, luxuriating in the comfort and lost in the glorious birdsong. Subconsciously, he knew that if he delayed his appearance at breakfast, the chances were that Uncle Samuel would have left on some business or other. At this moment, Will did not feel up to parrying his questions and being forced to justify his own actions.

Voices sounded below and the wheels of the carriage crunched on the gravel drive. Good, Will thought, perhaps we'll have a quiet day to ourselves. He turned over in his bed but sat up suddenly on hearing one high-pitched little voice. Unease swept over him as he crossed the room and leaned out of the window. Below him, the carriage and the greys stood in a state of readiness. From under the front porch the solid figure of Uncle Samuel appeared, making for the carriage door, and guiding little Samuel by the hand.

'Wait! Where are you going?'

Uncle Samuel peered up towards Will's window, scowling his displeasure.

'Twyford.' he snapped and took another step forward.

'Twyford? You can't take the boy to Twyford.'

'Why ever not? We shall return in three days. He will be safe with me. No need to worry. Say goodbye to your Papa, Samuel.'

The child looked up to where Uncle Samuel was pointing and smiled happily. 'Goodbye, Papa.' he called, waving to Will. They entered the coach and immediately Uncle Samuel gave the order to drive on. Will stayed leaning out of the window, watching the coach disappear down the driveway. He felt totally baffled. Why was his uncle taking such an interest in the child? Why was he stealing away in the early morning instead of informing Will properly and requesting his permission? The birdsong still continued but his pleasure in it had gone.

The three days passed slowly. Jane busied herself with the running of the house, sombrely carrying out the duties she had inherited from her mother, but every afternoon she sat down with Will and encouraged him to tell her all about his life in America. Tales of his family poured out. 'I can barely wait to bring Eliza to Beesthorpe, Jane. I know you will love her as a sister. When you are married to Marcus and whisked away to Muskham, the house will need a mistress.'

'I'm glad to hear that is what you intend to do. Father will be sad to be here alone and I know you will come back when the time is right.'

'How could I not return? I feel it is pulling me back stronger than ever now.' Will sighed and paced the floor. 'Jane, I am so ill at ease with little Samuel out of my care. I promised Eliza. I promised he would be safe and not out of my sight for a moment.'

Jane did her best to offer reassurance. 'He is perfectly safe, I am sure, though it is extraordinary that Uncle Samuel, who takes perverse satisfaction in disliking most of humanity, has taken such a liking to him. We must be thankful, Will. Really we must. It can only be a good thing.'

Will was not reassured. His father kept mostly to himself but when they were in each other's company at mealtimes, Thomas made the effort to provide congenial conversation. He did his best to inform Will of all the local news and gossip in Caunton and beyond. There was a lot of catching up to do.

Will visited the stables and knelt down beside Chaff. The dog lifted his head to be caressed and licked his master's hand. He went to the tack room where Dick sat perched on a stool, waxing the leathers. Will reached for the saddle, high up on a peg. 'I think I'll ride into Newark. See what changes have been made there.' Dick stood up to help and Will remembered his loyalty on the many occasions when he had found himself in trouble. 'I hear you have a wife now, and a house in the village.'

'Yes, Sir. And a child expected soon.'

Will smiled. 'A family brings responsibility and pleasure. I'm glad for you, Dick.'

The horse trotted down the road to Newark at a steady pace. At the top of the hill overlooking the town, Will reined in and stood staring down at the Trent valley below. The spire of the Newark church reared up out of the flatness and, looking to his left, Will strained his eyes to make out the great cathedral at Lincoln. Perched on a hill, it was often visible from this spot, but not today. The June warmth had provided a heat haze to block out the far horizons.

As he waited to pay his toll to cross the bridge which spanned the river, Will could see the horse-drawn barges upstream. The horses plodded slowly along the tow path, the bargeman fending off the bank with a long pole. When they came to a halt, workmen began to unload into waiting carts. Will decided that it was a consignment of coal that he could see, but he knew that often it was night soil from Nottingham. It required a strong stomach to load that on to carts for despatch to the local farms.

Will realised he was looking at Newark with new eyes. In his younger days he had thought it exciting, a place to be visited for diversion or a social event of some kind. Now he could only see its smallness and provinciality. Although there were smartly dressed citizens going about their business, by far the majority of the population sported the blue smock of the common labourer.

At the White Hind, Will left his horse at the stables and lifted the latch of the oak door. Little had changed here. Benches and stools dotted the stone floor and the low beams and small windows provided little light. Even the landlord looked the same, with his bushy side whiskers and dirty apron draped over his big belly. Will drank his ale and wondered if he remembered the night when someone had tipped off the constables about the Great North Road highwayman.

Having re-acquainted himself with a few tradesmen and towns-folk, Will had had enough of nostalgia and decided to make for home. Despite its industrial growth since his departure, with yet more breweries and dye works alongside the river, Newark seemed quaint to him now. He could never remember the tannery at the old castle smelling so strongly before. Perhaps it was bigger now, or it could be just the heat of the day.

The road north out of Newark had been improved and stoned, and all the while, Will remembered his last breakneck departure from the town. Even after all this time, it was etched deep in his memory. He realised now that he had been young and impressionable, yet even so, it was fact that Ned's friendship had greatly influenced events of his life. At Dark Turn, Will halted and studied the bank that they had leapt up on that moonlit night. In the light of the day, it seemed an impressive feat of horsemanship.

Uncle Samuel did not return on the third day, as he had promised, and Will grew anxious. On the fourth, he paced and watched until finally the carriage arrived. Little Samuel ran to his father to tell him all about his adventures. 'I've been fishing and riding. I have my own pony and I can ride by myself.' His eyes were bright and his cheeks flushed with excitement.

The carriage squeaked and swayed as Uncle Samuel stepped out. His bulky body staggered slightly as he regained his balance and made for the door. 'William, there are things we must discuss. I shall see you in half an hour in the library. Alone.'

Will's suspicions were aroused. Uncle Samuel was up to something. He presented himself as requested. Uncle and nephew sat in the high-backed chairs, facing one another. Tact and diplomacy were alien to the older man. He believed that if you wanted something, you should ask for it outright. 'The fact of the matter is – I am willing to bring up your son. I should like you to consider leaving him here, with me.'

Will stared in astonishment at his uncle and thought he could not have heard correctly. He hesitated for a few seconds. 'Uncle, my son belongs to my wife and to me. We need no-one else to bring him up.'

'You have plenty of money, do you? Enough to educate the boy properly? Give him all the advantages of social position? He is an intelligent child. There are things he should have – and I can provide.'

'I couldn't leave my son with you, Uncle. This trip home was for the benefit of my mother, that she could see her grandson before she died.' Will's hands had begun to sweat and he clasped his knees rigidly. As he looked directly at his uncle, his jaw began to ache with tension. He knew he was in for a long battle.

'Samuel enjoyed his time with me at Twyford. Ask him for yourself. I bought a pony for him. He loved being by the river. The servants doted on him.'

106

'All these things add up to no good reason why I should leave my son with you! His mother is expecting him to accompany me home.'

'She has other children, I believe. There are probably more to come. Do your finances run to providing for a large family? How could you deny your son the chance to be brought up with every privilege of an English gentleman? The best education? A career – in law, perhaps?

The barrage of Uncle Samuel's argument began to wear Will down. He clenched and unclenched his fists and jumped to his feet.

'Don't walk away, Will. Consider my words. Consider your son's future.'

Will stood at the window and looked down over the back garden. In the centre of a sunken area was a rectangular design of low-growing box, clipped to perfection. Beyond, to the left, were the orchards and, to the right, the grassy mound beneath which was the ice-house. The ice-house. Inside, Will began to feel just as cold.

Little Samuel was a delightful child with an easy temperament. He adapted without fuss and everyone loved him. It would break his heart to leave him behind. And yet ... was paternal love selfish or could it rise above the personal gratification of seeing one's child on a daily basis? Will turned to walk from the room.

'Consider your own future, Will, as well as your son's.' Will stopped where he stood. 'You are my heir. You will inherit all this.' Uncle Samuel waved his arm expansively and let the words sink in. 'You are fortunate. You have children. I do not. It has been a blessing denied to me. If I were to be allowed to shower benevolence on this fortunate child, I should be certain to look upon you most favourably in my will. Everything would be yours. I am an old man. This is a way I can help you.'

Will now felt simultaneously hot and cold. The chill at the thought of losing his son somehow became buried under the glow of hearing his uncle talk openly of leaving everything to him. His dream could be realised. He could bring Eliza home to Beesthorpe and be reunited with his son. If he played his hand right, he could have everything.

'We'll talk tomorrow,' Uncle Samuel said, dismissing him.

Tired and grieving though he was, when Will recounted the conversation to his father, Thomas' manner picked up. 'It's the only thing to do. You must leave your son. What will a few years' separation mean when compared to inheriting two estates?'

'But – Eliza. What could I say to her?'

'She will understand,' Thomas assured Will. 'Remember, her future depends on your uncle's generosity too. Do not anger him now, Will. There are second cousins he could settle his fortune on if he is displeased with you.'

Will sat on the fallen bough in Lockabeck Meadow and watched as the flow of water cascaded over boulders in the beck. It was one of the deeper pools and a good fishing place, but now the setting sun shone directly on to it from the west, turning it into an earthy orange. Above the man-made dam, he hurled twigs into the water and watched them plunge into the frothy turmoil below.

'I thought I might find you here.' Jane sat down on the bank beside him.

'Have you come to offer advice? I could do with some.'

'Poor Will. What a dilemma. I thought it odd – so unlike Uncle Samuel. We should have known he had a motive. He always does.' With a flash of her youthful impatience, she thumped her brother's arm. 'Don't be down. Let's work it through and come to the right decision.'

Will made no reply. Jane carried on. 'So, Uncle Samuel wants your child, and in return he is promising to leave you his fortune. In addition, he is going to care for and educate your son. Have you noticed how breathless he is lately? How high his colour? He may not live for many more years, you know.'

'Jane, please don't speak like that. I don't wish him ill. I just wish he didn't bully me so. He always backs me into a corner, and the only way out is to do as he wants. Papa thinks I should agree. Do you?'

'I know how hard it is, Will, but yes, I think so too.'

The water gurgled as it trickled lazily over the low stones before making a final rush and pitching over the dam, splashing noisily into the pool below. Will became mesmerised as he watched the never-ending flow. 'Very well.' His words were slow and deliberate. 'I'll write to Eliza tonight and catch the mailcoach tomorrow. It's vital that she knows before I return without

Samuel.' In the silence and the fading light, the sound of the bubbling stream intensified. To Will it suddenly seemed cold and accusatory.

After a fitful night's sleep, Will rose early and rode up to the coaching inn on Caunton Common, to ensure that his letter would be picked up by the mailcoach that morning. It had been a difficult letter to write, but he hoped that he had achieved the right tone of good fortune and opportunity for their son.

The scent of newly scythed hay wafted down the valley and, in anticipation of another sunny day, labourers were making their way to the fields to rake over the drying grass once more, before loading it up on the hay carts. So this valley really would be his one day. Somehow, Will couldn't quite enjoy the realisation as much as he would have expected.

When the two men met once more in the library, it was Will's turn to come straight to the point. 'If, as you say, Uncle, I am to inherit, then I would have no objection to your caring for and educating my son. I shall return to America and leave him with you.'

'Good. I'm glad the arrangement is satisfactory. I did take the liberty of calling on my solicitors during my journey back from Twyford and the necessary papers have been drawn up. They are on the desk if you would care to read them before you sign.'

'Papers? Why should we need papers?'

'For the adoption to be legal. You would not expect me to invest so much in the boy if you were free to take him from me as you wished.'

'We did not speak of adoption!'

'William, my dear boy, I have been in business far longer than you, and I know that it is vital, in any transaction, to know exactly where you stand legally.'

'This is not a business transaction. This is an agreement – concerning a little boy!' Will's voice had taken on a slightly hysterical note. Yet again, Uncle Samuel had snatched away the initiative from him.

'We are making a deal. You want to inherit my estate: I want your son.' His uncle sat there in his winged chair, heartlessly dictating the terms, his expression hardened and stubborn. He stared back at Will with compassionless eyes.

'Adoption or nothing. I'll not bend.'

In a daze, Will went to stand by the window but his eyes were unseeing. He rubbed his forehead and tried to think. So this had been his intention all along. But how would it really affect things? Perhaps hardly at all. The circumstances were exactly the same. It was just a piece of paper. The alternative was to lose his inheritance, for he knew with absolute certainty that if he crossed Uncle Samuel over this, there would never be a reconciliation.

Will found himself looking down at the solicitor's papers, sitting neatly on the polished desk. The words LEGAL ADOPTION were written in large, elaborate capital letters. His eyes could focus on little else. The quill and ink stood at the side. The clock ticked. Slowly, his heart beating heavily, he picked up the quill and dipped it into the dark liquid. A droplet splashed down on the edge of the document. With a shaking hand, Will Bristowe signed away his son.

He looked at his uncle. 'It is done.'

'Very well. A good decision. Now, say your goodbyes this morning. We leave for Twyford in the early afternoon. The boy's schooling must be arranged as soon as possible.'

Will had not thought it possible that he could be shocked by any action his uncle could take, but in this he had been cold and calculating beyond belief. From across the room, he could see that Uncle Samuel was barely able to hide a self-satisfied smirk. He was the victor and his eyes betrayed the jubilation he obviously felt. No handshake, no promises of love and care for the child. No message of reassurance for the mother. Just victory.

At that moment, a feeling that Will had never known before surged through him. Hate. He had laid bare his own weakness and this man, his blood relative, had exploited him fully. He felt the colour drain from him and, as if in a dream, he walked stiffly to the door. Their business was at an end. The deed was done. As he threw one last glance at the man who had stolen his son, Will had only one thought. I want this to be the last time I ever see him. He has only ever thought of himself, his needs, his wants. The only way I'll get Samuel back is when he dies. His death will free us all. I want it to come soon.

On the gravel drive, Will knelt down in front of his son. 'Your brother and sister, and your Mama and I, we shall all be coming to live in England very soon. Your Great Uncle Samuel has agreed to educate you and care for you.' The solemn eyes stared back at him and the knot in the pit of Will's stomach tightened. 'You will have new friends at your school and you will ride your pony over the Twyford estate – like a real gentleman.'

Little Samuel held out his arms and Will hugged him close. When at last he pulled back, the boy's lips were trembling and his eyes had welled with tears. 'I want to go with you, Papa.'

From the carriage, Uncle Samuel's harsh voice barked out. 'Enough! Bring him here now and we shall be away.'

Will carried his son to the carriage. Just for a few seconds he clung tightly and then let go. 'Be very good for your Uncle Samuel. Mama and I will write to you often.' He turned to his uncle for some words of solace or reassurance.

'Animals only miss their mothers for a few days, then they forget them. The boy will be the same.' Then, before further emotion could be displayed, Uncle Samuel banged his stick on the roof of the carriage, the coachman slackened the tension on the reins and the horses began to move off. Will hurriedly slammed shut the carriage door and caught the change of Samuel's expression as bewilderment and fear overcame him. Will just had time to smile encouragingly at his son. Then he was gone.

Under the porch, Jane stood quietly, her eyes brimming with tears. Thomas' face was hard and set. Will found that he could not look directly at either of them. When the carriage had disappeared from view, he trudged down to the beck and crossed over the stepping stones into Lockabeck Meadow. Disconsolate and wretched, he drew no comfort from the meadow now. He looked beneath the grass, and saw deep cracks in the soil. For the want of summer rain, the earth had opened up, changing the moist provider of nutrients into a hard and unyielding crust. If the lack of rain held for much longer, the grass would wither and die off – just as he felt he was now doing.

Will felt a desperate need for his wife, but a realisation slowly focused in his mind. Eliza would feel the loss as greatly as he, but perhaps even more so, and in the light of her reluctance to allow little Samuel to leave her side, she would heap blame and all her sadness on to him.

Will decided to stay at Beesthorpe for another two weeks, telling himself it was to enjoy the company of his father and sister. But he knew in his heart that it was to allow his letter time to be delivered, and for the news of the loss of her son to sink in and perhaps even be accepted by Eliza.

Chapter 13

The ship made a swift crossing from Liverpool to New York in twenty-four days. With every storm cloud or freshening wind, Will wondered if fate would intervene and he would be spared the difficult reunion with Eliza. If he should perish now, she would only think well of him for having left Samuel in England. This thought lingered at the back of his mind every day but the weather remained favourable and presented no danger to the little ship as they followed their course across the Atlantic Ocean. His emotions were churning as the ship crept slowly into harbour and berthed alongside the pier on a glorious September morning.

Despite all his misgivings, it was good to take in all the old familiar sights and sounds. Naturally, it was the Bristowe and Branagan warehouse that Will came to first. Seamus was delighted to see him and proudly reported a brisk trade and decent turnover. 'We've been busy and business has gone well, but it's a relief to have you back safe and well, my friend.' Seamus' smile was wide and he shook Will's hand vigorously.

Will looked his partner over. 'And at long last – a new set of clothes!'

Seamus stuck his thumbs under the lapels of his new jacket and assumed a self-satisfied air. 'Well, I decided that if it's a gentleman I'm to be, then I'd better start to dress like one. Feel the cloth here, Will. Have you ever felt such quality?' Will laughed, both at approval of Seamus' transformation and relief that all was well with the business.

'I never doubted you for a moment. I knew the business was in safe hands.' Will felt relief that all was well at the warehouse but sighed heavily at the thought of the meeting with Eliza. 'We'll go over the books tomorrow. Now, I must go home. Have you seen my family lately?'

'They are well, but anxious of course. Eliza has worried and fretted the whole time, just waiting for you to come home. Seamus suddenly realised the child was not with his father and looked around. 'Where is Samuel?'

Will's face clouded and he gripped his friend's shoulder. 'I'll explain tomorrow.' He picked up his trunk and set off.

From the end of the dusty street he could recognize Mary Ann by her dark curls as she sat on the steps of the tiny house, playing with her doll. She looked up and ran towards him, excitedly calling 'Papa, you are home, you are home.' He lifted her up and swung her around. Her face flushed with pleasure and she squealed in delight.

Unwilling to go through the door, Will waited on the street with Mary Ann jumping up and down beside him. The curtain was lifted and then the door opened. Eliza ran down the steps with her arms open wide. 'Oh, how wonderful! What a happy surprise!' Her face was full of joy and relief as she hugged and kissed her husband. Smiling happily, she pulled back to look behind him. 'Where is he? Where is Samuel?'

Will's stomach pitched down. This was his worst dread. The letter had not arrived. 'You … you didn't receive my letter? I … I wrote to you, telling you everything.' he stammered.

The smile slowly died on Eliza's face as her eyes questioned her husband. 'Everything. What is everything? What has happened? Where is Samuel?' Panic began to set in as she went behind Will to look for her son. She even looked up and down the street.

This was worse than Will had feared. His letter, so carefully constructed, had not arrived and now he must find the words to tell his wife that he had given their son away. 'Let's go into the house.' Eliza snatched her arm away from Will's grasp and stood defiant. 'Come,' he said quietly. 'Samuel is fine but there are things I have to tell you. We've much to discuss. We must go inside.'

Mary Ann had ceased her skipping around and stood watching the scene in bemusement. Her face resumed its melancholy expression and once more she picked up her doll and sat on the steps.

In the tiny parlour, Will looked around. He felt like a stranger. It didn't seem like his home, the place where he belonged. Eliza entered the room, hostility pouring out from her. She stood rigid, her face hard. 'What have you done?'

Will slumped into a chair. 'Please, sit down.' If anything, Eliza's body stiffened and she remained standing in the centre of the room, silently staring, waiting.

'Samuel is well and happy, you can be assured of that. My mother died just one week after my arrival in England but she asked me to give you her heartfelt thanks for allowing her to see her grandson.' Will clenched and unclenched his hands in agitation. His voice sounded strangled. He took a deep breath and searched for the right words. 'Uncle Samuel took a great interest in our son, and has offered to care for him and to educate him.'

'Uncle Samuel? The very same uncle from whom you found it necessary to escape and cross an ocean?'

'There appears to be a bond between them. Truly, my love, our son is not unhappy. He will be treated well and given the finest English education. You must understand there are advantages in the arrangement. My present financial state would be hard pressed to offer him any of these things. Uncle Samuel has shown himself to be generous.'

As if her legs could no longer hold her, Eliza sat down suddenly in a chair. 'Why did you agree? What hold did he put on you?'

Will was startled by the directness of the question. He studied his wife for a moment and decided to tell her the truth. 'He made it clear' he said slowly, 'that if I allowed him to adopt Samuel, then he would name me as his heir and I would inherit his estates. I understood that if I did not agree, he would cut me out of his will.' His eyes came to rest on the rug at his feet and he had great difficulty in forcing his gaze up to Eliza. When he did it was to witness a grief-stricken face, eyes brimming with tears.

'You sold our son for an inheritance?' Her voice choked on the tears. 'Do you know how dreadfully my heart aches for him? These past months I have dreamed of his homecoming, his running into my arms. I've imagined how much he might have grown and what he would have told me about England.' Eliza gave way and wept openly.

Will crossed the room and tried to hold her. She rebuffed him. 'I had to make the decision alone and I decided to do what was best for Samuel. My uncle is not a well man and he probably won't live for very long. This way is the best for us all.' The silence in the room was broken only by Eliza's sobs.

Eventually, Will remembered that he had another son. 'How is baby Simon?' No reply came. 'I shall go up and see him.' In the little room up the stairs, Will stared down into the crib of the sleeping child. He had grown a great deal in the summer months. His plump face was crowned by fair hair and his fingers lay curled contentedly by his cheeks. Strong paternal love overwhelmed Will and he turned away as he felt his eyes begin to prickle. So small, so vulnerable. He sent up a silent prayer that poor Samuel, bereft and alone, would be treated well and loved.

Eliza was inconsolable, refusing to converse or even acknowledge her husband, so eventually Will decided to leave the house for a while. After all, she needed time to come to terms with such a family wrench. Deep down, though, he realised that it was possible she never would. He decided to return to the warehouse. At least all was well there, and just catching up with Seamus' dealings would keep him occupied for the rest of the day.

Instead of going directly to the office to check the ledgers, Will slipped quietly in through the side door and let his eyes adjust to the gloom before moving on. He had learned long ago that shins were easily skinned in the windowless storage areas. As he stood peering in the dim light, he thought he could hear low voices on the next floor. There was nothing unusual in that. Labourers would be up there, shifting and organizing bales and casks.

Will looked around. Hessian sacks were piled high to one side and although they gave off the usual pungent aroma, he sniffed the air, trying to distinguish the other smells permeating the warehouse. Cotton, skins, leather, tobacco – he knew them all, but today it was different. The door banged shut behind him and he walked towards the wooden steps. A startled face appeared above him. 'Will! What are you doing back here so soon?' Seamus ran quickly down the stairs towards Will.

'Much to do to catch up. Can't have you doing all the work.'

'Don't you trust me?' Seamus' smile seemed forced and his eyes anxious.

'Of course I trust you. It's just that I had to tell Eliza that I left Samuel behind in England and she needs time to come to terms with it. Better for me to be out of the house for a while.'

The explanation brought relief to Seamus' face and he nodded. 'Yes. Of course, I can see that.' He put an arm around Will's shoulder and began to guide him to the door. 'Why don't we go over the books together, in the office?'

Will stopped abruptly and looked at his partner. He was agitated and uneasy, not at all his usual self. Something wasn't right. 'What is on the next floor that you don't want me to see?'

116

Seamus shook his head. 'Nothing. Just the usual stuff. Well maybe a few extra casks of undeclared brandy.' He attempted a mirthless laugh.

Decidedly ill at ease now, Will turned towards the steps.

'No! Don't go up.' Will turned to look at Seamus just once before his boots sounded on the first step. 'Please, Will. I can explain!'

As he climbed higher, the smell became more acrid. There was an occasional clink of metal and Will's apprehension intensified with each step. At the very top, he could see nothing. He wasn't even sure if he could hear anything beyond his own breathing. But something was going on, so with a considerable sense of foreboding, he inched his way sideways to the window that had been shuttered. He forced up the heavy latch and swung the wooden shutters wide. Light flooded in.

Will's heart lurched at the scene before him. On the second floor of his warehouse, crammed and chained tightly together, sat an endless number of naked, black slaves. Some shielded their eyes from the sudden light, some stared back dispassionately, some accusingly. Black arms and legs protruded from the lines, deep sores showing bloodied and infected beneath the shackles. Such shameful misery.

'How could you?' Will hissed, fighting down the urge to retch.

'A few more days and you would never have known.'

'They are men! Humans! Just like us. How can we buy and sell them? How can we keep them in such a miserable state, worse than animals? Tell me, Seamus, how can it be right? How can it?'

'We'll talk about it. Just keep calm and we'll talk it through.'

'We have talked about it, remember? We agreed on it. We agreed never to do this. For God's sake, how many of them are there?' Will could not bring himself to look again at the bowed black heads and shackled limbs.

'Ninety-one. I bid for a hundred but they had extra casualties.'

'Casualties! You mean they died in vile and inhuman circumstances.' Will's hand trembled as he passed it over his forehead and rubbed the side of his face. If only this were a bad dream and he could wake up.

'We unloaded just today. That's why they look so bad. We clean them up, feed them well and find them clothes. By the end of the week, they'll be ready for the slave market. This is how it's done, Will. If we didn't do it someone else would. It's the way to make money.'

In a sudden surge of rage, Will turned on Seamus and slammed him against the wall. 'You know how I feel about slave trading. It turns my stomach. I thought you felt the same. We discussed it. Remember?'

'I know. But it happens. People need slaves and we can get rich selling them. A prime field slave can make nearly two hundred dollars. Just imagine that!' Seamus squirmed free from Will's grasp. 'When you've got used to the idea, you'll see.'

Will shook his head, threw his partner a look of hatred and marched out into the sunshine and the comforting familiarity of the quayside. He tried to gather his thoughts to the gentle lapping of the water against the wooden piers. After a while, Seamus came to sit silently by his side. Eventually he said quietly ' 'Twould be a shame for our friendship to end over this. We've found a way around our other differences and been good for each other, don't you think?'

Will could find no words. What a hideous day this was. Slavery had always been abhorrent to him. It had troubled him since he first arrived in New York, and he had been happy to sign petitions and give his support to the growing number speaking up against it. But then guilt began to creep into him. Was he any better than a slave trader? After all, he had sold his son. He had deprived him of a warm and loving family, so that he himself would one day become a rich man. No, he was no better. Self-loathing he would have to live with, but not self-delusion.

'The difference between us is that I know that in this life you don't get a second chance,' Seamus continued his argument. The longer Will listened, the more chance he had of bringing him around. 'Men don't get rich by being nice to everyone and always doing the right thing. You do what you have to. We're traders. We trade and slaves are a commodity. And there's something else you should know.' Seamus' voice changed and Will looked at him closely, trying to guess what further revelation there could be. 'I took a risk. A cargo of furs ... just a short hop down the coast was all. I ... I didn't insure. Stupid, I know, but if the ship hadn't gone down we would have made a tidy fortune. Anyway, it did go down and these slaves were to put us back on track. A few more days and you would never have known. But now you do. Don't you think you owe it to your family to do the best by them? It will only take a few bad debts now, and any more lost ships will put us on the street too. Do you want that?'

Will mulled over the admission of guilt from Seamus. He knew they had taken a few risks early on with insurance, or rather without it, when they really couldn't afford it, but Seamus should have known better. 'Show me the ledgers.' he said finally.

Will ran his finger down the columns and sighed. The lost ship had indeed robbed them of security and cash flow. He had to admit that a quick and lucrative turnover would be the answer.

'Think of the family, Will,' Seamus pressed on, oblivious to just how closely his words hit their mark. He was right, Will thought. Financial security is what life is all about. Lose that and the rest starts peeling away. How many more children would he have to give away? Eventually he rewarded Seamus' patience. 'When do we take them to the market?'

'Friday. Three more days. But I'm thinking we could forget the slave auction. They take a big cut and I've a contact who is supplying slaves for the mills. It's a good price for them if we sell directly, and we could increase our profit by a sizeable margin.'

Will stood up. 'I'll leave the dealing to you. Just make sure you treat them well.' He started to head towards the office but stopped himself. He felt cold and empty and knew he hadn't the heart to do anything else today. 'I'll be back early in the morning.'

Seamus nodded. 'I'll see you then. I've plenty to tell you.'

'No more surprises?'

'No more surprises.'

As he turned into his street, Will wondered at the reception he would receive from his wife. As he imagined, it turned out to be ill-disguised hostility. The tears had dried, but the resentment poured out of Eliza with every gesture. Will cuddled the now wide-awake baby Simon, as he listened to a running commentary of their lives from Mary Ann. Eliza presided over the modest evening meal in silence.

As they retired to bed, Will hoped they would resume the love they had always shared, but Eliza turned coldly away from him. He ached to feel her arms around him, to enjoy her warmth and comfort, but there was no love in her for him. Though exhausted, sleep evaded him. His life seemed to have broken into a million pieces. He had lost so much in such a short time and his mind was a turmoil of shame.

The next three days were spent organizing food and clothes for the slaves. Will had wanted no part of it, yet found himself checking that details had not been overlooked. Even so, he couldn't bring himself to go near this human 'commodity'. He knew they would feel his shame. They might look into his eyes and see into his soul, and he couldn't bear the thought of such personal exposure, even to such miserable wretches. He was responsible for selling them on to live a life of God knew what torment. Best to keep his distance, try to think of them as a commodity rather than acknowledge them as men. The introduction of washing and hygiene at the warehouse helped and gradually the smell became less repulsive. Seamus went off to meet his contact to discuss the deal.

On studied inspection, the ledger books tallied and really did show a decent return, until the fateful sinking. Seamus'dealings had served them well. Money had been lodged at the bank and the much needed slave deal could boost profits considerably.

Even so, it was not enough. Will made a mental note to call and see Josiah Bonham very soon. The five years were almost up and it was time to make the deferred payment for the business. It would not be possible to release the money and carry on trading without a further loan. If he could be persuaded to give them another year's grace, it would make all the difference to their trading capacity.

Seamus returned triumphant from his meeting. They were to deliver the slaves themselves, walking them north out of the city on Friday, and avoiding the slave market. Shackles were removed and replaced with rope, and warm clothing bought and distributed. Preparations were made for the journey of about twenty miles.

They left the city very early in the morning. Will and Seamus rode and a labourer drove a cart with basic provisions. Tied together in tens, the slaves trudged quietly through the streets, their fate and destination unknown. Will had conceded that they could not risk an escaped slave, so Seamus had appeared with two pistols and a bullwhip. He just hoped to God in Heaven that they wouldn't have to use them. The morning was pleasant and good progress was made, but as midday came, and they stopped to eat bread, dark clouds gathered overhead. Barely had they started again when the weather broke and heavy rain lashed down in driving bursts. Slaves and masters put their heads down and plodded on.

Darkness had fallen when they reached the appointed place – a ramshackle cluster of wooden buildings close by a river. The overseer came out to them, whip in hand. He cracked it and pointed to a low shack. 'Put 'em in there.' Seamus led them to the door and one after the other they disappeared inside. Will opened his mouth to speak, to complain to the overseer that there were too many of them for such a small building. It would be far too crowded. But he stopped himself.

Seamus accepted the bag handed to him and stooped under a lamp to inspect the contents. 'It's all there,' the voice growled.

'Then our business is complete.' Seamus held out his hand and the overseer shook it.

'I may be wanting more fairly soon. They don't tend to live too long here.' The cruel voice made Will shudder and he mounted up, anxious to be away from the place. As they trotted back down the road in the darkness, both men stayed silent, each with their own thoughts. The money was good and much-needed, but neither felt proud of their day's work.

It was daylight by the time Will arrived home and walked in through the door. He was weary, stiff and saddle sore. His clothes had dried on him and the caked mud still stuck. His hand shook as he poured water from a pitcher and drank deep to slake his thirst. He stooped down and attempted to resurrect a fire from the previous night's ashes. Eliza came in, wrapping her shawl around her. She had still not spoken freely to Will since his return, and the set expression on her face gave him no reason to hope now. But she took the poker from his hand and began to lay sticks on the hot embers.

Will sat heavily on the chair. His limbs were leaden but inside he felt even worse. He fumbled in the cupboard and found the brandy. Ripping off the cork, he put the bottle to his lips and tipped the fiery spirits down his throat. His hands began to shake. Try as he might, he could not control the tremors. Guilt? Exhaustion? 'We delivered a consignment of slaves last night,' he said loudly, so as not to allow any cracks in his voice. 'I thought you should know just how low your husband could sink. He'll do just about anything for money.' Will took a huge slug of brandy and began to feel its comforting warmth. Eliza began to prepare breakfast.

'Poor devils. Sold into slavery. Nothing but pain and misery for the rest of their lives, however long that may be. And I delivered them. Just like I delivered my son.' Will bowed his head down low over his folded arms. Exhaustion and alcohol lowered his defences. Suddenly, he laughed – a humourless, harsh sound. 'So you may take it, my love, that your second husband is a truly wicked man. He is weak and easily used. And will do anything for money!'

Eliza stood by the smoking embers, her body rigid. Her husband's rantings alarmed her.

'It is so tragic, especially since your beloved Eduardo was such a virtuous and honourable man. And I know that you love his memory more than you've ever loved me. You thought I didn't know that. I know about the silver locket you treasure so dearly, and I know that it's a lock of his hair you keep inside.' Self-pity washed over Will. He felt demeaned and devalued and at that moment it was easier to cast the blame on Eliza for his misery. Having lost her already, there suddenly seemed no point in holding back and so, liberated by the alcohol, he carried on speaking all his secret thoughts aloud. 'So perfect, your first husband, the gallant Eduardo. He gave you everything. All I ever wanted to do was make enough money to give you the same things. But you don't want me anyway.' He waved his hand in Eliza's direction and picked up the bottle again.

His head was spinning and he felt nauseous. He closed his eyes to block the light, to hide, to withdraw from himself and from Eliza. Sleep began to beckon. Will wasn't sure if he was dreaming when he heard the soft voice. It seemed to float around in his head and he struggled to concentrate on the words. The voice was flat and low and he knew from the tone that he must listen and not drift off into the blissful sleep that he so yearned.

'Eduardo wasn't perfect. I discovered, after his death, that there were certain things that he had kept from me. It's true, I did love him very much, but he loved the sea.'

Will forced his eyes open and tried to stay alert, to take in what she was saying. This was, he realised, the first time Eliza had ever spoken of Eduardo, and he suddenly understood that all his impressions and opinions of the man had been formed from scant factual knowledge, and derived mainly from the hurt of the treasured locket with the precious curl of black hair.

'I always knew how you felt about slavery – and there's something I haven't told you. I was too ashamed. When Eduardo's ship, The Betsy, went down off the coast of Jamaica, the cargo went down too. They were slaves, chained together in the hold. It's a picture I have difficulty in erasing from my mind.' Eliza took a deep breath and her voice was barely audible. 'My husband was the captain of a slave ship. I didn't know until after his death.'

Will took a few moments to allow the meaning of the words to sink in. He blinked rapidly as confusion turned to blinding clarity. So, the dearly loved Eduardo had been the conveyor of hell. He had sailed the seas not as an honourable captain, but as an overseer of misery, degradation and death. The knowledge of Eduardo's shame actually cheered him a little, allowing him to feel slightly less tainted. Eliza had shared her burden and in so doing had eased his own. Hope edged into his heart. He raised himself out of his chair and slowly moved towards her. Tentatively, he touched her arm and, feeling no resistance, he enclosed her in an embrace. 'We all have to live with our regrets,' he whispered. Exhausted though he was, her closeness aroused him. He stroked her hair and soft cheek, not daring to look directly into her eyes, fearful that this momentary softness would evaporate and the distant, unforgiving Eliza would return. 'You are everything to me, Eliza.' His voice wavered and cracked a little. 'I only wanted to provide the very best for you and the children, but I know I've made some terrible mistakes. Can you find it in your heart to forgive me?' Will bent to kiss her lips and the kiss was returned.

Chapter 14

Determined to have nothing more to do with the hideous trade of slavery, Seamus and Will concentrated fully on the business. Furs from the north and cotton from the south continued to be a lucrative source of income, but expenses were high, insurance being the biggest expense of all, and one without which they could not afford to trade. Reading the market wasn't always easy. Prices fluctuated and there were times when they were forced to sell a cargo for less, or little more, than they paid for it. They had certainly had a few disappointments over the years, yet the foundations of a sound business had definitely been laid. One more year of grace before paying back their benefactor was all they needed.

Will knocked on Josiah Bonham's door and shivered in the cutting autumn wind as he waited. He glanced around him at the smartly paved street and well proportioned houses. After quite a time, the huge door opened and the flustered face of a servant girl appeared from behind it.

'William Bristowe to see Mr. Bonham.' At first, the girl seemed not to understand the request but after a few seconds her face began to crumple and she dabbed her eyes with her apron. Will waited uncomfortably.

Suddenly the housekeeper appeared from behind the girl and, recognising the visitor, sent her off and took charge. Her robust figure filled the doorway and for a moment Will thought he was not going to be invited into the house. 'Please step into the hallway, Mr. Bristowe.'

Will did as he was asked and waited awkwardly for the cause of the domestic tension to become clear. 'You have called at a difficult time, I'm afraid. The doctor is with Mr. Bonham, and has been calling daily for some time now.'

'I'm so sorry. I had no idea that he was unwell.' The housekeeper inclined her head in acknowledgement of the apology. Will turned towards the door. 'Perhaps you would be good enough to tell Mr. Bonham that I called and to wish him a speedy recovery.'

The housekeeper held open the door. 'I am afraid there will be no recovery.' she said flatly. 'The doctor has told us it is simply a matter of time. He is already unconscious, you see. Quite simply a matter of time.'

Will had been courteously dismissed and found himself out on the street, his hat in his hand, still murmuring apologies. Carriages rattled by and servants scurried to and fro whilst jumbled thoughts raced through his mind. Josiah Bonham was dying. The debt would have to be paid to his estate. Will remembered the legal document he had signed, pledging the payment in full after the duration of five years. In just six weeks time, those five years would be up.

Deep in thought, Will walked back down the wide street. No traders' cries here, no heavy carts making deliveries – just the quiet dignity of an affluent residential area. Whilst it helped to calm his mind and focus his thoughts, it also depressed him slightly. Eliza should be living in a street like this, not the noisy, claustrophobic atmosphere of their district. Not that they found it easy to pay the rent even for that. Whilst he had been in England, household bills had mounted up and he was unwilling to take more personal expenses out of the business. He had already decided that he would pay half of all the bills, thereby ensuring that the traders would still allow him more credit. The imminent death of Mr. Bonham was certainly a blow, and their chances of successfully holding on to the warehouse seemed to diminish with every step Will took.

Heading back, as he turned into each street, the rougher the area became, until finally he had reached the familiarity of the infamous dockside. Murders, robberies and brawling were commonplace here, but if he were forced to give up, Will knew he would miss it dreadfully. Seamus was in the office.

'I paid a call on Mr. Bonham this morning. You know that the agreement we signed means we have to make full payment in six weeks time.'

Seamus nodded. 'Did you ask him for an extension? What did he say?'

'I couldn't see him. I only spoke to the housekeeper.' Will sat down. 'She told me that he is dying. That it is just a matter of time.'

Seamus thought through the implications.

'We will still have to pay,' Will went on. 'It will be part of his estate. The document will be in his lawyer's office. If you remember, the wording was for payment in full or the warehouse would revert to Mr. Bonham. I should have asked him for an extension before I left. He would have agreed, I'm sure he would.'

Seamus crossed the room and pulled out the leather bound account book. 'So, we've six weeks to deal our way into a position to pay.'

'Or take a loan from the Bank of New York.'

'The charges they make – have you any idea what a decent loan would cost us?'

'But we would pay it back out of profits. It would just set us back a few years, that's all. There's really no alternative.'

'There's always another way, Will. The only question is whether or not you're brave enough to take it.'

'No. I'm not prepared to risk our business.' Will's voice grew harsh. 'We've come a long way. Think of the years of hard toil we put in when we first came here. Could you go back to that? It's a loan we're taking. No risks.' The discussion was over, the finality signalled as Will abruptly left the office.

Sitting outside, watching the ships leaving the harbour and negotiating the estuary under full sail in the stiff breeze, Will grew cold. He was on the point of going inside when Seamus came and sat beside him. Neither felt inclined to renew the argument yet it had to be faced. Both men churned over the dilemma.

'What do you want out of life?' Will said eventually. 'Don't you want a wife and family? A house of your own? We came here with dreams of prosperity.'

'I remember. And if you compare my life now with what it was in Ireland, well it's like a king I'm living. But you must trust me, Will. I can make deals. It's what I do best.'

Not wanting to hear, Will poured out his thoughts. 'When you really love someone, you want the best for them. I want the best for my family.'

'You mean before you go home and claim your inheritance. You see, it's always there – a soft landing for you when things go wrong. Well my sort don't have that, so we live by our wits. It gives us the edge – all or nothing. It's a gamble.'

'Yes, I suppose you're right. I need security and permanence. My place. My inheritance. But sometimes those things come at a price. Do you know what I did, Seamus?' Will suddenly felt the need to share his weakness. 'I sold my son for the promise of assured wealth. When I left him in England, it was so that I can rest in the knowledge that I shall inherit the estates. Yes, if all fails and we lose the business, I can go home.'

Seamus saw his chance and moved in quickly. 'Will, I want you to listen to what I'm saying. Don't interrupt and don't walk off. I know how you felt about the slave dealing, but you must agree, the accounts looked healthier as a result. It was a good few days' work. Our investment paid off.'

'Your investment, Seamus. Your investment – not mine.'

'Alright. But it worked out. You know, a few more shipments like that and our prayers would be answered.'

'No.' Will turned from his friend to stare across the bay.

'Just think about it. I've made some good contacts, cutting out the market dealers. They aren't happy, of course, but that doesn't bother me.'

'What do you mean?'

'Nothing. Well just a few threats is all. Sure they don't like to lose their cut, but I'm not worried.'

Will turned to stare closely at Seamus. 'Don't do anything foolish.'

'You asked me what I want out of life. Well, I do have a dream. And the only way I can have a chance of making it come true is to take risks. I want to go south. Buy a plantation – grow cotton and sugar cane, and build myself a fine house.'

'Will you have slaves?'

'Of course. It's the way things are. And when I've done all that, then I'll find myself a good wife. But if I'm to make that sort of money, I need to make good deals, in the things that pay the best – slaves.'

That night, Will tossed and turned in his bed, his brain formulating arguments and alternative solutions, endlessly mulling over the predicament. Seamus was right: to make an impact on your life and do what you really want to, you have to take the initiative. Hadn't Uncle Samuel told him as much? His thoughts turned to his son and the usual guilt crept up on him. If he could barter away his own child's life, would it really be so bad to sell on black natives from another country? After all, he hadn't turned them into slaves, and if he didn't do the dealing, someone else surely would.

By morning he had made up his mind, but decided against discussing it with Eliza.

Within a few days, word came that Josiah Bonham had died. Will and Seamus attended the funeral in the newly completed stone church. There were few mourners, just a handful of friends, distant relatives and business associates. Will found himself wondering which one was the lawyer, which would be the one to confront him with the legal agreement and demand immediate payment.

The coffin was lowered into the ground, just outside the imposing church door. Headstones in this part of the graveyard were large and impressive, the area obviously being reserved for the most prestigious members of New York society.

Silently, Will said his goodbye and his thanks to a good man who had shown great faith in him and given him the opportunity to become a businessman. Even so, despite himself, he couldn't help but see the irony of the situation and wished that Josiah Bonham had managed to stay alive for just a little longer.

As they left the churchyard, Seamus chose his moment. 'There's a shipment due in any day and we have bought it.'

'Bought it? Sight unseen?'

'We pay a fixed price per head, but I've already negotiated the sell-on price. More than double,' Seamus could not hide the eagerness in his voice. Will nodded but could not bring himself to smile.

The deal went ahead as planned. Once more, the slaves were housed, cleaned up and fed, and marched away to their fate. Barely had the warehouse been sluiced down before Seamus had another deal on the go. One evening, just as they were preparing to leave and go home, there was a loud banging on the door. Seamus instantly looked uneasy but nevertheless went forward. Before he had reached it, the door burst open and the office was invaded by ruffians wielding cudgels and carrying pistols. The leader made straight for Seamus whilst two others pinned his arms behind his back. Will was thrown against the wall and held there with a knife at his throat.

'This social call is long overdue.' The leader's voice was restrained yet full of menace. He pulled back his fist and thumped Seamus hard in the stomach.

'Stop!' Will shouted. 'What is this about?'

After raining a few more blows to Seamus' body and head, the man seemed to grow bored, and turned towards Will. 'This is about trade, my friend. Fair trade. In trade everyone gets to take a cut of the deal. When you try to out-manoeuvre the system, people become very unhappy.'

'Who is unhappy? Will struggled to speak above the knife held at his throat.

'You know well enough. Mr. Bailey expects all slaves coming into this city to go through his market. Even if they're sold privately, it's still through him. How else can he take his cut?' The man's face was inches away and the full force of his evil breath filled Will's nostrils. He could study close-up his blackened teeth and the wiry hairs of his beard partially concealing the criss-crossing of scars on his face.

Seamus began to cough and the man turned around. 'You, you're the one who does the deals. Mr. Bailey said to tell you that this is your one and only warning.' He pulled Seamus' head upright by his hair and aimed one last punch. Seamus slumped to the floor, blood trickling from his mouth. The man holding the knife spat at Will and retreated. Suddenly they had all gone.

Will ran across to Seamus. He was dazed and moaning. After a while he was able to sit up and Will propped him against the wall. 'I should have warned you.' he croaked through bloodied teeth. 'I thought they might come.'

'We stop this right now. Tell them in the morning, we'll have nothing to do with the next consignment.'

Seamus winced and cradled his ribs with his hand. He reached up his other arm to touch Will's shoulder as he crouched on the floor alongside him. 'That's my Will. I knew you'd say that. It must be true that all bloody Englishmen are cowards. Where's your fight, man?'

'In case you are unaware, we don't employ thugs to fight our cause. We are just the two of us, and this Mr. Bailey has these rogues and probably more besides to do his dirty work. Or is it true that all bloody Irishmen just love a fight for the sake of it?'

Seamus grinned. 'Think of the money, Will.'

'There's precious little point to being rich and dead. Come on.' Will put his arm under Seamus' shoulder and helped him to his feet. 'You're coming home with me.'

Eliza attended to the cuts and bruises. Shooing the children away, she ministered to Seamus whilst aiming all her questions towards her husband. Will answered evasively and eventually she grew tired of the game, knowing that she would not be told the whole story. After Seamus was bandaged and put to bed she resumed her persistence. 'You know who did this and why. Is it too much to ask that you confide in me? Don't I have the right to know if you're in danger?'

Will gave in. 'We've been trading directly and cutting out the slave marketeer.' His voice was flat and unemotional. 'They don't like to lose their cut. That's all.'

Eliza sat down. 'You said you would have nothing more to do with slave trading. Have you forgotten so soon?'

'We have no choice. We must pay the bill in full for the warehouse in a few weekss time. Without the extra revenue, we won't be able to trade. We would be finished.'

'You could take a loan.'

Will found it hard to look at his wife. 'We've agreed on it. Just one more consignment. That's all.'

Mary Ann opened the door and stood watching her parents. She had seen Seamus being helped into the house, bent over double with blood pouring from a gash on his head. She ran across the room to sit on Will's lap, needing reassurance.

'It's alright, little one. Nothing is wrong.' He held her tight and she snuggled against his chest. Eliza sent a withering look of contempt across the room as she cleared away the bloodied water.

In a couple of days Seamus had recovered sufficiently to leave. Whilst nursing his bruised ribs, he had suffered Eliza's disdain and moral lecturing, and was relieved to be up and away. 'We'll do everything under cover of night.' he said to Will once they were back at the warehouse. 'We'll unload in darkness and there'll be no walking them through the streets. We'll hire wagons to hide them in when we rendezvous. Just a few extra precautions and no-one will know.'

Will was worried. 'I hope you're right. We don't want to see Bailey's men again.'

Four days later, the ship sailed into harbour. Seamus hurried down the pier to talk to the captain and explain the need for secrecy. For the price of a couple of brandies, the crew were bribed to tell no-one of the cargo they carried.

It was after midnight when Will and Seamus boarded the boat and the captain unlocked the hold. In the still of the night, the rattling chains seemed incredibly loud as the slaves staggered up on deck and Will worried that the sound would carry across the water. In the darkness he hurriedly organized them in rows and they followed him down the quayside.

The alehouses had closed and the prostitutes gone home. All was quiet but for the gentle lapping of the water against the stone wall of the quay. Nervously, Will looked around. The moon was hiding behind the clouds and his pupils were fully dilated as his eyes struggled for vision in the darkness. Without the aid of a lamp, they negotiated the causeway without mishap. Any sailor on watch would have seen nothing, the gentle rustling of chains as each bare foot took a step forward being the only indication of enslaved men passing by in the darkness.

As they reached the side door of the warehouse, Will hastily unlocked it and ushered them up to the second storey. After the door was closed, he lit lamps and took stock of the results of Seamus' bargaining. Holding the lamp high, he walked along the lines of chained, naked slaves. They were dirty. Vomit and excrement stuck to their black skin and their eyes were wide and fearful. 'When were they last given food and water?' he said to Seamus.

'Yesterday.'

Will grimaced and walked towards a bucket of water in the corner. Dipping a tin cup into it, he went down the line for each man to receive a drink. Much as he tried to control it, his hand trembled and water splashed this way and that. Towards the back of the group, he realised there were about ten women. He stared at their black, naked breasts and felt a huge pang of guilt. Some were quite mature. They probably had children whom they would never see again. Their lives would be a marathon of misery and endurance – just so that white men could grow rich. Will offered them the water, but could not look into their eyes. Shame, he knew, was written clearly on his face. He couldn't wipe away the overpowering thought that, sooner or later, there would be a price to pay for this.

In the morning, Seamus brought in baskets of bread, along with water for washing and rudimentary clothing. The smell in the warehouse was fast becoming overpowering. 'We'll get them out tonight,' he said. 'I've two wagons organized and sent a messenger with the plan for the rendezvous.'

'Two wagons won't be enough,' Will said.

'It'll have to be. I've only two drivers, and horses for ourselves. We'll get them in somehow.'

They stayed with the slaves all day, furtively coming and going in order to complete their tasks before nightfall. By mid-afternoon, as they passed by, the priest was perched on his crate and preparing to embark on a sermon. He hailed Will and Seamus and they briefly acknowledged him before scurrying on. When they returned from their errand Father Kennedy was in full flow, and the crowd had fallen silent under his persuasive Irish eloquence. He was animated and delivered his argument in a passionate denunciation to the assembled crowd. Seamus lowered his eyes and his head, for as he drew near he realised that the subject of the lecture was the evil of slavery. Will felt the words burning into his soul.

They were reasonably confident that their activities had not been observed. The noisy chains were replaced with rope and they waited anxiously for the bars to close and the city to settle down for the night. When Seamus judged the time to be right, they emerged into the darkness.

Roped together, the slaves stumbled on down the narrow alley. Will could feel his heart thudding in his chest. In the inky blackness, he almost walked into the first wagon, placed as it was right at the junction to the street. With hissed orders, the drivers urged the slaves to climb up into the wagons. Long after each was full, they pressed them in, risking broken limbs or suffocation, until finally a heavy canvas was drawn over to conceal them from view.

The teams of heavy horses set off, negotiating the narrow streets until they eventually left the city behind them. Will and Seamus rode alongside. Despite the moonless night, the drivers picked out the way easily enough and the creaking wagons rumbled along the hard baked road with little trouble. After an hour the track took them through dense woodland and the path, littered with leaves, became less defined. The smell of decaying vegetation was all around, putting Will's mind to thoughts of death and morbidity. But he told himself it was only the smell of autumn. Seamus lit a lamp and rode ahead of the first team to light the way.

'How much further do you think?' Will asked on coming alongside.

'As soon as we're through this woodland, we've about a half-hour to do on the open road again. Then we take a right turn at a crossroads and come to a shack.'

Will was nervous and could feel his stomach starting to churn. He daren't allow himself to think about the suffering of the slaves crammed into the wagons. Yet he knew that worse pain awaited them at their destination.

Eventually, they emerged from the woodland and simultaneously the sky cleared to reveal the moon. Layers of wispy cloud still drifted by but the glow showed them the way and soon enough they reached the crossroads. The wagons lurched to the right but Seamus called a halt. 'Wait here. I'll go ahead alone first. Just as a precaution.'

He disappeared and Will turned in his saddle to check the wagons. With no thud of hooves or creak of wheels, a heavy silence descended. An owl hooted and a rustle of bushes nearby caused Will's head to jerk around and his eyes to strain for movement. There was none. Even so, his mouth felt dry. Only the occasional snort from a horse or jingling of harness punctuated the still night as they waited.

'Everything looks alright.' Seamus said as he returned. There's a light in the shack and I've scouted around. Let's go.'

The driver slapped the reins over the horses' backs and they moved off again. The door to the shack opened as they approached and light flooded out. The bulky form of the slave master stood in the doorway, bullwhip in hand. Will was glad to let Seamus go forward to do the talking. As he watched the two men, illuminated in the pool of light, he noticed that Seamus did not dismount. From the saddle, he nodded and then indicated for the drivers to unload.

As the slaves lined up, still tied together by their necks and hands, the slave master held high his lamp and walked up and down the lines, inspecting them closely and counting. Finally satisfied, he strode back into the cabin and emerged with a leather satchel. Still astride his horse, Seamus slowly rode up to him and took the bag. He looked inside and then nodded.

As he turned his horse back towards Will, there was a shout from the side of the shack and suddenly horsemen burst into the clearing. The horses milled around, blocking their retreat, and above the shouts and orders, Will heard the click of pistols.

The slave master lurched forward, holding high the bullwhip and reaching out to snatch back the satchel but Seamus was too quick for him. As the horse reared and took him off guard, Seamus leaned down and grabbed the whip from his grasp.

'Stand still or we'll fire!' a deep voice bellowed out of the gloom. 'You're outnumbered and surrounded.'

Will and Seamus wheeled their horses around, desperately looking for a way of escape. There was none. The slaves cowered together by the wagons. Seamus tossed the satchel to Will and lifted the bullwhip high above his head. The trailing hide whistled as it flicked through the air, cracked like a gunshot and snaked out towards the slave master, opening up a bloodied gash on his cheek. He gave a mighty roar of pain and rage and lunged forward.

'Ride!' shouted Will as he kicked viciously into his horse's flank and whacked the satchel down hard on its rump. The horse leapt forward, Will spotted a narrow gap and set his horse towards it. Seamus was right behind him and they kicked on hard towards their startled attackers. Hastily aimed shots rang out as they charged through the ranks and galloped on towards the trees. With every muscle and sinew straining to widen the gap and make good their escape, Will knew they had to make it to the cover of the woodland. The screen of safety lay just ahead and he prayed that the confusion behind would give them the advantage of a few moments' lead.

Just a few yards short of the precious sanctuary, Will risked a glance back and saw the flash of a pistol. Instantly, Seamus cried out and slumped forward in the saddle. Will urged his horse in close and snatched the reins as, side by side, the horses galloped on. 'Hold on.' he shouted. 'We're almost into the woods. We'll find somewhere to hide.'

Seamus did not reply. His mouth was open wide as he gasped for breath. He lay over the horse's neck and twisted his hands through the mane as he clung grimly on. From behind came shouts and the sound of pounding hooves. In desperation Will urged the two horses on but within a few more yards the effort to stay in the saddle became too much for Seamus and he slowly began to slide to the ground. Will's horse reared as he yanked it to a halt and leapt down to reach his friend lying face down in the road.

'Seamus, Seamus,' was all Will could say as he knelt down and gently turned him over. At that moment the clouds parted and a bright full moon shone down on the injured man. Seamus' eyes were open but his breathing was shallow. Will could feel his own heart hammering fast as he fumbled to unbutton his friend's jacket and felt the warm blood oozing between his fingers. The dark stain on Seamus' chest crept wide. Oblivious to the shouts and commotion about him, Will cradled him in his arms. He could hear the tremor in his own voice as he struggled to reassure him. 'You'll be alright. We'll get help. Just hold on, Seamus. Hold on.'

Seamus made no sound but his eyes locked on to Will's, desperate not to let go. His lips worked to form silent words and Will bent nearer to catch them. He shook his head. 'Save your strength, Seamus.' Within seconds bubbles of blood began to escape from the side of Seamus' mouth but still his eyes bore fiercely into Will's.

Helpless to offer any aid other than his arms to hold him and his own force of willpower to keep him alive, Will prayed that Seamus' stubborness and ambition would keep him going until he could get him to a doctor. 'Remember your plantation, Seamus. You'll get it one day, I'm sure you will. Don't leave now. It's too soon. We've so much still to do.' Horses stamped all about them, but Will kept his eyes locked protectively on his friend. When exactly it happened, Will never knew, but as he pleaded with Seamus to stay, talking of anything he could think of to cause a spark and help him resist the seductive darkness, the chilling realisation slowly swept over him. Although his eyes were still open, they were staring and sightless for the life had gone right out of them. His head fell against Will's chest and his hand fell limp to the ground. Seamus was dead.

Chapter 15

The pursuers encircled Will as he remained motionless on the ground, cradling Seamus in his arms. Moonlight glinted on pistols aimed at him but Will didn't even look up, hunched as he was over his dead friend. Shock numbed him and tears stung his eyes. They had come so far together, and taught one another so much. Their differing status in society had mattered little, merely serving as a means with which to upbraid or tease one another. What cruel irony that their only difference had been over this venture. Nothing else had ever come between them.

'Shall we finish him off, Mr. Bailey?' There was the click of a cocked pistol.

'Let's get a good look at him first. Stand up!'

Will raised his face in the direction of the voice. All he could see were shadows looming over the legs of the milling horses surrounding him. Gently he eased Seamus to the ground, ran his sleeve over his cheeks and stood up. The voice of Mr. Bailey barked out from the darkness. 'What is your name?'

'Will Bristowe.'

There was a lengthy silence. 'Shall we shoot him now, Sir?' The thugs were anxious to complete their night's work.

'Bring him into the cabin, where we can get a good look at him.'

Roughly, Will was grabbed and propelled towards his horse. Back at the shack, he was marched inside and forced into a chair. He blinked as the lamp was held up close to him, but the faces of his persecutors remained in the shadows.

'We could cut him up a little first.' a voice suggested. Will recognized it was the leader of the gang who had come to the warehouse to warn them, but clearly it was Mr. Bailey who was in charge.

The chill of fear swept through him. He was about to die – and for what? They had knowingly evaded the established system, however corrupt that may be, and had ignored the warning. Slavery had been against his principles, but principles counted for nothing when money was to be made. He thought of Eliza. She would be a widow again. Perhaps Mr. Bonham's lawyers would allow her something out of the sale of the warehouse, or maybe they would choose to interpret the exact terms of the agreement, and she would be left with nothing. How would she feed the children? Would she have the courage to write to Uncle Samuel? Would he have the decency to help her?

Minutes seemed to tick by, or was it seconds? And still no-one spoke. His mouth was dry, yet sweat broke out and ran down Will's back in rivulets. What would they do to him? At least this Mr. Bailey was giving some thought to the small matter of Will's life. But the thugs were getting fidgety.

'Leave us.' The deep voice of authority came out of the gloom. No-one moved. 'I said leave us, now.' The thugs shuffled out through the doorway, looking back uneasily and thrusting pistols and knives into their belts. One figure remained at the far side of the room. Where the light of the lamp shone down, Will could see his boots – well cut, leather boots shining black against the dusty floor. He was tall and loomed high over the lamp, features still hidden. Will thought of getting up from the chair, but realised he should do nothing unless he was told.

'So.' Mr. Bailey finally spoke. 'Will Bristowe is it? Would this be Will Bristowe of Beesthorpe Hall?' Will's head snapped up and he squinted into the gloom, trying to get a clear view of the man. The boots came nearer.

For the moment, curiosity overcame fear as questions surged up in his mind. How did this Mr. Bailey know him? Who was he to have this knowledge of Will's background? After a few moments of bewilderment, Will finally found the courage to stand up so as to be on a level and have a proper view of his tormentor's face. With a sharp intake of breath, he stared, aghast. He must be dreaming. It was not possible that this was the man standing before him. But he knew he was not mistaken and this was no dream. What is more, Will had no doubts about the true identity of Mr. Bailey.

'Ned. It really is you, isn't it?'

'Oh yes, Will. It really is.'

The face was fuller, and harder, Will thought, but the dark eyes and black hair tied back were just as he remembered that grey morning they bade each other farewell in Hare Hills Wood. 'I had been led to believe you were dead,' Will began.

'You were meant to think I was dead. And although it was not planned that way, it suited me very well. Sit down. We'll talk.' Ned pulled the chairs up to the table and took down a bottle and glasses from the shelf. He poured generous measures and Will took a good slug of the rough whisky. He had never needed a drink more in his life.

'Still living by your wits then, even in a new country. Not quite the respectable, law-abiding citizen.'

Ned shrugged. 'That depends upon your point of view. But it probably is true enough, especially with regard to your rather difficult predicament.'

'So how did you manage it? How did you give them the slip?'

'It was the hand of fate, Will, but I'll tell you how it came about. You know I always worked alone. Well, a chap called Jack Smith met me from time to time – in much the same way as our friendship came about – and he wanted to be my accomplice. I wouldn't have any of it, for I preferred to work alone, but for months he kept asking and eventually I gave in. The stagecoach was due and one night we hid in woods just south of York. It was almost dusk and you could see the driver was nervous from the pace he was going. The coach was swaying and the horses straining – desperate he was to be out of those woods before dark.'

Ned's face was alive with the memory and Will realised that this was probably the first time he had ever told anyone the story.

'Well, we halted the coach and Jack took a fair haul. I stayed back near the tree line, watching for outriders, but a passenger grew bold and fired a shot from his pistol. He only winged Jack but his horse reared and unseated him. At that moment, fifty yards down the road, came a half-dozen riders, firing even from that distance. The game was up for Jack. My escape was easy.'

'So why did they think it was you?'

'They appear to have not realised there were two of us. And of course they were after a lone highwayman. Little did they know it was the first time I had taken an accomplice. Poor Jack. I'd lent him a pistol, acquired on the road only the previous month, with elaborate inlaid handles. Belonged to some noble lord or other. They seemed to take that as proof. When the newspapers heralded the capture and subsequent hanging of the notorious Great North Road robber, well, I decided to take it as an omen. Changed my name and sailed for America.' Ned laughed aloud with pleasure at the irony of having as a prisoner the only man in the world who knew that he had been a highwayman.

Will listened to the story, but had not forgotten his precarious situation. One word from Ned and he would be as dead as Seamus. 'So, what happens now?'

But Ned would not be rushed. 'Tell me about yourself. You followed my advice, though I'd never have thought it. How long have you been here?'

Will had no desire to recount the story of his life in America, considering his friend and partner lay dead outside, but he sensed it may be his only hope. His life probably depended on it. He took a deep breath. 'You remember the day we said goodbye, after being chased out of Newark?'

'I remember it well. You were anxious to get home without being seen by your father,' Ned chuckled.

'I didn't manage it. He was furious. The constables combed Caunton Woods all night, looking for us. My uncle came that day, demanding to know how I was intending to earn my living. I just told him I was going to America – to seek my fortune.'

'And have you?'

'I've worked hard and had some degree of fortune. My partner, Seamus, and I ...' Will hesitated and swallowed hard, acutely aware that it was nothing short of bizarre to be cosily chatting and catching up with one another's lives whilst Seamus lay dead outside. It was hard to concentrate and find the right words, while all the time his thoughts silently raced along, bitterness clashing with sadness, fear over-riding relief. He took a deep breath and forced himself to continue. 'We own a warehouse. We mostly trade in furs and cotton, but a deferred payment date is looming and our benefactor died – somewhat inconveniently. That's why we did the slave deals. This was to be the last one. I don't even hold with slavery.' The two men fell silent and Ned poured another drink.

Emboldened by the fire of the crude whisky as it hit the back of his throat, Will carried on. 'If we don't make the payment, my wife and family will probably be put out on the street, and then we shall be forced to go to England and live on the charity of my uncle. Not something that rests easily with me, as I am sure you understand. In fact, it's the very last thing on earth that I want to do.'

Ned looked down at his glass and tapped his finger repeatedly on the table, deep in thought. 'We have a problem here, you and I. Did your friend have a family?'

'No. His dream was to go south and buy a plantation.'

'Ah. Well, I am truly sorry for his death, but you know, you shouldn't have ignored the warning you were given.'

Outraged by the arrogance of the rebuke, Will stood up, fists clenched. 'And what gives you the right to dictate terms and conditions of trade? You haven't come to America to earn a decent living and become an honest man. You're still the highway robber, and you're no better than the murderous cut-throats you pay to do your dirty work.'

Ned leapt to his feet and sent the chair toppling over. The vaguely friendly nature of the previous conversation instantly turned to ice as they squared up to each other with tempers taut and hard eyes blazing. The door burst open and men piled in, pistols at the ready. Ned raised his hand. 'It's alright.' he said quickly. 'It's nothing. Go.'

Warily, the two men sat down again.

'It seems to me that the only card you hold, Will, is our past friendship. You will agree, I'm sure, that the upper hand is mine. But we must think this situation through. You'll not be trading in slaves again, you say?'

'No. Never. I just wish to God I hadn't let Seamus persuade me. I should have been stronger.'

'Right. Then that being the case, take your money and go home, back to your wife. We've both lost tonight.'

'What about Seamus?'

'No family, you say? We'll bury him in the woods. No awkward questions then.'

'No.' Will shook his head. 'I can't leave him here. He was a Catholic. The priest should say the right words for him. I'll take him back with me.'

'Then be sure to pay for this priest's silence. I mean it, Will. We don't want to be answering awkward questions, any more than you want these dealings to become common knowledge.'

They went outside and the men covered the body and laid Seamus in the wagon. So that was it, Will thought. A risk, a gamble in the pursuit of money and Seamus had paid the ultimate price – his life cut short, just as the future was beginning to come into view. No children to hold dear his memory in the years to come, no wife to weep. Such a pointless, stupid waste.

As daylight spread, the slaves were re-grouped and led off down the road. Will watched them go. As they passed by him he looked at them properly, for the first time. It seemed the only gesture he could make, to simply acknowledge their presence. Whatever their fate, he knew he was partly responsible. The guilt that he had managed so conveniently to over-ride now consumed him. He had failed them. No human being should belong to another, be deprived of his freedom, be put to work like a common beast of burden, suffer abuse and be treated with contempt for his humanity. 'Are we not brothers?' the abolitionist chant rang in his ears. No futile excuse of caring for his family's future would ever redeem him from this act of human betrayal. As the slaves shuffled past, eyes fearfully cast down and faces set, a shaft of pain pierced Will's heart so deep and swift that it took his breath. It tightened its grip and wrenched so violently that his eyes stung and he staggered forward. The slave master cracked the whip, splitting the air above the slaves in domination, venting his anger and humiliation for his sliced cheek. As the whip snaked out and whistled down to the ground, the tip bit viciously into the soil, sending up fiendish clouds of dust, a foretaste of the life of barbarous atrocity that lay before them.

Ned offered Will his hand. 'It's been a strange night. And another goodbye, Will.'

Will stared unseeing for a moment, lost as he was in the picture of violent domination before him and his own guilt-ridden misery. He was reluctant to shake the hand of the man responsible for Seamus' death, but after a considerable hesitation, he eventually accepted it, and wearily turned to mount his horse. 'I shall never forgive you.' he said quietly. 'Seamus was a good man, but even so ... even so, I'm glad it wasn't you on the scaffold at York. Maybe we shall meet again. Who knows?'

'Who knows?'

With Seamus' horse tied to the wagon, Will rode on ahead down the track. He had never felt more worthless or alone.

Will arrived home in a state of exhaustion and, with barely a word to Eliza, fell into his bed and slept for hours. When finally he awoke, she brought him a drink and sat on the bed, awaiting an explanation.

'Seamus is dead.'

'No!' Eliza's hand flew to her mouth as she recoiled at the news and her eyes were wide and incredulous. Slowly, Will recounted the events of the previous night, sparing her little detail, yet omitting the facts of Mr. Bailey's true identity. 'I left his body in the warehouse. I have to go and make arrangements with the priest, Father Kennedy. It must be a proper burial sanctified with the holy rites of the Roman Catholic Church. That is the only thing I can do for him now.'

'Won't the authorities be asking questions?'

'I'll make a donation to his church and ask the priest to be discreet. It happens all the time.'

'Poor Seamus. It's so hard to believe we'll never see him again. He had such plans, and was always so optimistic and eager to do his deals. How has it come to this?'

Will pulled Eliza towards him and held her close. Her tears spilled over. 'Oh, Will, I know I shouldn't say this, because I was so very fond of Seamus. But what would I have done if it had been you? I can't bear to think about it.'

'I know, my love. I know.'

With the repayment at the forefront of his mind, it was no surprise to Will to receive a letter from Mr. Bonham's lawyer, asking him to be so good as to present himself at the office. Will spent hours poring over the ledgers, endeavouring to portray the business in a good light so that it may be looked upon favourably. With another shipment due, even an extension of just a few weeks would be acceptable.

Will stood outside the office, situated in a wide, fashionable street. Wendle and Monkpeace, the sign announced. 'I'll tell Mr. Monkpeace that you're here,' the clerk said. Will stood in the outer office, smoothing straight the stock at his neck and brushing bits off his sleeve, conscious that he had come straight from the warehouse.

'If you would be so good as to step this way.' Will followed the clerk into the office. Mr. Monkpeace rose to his feet behind an enormous desk and extended his hand. Will recognized him from the funeral. An elderly man, probably of a similar age to Mr. Bonham, he wore small, round spectacles and a generous, grey wig. His manner was unmistakably serious, an air of gravitas being applied even to the task of bidding Will welcome to his office. From a large pile of papers to his right, Mr. Monkpeace selected the top scroll, tied with black ribbon. He undid it and with his hands he smoothed flat the vellum on the table.

'I have here' he said gravely, 'the last will and testament of my client, Mr. Josiah Bonham.' Will nodded acknowledgement.

Mr. Monkpeace extended his right hand once more and picked up another scroll, tied up with red ribbon. Flattening it out alongside the will, he said 'And I have here a document, an agreement signed by Mr. Bonham and yourself, Mr. Bristowe.'

Will nodded again.

'The document is dated five years since, and states that payment for the warehouse on the quayside should be made in full by the end of September in the year eighteen hundred and three.' The lawyer paused for effect and peered over his spectacles. 'You are aware, no doubt Mr. Bristowe, that we have but one day left of September eighteen hundred and three.'

Will opened his mouth to speak but the lawyer held up his hand for silence.

'This document, I should remind you, states quite clearly, that should you be unable to meet this payment, in full, the property will automatically revert to the ownership of Mr. Josiah Bonham, or his estate, with immediate effect.'

The control that the old man held over the meeting was as absolute as that of Uncle Samuel's. Silenced by the authority and precise wording, Will resigned himself and waited to be invited to speak.

'Now we come to the will.' The lawyer clasped his hands in front of his chest and peered down at the wording. 'As you might imagine, a businessman as successful as Mr. Josiah Bonham must give considerable thought as to what and to whom his bequests are made. I shall, therefore, not read the will in its entirety, but cut to the section in question, wherein your name appears.'

It seemed to Will that Mr. Monkpeace took an age to find his place in the document before him. Finally, the words were slowly and precisely read out to him. 'and I, therefore, leave the building known as Number Three Warehouse, on the quayside of New York to my former employee, Mr. William Bristowe.'

Regarding Will over his spectacles, he waited patiently for a response. 'Did you understand the meaning, Mr. Bristowe? The payment transaction you thought you were about to make need not take place. The warehouse now belongs outright to you.'

'Thank you. Yes. I did understand.' Will's words were spoken quietly, but all the while a voice raged in his head. How could you have been so stupid? Where was your trust? Why didn't you go to see him earlier? He wanted the lawyer to repeat it but couldn't quite find the courage to ask, so he sat silently.

'I imagine the news has taken you aback, somewhat.'

'Yes. A little. It is so unexpected.'

'Of course.' Mr. Monkpeace stood up to signify the end of the meeting. 'If I can be of service to you at any time, please do not hesitate. Good day to you, Mr. Bristowe.'

'Good day, Sir.' In no time at all, Will had been shown out of the office, was back outside the door, and standing on the street in quite a daze. He knew he should feel elated, for it was the most wonderful and unexpected thing to have happened. The longed-for security of a stable business was now his. He set off down the street, heading for home and Eliza.

Yet, somehow, he could find no joy. Quite the contrary. The voice in his head still ranted, nausea crept over him and his legs felt heavy. If only … if only he had known. He would never have sanctioned the slave deals, never have put their lives in danger, and Seamus would be here now, to laugh and joke and raise a tankard of ale in celebration. And then, his worst sin of all. Samuel. If he could have foreseen even the slightest glimmer of hope that by the last day of September 1803 he would find himself a rich man, with outright ownership of a prime warehouse, he would never have given his son away. He had traded him just as callously as he had traded the slaves. The legacy was a punishment.

Will's footsteps slowed and he found himself outside the new stone church. Just across from the doorway, next to the path, Josiah Bonham lay entombed in his vault. Will looked down at the freshly chiselled stone in a confusion of guilt and despair. When the old man had written his will, he must have imagined the pleasure and excitement his bequest would give Will and his family. They could move to a big house in a smart area, and the children could receive good schooling. He knew Mr. Bonham had always liked and admired Eliza. This legacy was for her too.

Will stepped into the cool of the church. The elaborately carved pews on either side of the wide aisle were empty. He slipped into the nearest one and knelt down. Almost a full hour later, his burden of guilt no lighter, he emerged into the churchyard, and it was raining.

Chapter 16

Eliza heard the maid's footsteps, solid and purposeful as she crossed the tiled floor of the wide hallway on her way to answer the front door. It was three o'clock in the afternoon. Mary Ann was still at her lessons and Simon asleep in the nursery. It being a sultry day, little air circulated through the house and, although her chaise was close by the large open window, Eliza felt the need to waft her fan to cool her face.

She glanced idly around the room. The vast gilt mirror above the marble fireplace reflected the red velvet drapes and the oil painting on the opposite wall. The book in her lap remained closed. It had not held her attention for long. She had found it hard to concentrate on anything for the entire day. It had been a difficult week and both she and Will had been ill at ease and withdrawn. Seamus had died exactly one year ago.

The maid knocked lightly and entered the room. Approaching Eliza with a silver tray, she curtsied and placed it on the small table by her side.

'Thank you, Sarah.' The maid retreated and Eliza still stared at the letters piled there. The ritual was almost like a game, but the outcome was always the same. How different from the first few months. Then she would snatch up the letters instantly, sifting through for a sign that one was from England, and perhaps with childish handwriting. Such a letter never came.

After months of disappointment, Eliza attempted to adopt a calmer approach to the lack of communication regarding her son. She had been forced to rely on information reaching her through letters from her sister-in-law, Jane, or very occasionally, Will's father, Thomas. Despite repeated letters to little Samuel, and heartfelt pleading to Uncle Samuel himself, no word had ever been forthcoming from Twyford Manor. The deliberate intention, she knew, was that there should be no contact.

With faintly trembling hands, Eliza picked up the silver letter opener and studied the first envelope: an invitation. It was a testament to Will's ascendancy in the social hierarchy of New York that the mantelshelf was almost constantly adorned with offers of hospitality. Not that this displeased Eliza in any way, for their new-found wealth had brought many pleasures and diversions. Her delight in expensive and exquisitely made clothes in fashionable styles made them the perfect guests to grace any social occasion.

Today, however, not even the invitation to attend the official laying of the foundation stone for the much talked about City Hall could raise Eliza's spirits. Slowly, she traced the tiny ridges of the velvet covering of the chaise with her finger. She knew in her heart that she shouldn't blame Will. Yet sometimes her bitterness spilled out and angry words were exchanged. The events of the previous year had done much to dampen the joy of the unexpected inheritance. If only Will had not taken Samuel to England. And if only he had not agreed to one more slave deal.

Eliza remembered vividly the day she had accompanied Will to visit Uncle Daniel and Aunt Kathleen to inform them of Seamus' death. She had often wondered since why she had felt it necessary to go, but her feeling at the time was that Will's grief for his friend had rendered him fragile, and she had to be with him to give him the strength. Certainly, he had given them an honest account, explaining how they had struck a slave deal, and lightly skimming over the details of the 'accidental' death.

'Seamus liked his deals. Never saw the danger in them.' had been all that Uncle Daniel said. Will promised to pay the share Seamus owned in the business as soon as the lawyer had settled on it.

All that was a year ago now. Their move to a fine house on a prosperous street had occupied their time and Will had taken on extra staff to help at the warehouse. Plunged into a social and business whirl, Eliza and Will had each tried to come to terms with the loss of both their son and their friend. On the occasions when they managed to talk about these things, they could offer comfort and support to each other, but sooner or later a chance remark would incur bitterness and recriminations. Their fragile relationship teetered like a child's see-saw.

The door opened again and Mary Ann's solemn face peered round. Seeing her mother lying down, she crossed the room to her. Eliza opened her arms and, with her usual motherly smile, welcomed her daughter to her. Mary Ann showed no pleasure on her face. She just quietly nestled into the space beside her mother.

'Did your lessons go well today?'

'Yes thank you.'

'What did you do?'

'The usual things.'

Eliza sometimes felt despair when she thought about the sort of young woman her daughter might turn out to be. She could be wrong, of course, and she sincerely hoped that Mary Ann would soon begin to show some sign of a friendlier demeanour, but as yet her face rarely registered happiness. Mostly she wore a serious frown, but this turned into a scowl when she was displeased. In fact 'Don't scowl, Mary Ann' had become a much repeated phrase in the household.

This is not to say that Mary Ann was an unhappy child. Nature had not blessed her with angelic features, but at the age of eight she often showed an understanding beyond her years. She adored her baby brother, Simon, and would keep him happily entertained for hours, but after the initial questions concerning Samuel's welfare in England, she rarely spoke of him. Eliza knew how much she missed him, for they had been very close, yet Mary Ann knew that the subject of her brother's whereabouts caused pain and acrimony between her parents. Consequently, she rarely mentioned his name.

Eliza attempted to tame back her daughter's dark curly hair with her fingers. The ribbon had come undone and the mass of frizzy curls sprang out wildly. With her dark complexion and watchful eyes, and her reluctance to smile, Mary Ann seemed serious and sombre.

'When is Papa coming home?'

'Perhaps he won't be too late today. But you know how busy he is.'

'I don't like it when he's late.' Mary Ann's voice was petulant.

Eliza smiled. It always gave her pleasure to witness the special bond between her daughter and Will, who was after all, not her natural father. One day she would have to tell her, but not yet.

At the sound of a coach drawing up outside, Mary Ann rushed to the front window. There, stepping out of the shiny black carriage pulled by matched chestnut mares, was Will. Looking every inch the successful businessman, he handed his top hat to the maid at the door and then held out his arms to greet Mary Ann. She bestowed upon him a rare smile of pleasure. Leading him by the hand, she proudly announced his arrival to her mother.

'For once, everything seems to be in order,' Will said by way of explanation for his early arrival home. 'The new clerk appears to be very able.'

'I'm pleased.' Eliza looked at her husband and for the first time noticed that his face had changed. Worry lines seemed to have appeared overnight, giving him a more mature appearance. He had also filled out slightly, no longer presenting the boyish figure he once had. But Eliza knew that when he looked at her, it was with the same intensity and love as always. It was a depth of love which she knew she could never return. She gave him a quick smile.

'It's ages, Papa, since you told me stories of Beesthorpe,' Mary Ann wheedled.

'I have no new stories to tell. You've heard them all so many times.'

'But if we're to go there one day, I need to know everything.'

Will smiled indulgently as Mary Ann clung imploringly to his leg. He released himself from her grasp. 'I promise we will talk of the estate before you go to bed, but for the moment I must speak with your mother.'

'Why don't you go and see if little Simon has woken up from his afternoon nap?' Eliza said. Mary Ann looked solemnly at her parents, watching for signs of underlying tension. 'Don't forget, Papa.'

'I won't.'

When the door had closed behind Mary Ann, a slightly uncomfortable silence developed. Eliza lay back on the chaise and Will began to slowly patrol the room, picking up objects and studying the furnishings closely as if seeing them for the first time. In fact he had spent little leisure time at home since their move to the big house, and some of their possessions were unfamiliar to him. Finally, he sat down opposite Eliza and sighed heavily. 'I've been thinking about Seamus all day today.'

'Yes. So have I.'

'The lawyer has finally completed his calculations. Seamus' share of the business comes to five hundred dollars. It rightly belongs to the family in Ireland.' Will shifted his weight uneasily in the chair. 'Of course I can't be sure that it won't go to the rebel cause, but Seamus only spoke of the one brother involved with the

149

United Irishmen. The trouble is – I feel a responsibility to his family.'

Eliza waited.

'I think I should deliver it in person. It's too risky sending it. What if it fell into the wrong hands and they were cheated? They are simple people – unable to read even. No experience of business and banks, I'm sure.'

Eliza's mind started to race. If Will made a trip to Ireland, he could continue on to Derbyshire and see Samuel. They could have first hand knowledge of him. Will watched her face and held up his hand. 'I know. I'll go and find Samuel, too.'

Eliza stared unseeingly at the fireplace. Her fingers played around her mouth as she gave thought to her son. Will could report back fully. She needed to know so many things – Was he happy? Had he grown much? Were his fair curls still bouncing on his shoulders or had they been cut off? Did he have friends at school?

'Yes. I think you should go. But when?'

'Either I leave immediately, that is before the winter storms begin, and possibly be forced to stay the winter in England. Or I wait until spring, and sail over and back again quite quickly.'

The thought of enduring the whole winter without word of Samuel plunged Eliza into despair. 'It would be wrong to leave Seamus' family in poverty for the winter, if you could find a berth to Ireland this autumn.' she said, only too aware of her duplicity.

'I agree. There's a ship calling into Galway and it sails next week. I'll book a passage.'

'Will the business manage without you?' Eliza was suddenly concerned, for though this lavish lifestyle had been only recently acquired, she had no wish to relinquish it through ill management.

'Ah, now, as for that, I wondered how you would feel about calling in at the office every few days – just to check that everything is as it should be. A formality really. You remember that you helped with the books before Samuel was born? You were good at it. Even Mr. Bonham was impressed.'

Eliza smiled at the memory of those difficult days, filled only with hard work and hope. 'Yes, I think I could do that. I might even enjoy it.'

Will gave a small sigh of relief. 'That's settled then. Come down to the warehouse with me tomorrow and I'll show you the new ledgers.' He reached over and squeezed his wife's hand. 'Everything will be fine.' They both knew that 'everything' really referred to Samuel.

After Will had gone to make his peace with Mary Ann, Eliza raised herself from the chaise and began to wander about the room. How strange, she thought to herself, that this magnificent house and all its attendant luxuries should bring so little pleasure. Equally perverse were her thoughts constantly straying to her two dead babies and lost child. Mary Ann and Simon meant the world to her, but the truth was that her mind was mostly occupied with longings for her lost children.

She felt grateful to Will for his action. For him to go personally to Ireland was a noble gesture, but to go in search of their son meant so much more. It had given her hope.

The elite of New York society gathered for the official ceremony. Carriages lined up all along the wide street and well attired businessmen circulated amongst the crowds, always mindful that being seen at a civic function may bring some new business their way.

Will and Eliza strolled around the appointed site and viewed the elaborate plans for the marble-faced building. The new City Hall was designed to be vast and imposing, a reflection of the importance of the constantly expanding city, and would, they said, take years to complete. Will raised his hat to businessmen and acquaintances, and, on his arm, Eliza inclined her head and smiled sweetly. This was their last day together, as Will was to sail the next day.

As they listened to the speeches and gathered around the foundation site, Will glanced across the crowds. With a start he realised that Ned was close by, watching him. Their eyes met and each nodded slightly. It was the first time they had seen one another since the incident a year ago and both looked uncomfortable. Even so, when the speeches concluded and Eliza became engaged in conversation, Will made his way through the crowd in Ned's direction.

'It will be a fine building, don't you think?' Ned remarked.

'Yes, indeed. New York is a wealthy city.'

'Is trade going well for you?'

'Very well, thank you. And you?' Will's eyes shifted uneasily. He had no desire to hear news of the slave market and it pained him to even think of it.

'I shall soon be out of New York. I've plans to buy land in the south. A plantation. My own estate. Just like you, Will.' Ned looked directly at Will and they both remembered the night spent in Hare Hills Wood, when Ned had been a homeless fugitive. 'I've lived by my wits long enough. I'm tired of it.'

'A plantation.' Will's voice tightened and he shook his head with the irony of it. 'That was my partner's dream. You remember Seamus, my partner? You had him shot in the woods.'

Ned looked around anxiously, in case they were overheard. 'You know that wouldn't have happened if I'd known it was you. I swear I was just as shaken as you that night.'

'Well, you'll have plenty of slaves to run your plantation, no doubt.' Will turned to finish the conversation but Ned continued.

'Oh, I know the growing feeling against slavery here. Legislation will come along soon enough. It's time to move on now. So tell me, when will you be going back to England to claim your estate?'

Will sighed, 'When my uncle dies, and not before, though he seems to hold on to life with such tenacity that I truly believe he will live to be a hundred.'

'Ah, we all have to play the cards life deals out to us. We can only do the best we can and hope fortune smiles on us.' Ned held out his hand. 'Good luck to you.'

Will slowly shook the hand offered to him and looked up at Ned. 'Goodbye. I hope you find your plantation.' Ned turned and made his way through the crowd.

'Who was that handsome man I saw you talking to?' Eliza came up just as Ned disappeared out of sight.

'Just someone I used to know.' Will took Eliza's arm and steered her back to their carriage.

Once more, Will watched the city of New York disappearing in the distance as the ship sailed out into the Hudson River and on into the Atlantic Ocean. The journey, uneventful and tedious, gave him plenty of time for reflection, which is not a good thing when past mistakes loom large. Diversions were few and Will's mood remained melancholy throughout the voyage.

In due course, the majestic sweep of Galway Bay and the Connemara Mountains came into view. Relieved at the opportunity for exercise and action, as well as fulfilling his duty, Will went ashore and set about finding Seamus' family.

He hired a horse, asked directions and, in the early morning, set off south into County Clare. With the mountains to his left and the craggy coastline to his right, he followed the stony road through tiny villages and past isolated cottages. These rural settlements, or clachans as Seamus had called them, were desperately poor. The mud-built dwellings were crude and clustered together and every child playing outside was dirty, barefoot and clothed only in rags and tatters. As Will trotted by they stopped to stare or ran for the cover of a doorway to watch from a distance.

The beauty of the landscape was more intense than he had imagined, but it was harsh and had an unforgiving wildness to it. A keen wind blew in off the sea and, in a sky full of menace, heavy clouds threatened. Peasant farmers, poorly clothed and usually bent low under the strain of a heavy load, struggled along. They regarded Will suspiciously, for a horseman would not be one of them.

Will reined his horse back to come alongside a man leading a mule and small cart piled high with squares of cut peat. 'Can you tell me if I'm on the right track to find the Branagan cottage?' The reply was a long time coming and Will felt acute distrust emanating from the man as he was closely scrutinized. When eventually he spoke, the words were delivered in such a strong dialect that to Will his reply was almost unintelligible. But with the help of gestures he managed to confirm the direction and trotted on once more.

Eventually, the boulder-strewn landscape gave way to a kinder soil and there was evidence of tiny strips of cultivation. Occasionally he came across a cow tethered on a patch of grass or being led along to better grazing. On one unusually flat section, a mule pulled a plough. The farmer struggled to keep the point under the hard ground, as time and again it hit stones and reared up out of the earth. His progress was slow as he was frequently forced to halt, stoop down to lift the stones and roll them aside before grasping the handles of the plough and urging on the mule once more. A sizeable pile of stones at the edge of the field gave testament to the tortuous procedure. Will remembered John Greaves complaining of the skerry he constantly had to contend with when he ploughed Bark Hill, but it had been nothing compared to the back-breaking labour of this farmer's toil.

It almost felt to Will, as he rode along, that Seamus was with him. He used to speak so fondly of this landscape, and although it held no emotion for Will, he could understand Seamus' homesickness for it. Poverty had driven him on and caused him to make difficult decisions, but Seamus had never forgotten his homeland. He had probably dreamed of coming back one day, a rich and successful man. That he would have been rich and successful Will was quite sure, but for that bullet – and a man called Ned Hobbs.

The little valley in which Will now found himself was sheltered from the wind, and the horse picked his way carefully along the stony track. Will kept his eyes fixed ahead scouring the hillside for a sign of a dwelling, but it was as deserted a landscape as he had ever seen. At last he made out, in the distance, a column of smoke spiralling up from a chimney. He drew nearer, and the rocky ground to his right suddenly dropped away, affording him an uninterrupted view of the bay. A reluctant sun struggled to emerge through the clouds, and the sea shimmered delicately beneath its weak rays. Will halted for a moment and stared at the scene before him. It was just as Seamus had described.

Will slowed down as he approached the cottage, uncertain as to whom he would find, and what his reception might be. Apart from the smoking chimney, there was no sign of life. He dismounted and found a low tree to which he tethered the horse. Vegetation was sparse and stunted and twisted branches leaned heavily into the hillside, pleading for mercy from the relentless wind. The mud cottage had two windows and a door and nestled back against the hillside as though clinging for protection. Will knocked on the door, removed his hat and stood back. Out of the corner of his eye he caught a movement, and looked around just in time to see the disappearing backsides of two ragged boys.

After a few moments he could hear movement inside and the latch clicked. With the door opened just a few inches, he could make out the face of a woman – not old but not young either. 'What are you wanting?'

It was difficult to begin the conversation through such a tiny gap in the door but Will did his best. 'Good day to you. My name is William Bristowe and I was a good friend of Seamus. Seamus Branagan. In fact, we were in business together.'

The woman looked at him. She seemed to be processing the information for a moment and then shut the door. Inside, there were voices. First a high, thin voice and then a rough, masculine one. Will waited. There was no sign of the boys.

When the door opened again it was an old woman who stood there, stooped and peering. Her heavy shawl was tied tightly around her and her black skirt was worn and dirty with years of wear. Wisps of grey hair straggled loose beside her face but her eyes were blue and steady. She pushed the door wide and scrutinized Will. 'You knew my son?'

'Yes, Ma'am. Seamus was my good friend and partner.'

The woman nodded. 'He told us of you in his letters. The Englishman.'

'I should like to talk to you. May I come in?' The woman turned and hobbled inside, leaving the door open, and Will bent low to follow her. The dirt floor, mud walls, smoky fire and low ceiling made for a gloomy atmosphere, but it was neatly kept and warm. In a chair by the fire sat an old man, his long grey hair reaching down to his shoulders and his white beard resting on his chest. With his bony hand holding a long, clay pipe, he indicated for Will to take the other chair.

Steam rose from the bubbling pan on the fire and Will caught the sickly sweet smell of rotting vegetables mixed with burning peat. Two children wearing little more than threadbare tatters sat silently on the floor, their eyes fixed on the stranger.

Will cleared his throat. 'I came to see you in person because I have something to give you. I know Seamus sent some money back to you, for his brothers, but you see, he was a very hard worker and we were in business together. When he died, he owned a sizeable share, and I have come to pay you the money that is owed.' Not a word was uttered in response. Will wondered if they had understood him. He reached into the bag slung across his shoulders and drew out a piece of paper.

The latch clicked and in the doorway stood a man. He stared suspiciously at the stranger in his house and Will, startled by the sudden arrival, stood up and stared back. The stocky man had dark hair and weathered skin. His clothes were worn and much mended and he exuded an earthy smell, as if he had himself become a part of the Irish soil over which he laboured.

'This is the Englishman. The one Seamus spoke of in his letters.' The old man spoke slowly. Turning to Will he explained 'This is Michael, Seamus' older brother.'

Will nodded to him and held up the paper in his hand. 'This is a bank draft. For five hundred dollars. That is the share in the business which belonged to Seamus when he died. The money will make a difference to your lives, I'm sure, but for safe keeping it must be presented to a bank with a proper account number.'

'You're giving us money?' Michael Branagan had closed the door but remained standing by it. He glowered from beneath his dark eyebrows and his words were heavy with suspicion.

'No. It's not my money. It was earned by Seamus and now rightly belongs to you. I was sailing to England and thought I would deliver it in person – to be sure you received it.'

Seamus' brother stepped forward and slowly reached out to take hold of the bank draft. He held it in his dirt encrusted hand, staring down at it. His face registered nothing and Will wondered if he could make out the figures. 'It is for five hundred dollars.' He said again.

Everyone in the room stared at the paper and the silence continued as if Will had been the bearer of bad news. 'I should be happy to accompany you to the bank in the town to make sure that it is safely lodged.'

Michael shook his head slowly. 'No. That won't be necessary.'

'I think it would be wise.' Will persisted. 'The bank may become suspicious as to how it came to be in your possession. I shall be staying at the inn overnight. Perhaps I can meet you in the morning. Eleven o'clock?'

Michael thought over the proposal. 'Eleven o'clock it is.'

'Good. Then I shall bid you good day.' Will started towards the door and the movement seemed to break the spell. The mother was the first to speak. 'God bless you, Sir.' Her voice was high and quavering and Will could see the tears working their way down her lined face.

Seamus' father levered himself up out of his chair and stood shakily on his bent legs. He extended a trembling hand and as Will crossed the hearth to take it, he could see that the old man's pale eyes were brimming . 'Thank you, Mr. Bristowe,' he said in a voice full of emotion and barely above a whisper.

'You are most welcome.'

Seamus' brother still stood in the middle of the room. 'You are the one who taught him to write?'

Will nodded. 'And Seamus had a lot to teach me, too. We were a good partnership.' He shook Michael's hand and walked out into the fresh air and sunshine. He stood for a moment to take in the view. Little stony fields led right down to the sea where white-topped waves crashed in on a wide beach. It was just as Seamus described it. With the debt honoured, a little of the guilt ebbed away.

By the time he had mounted his horse, the entire family were standing just outside the cottage doorway. 'I'll see you outside the bank at eleven tomorrow.' Michael nodded and Will waved to the stunned little group. He turned the horse back up the track towards the town. As he trotted along he smiled as he wondered what they would do with the money. They may emigrate to America themselves or they may use it to maintain their existence there. If he were a betting man, Will decided that it would be the latter. It had seemed to him that the family were as much a part of Ireland as the landscape itself.

The next morning Will watched the approaching figure of Michael walking down the street towards him. He had washed and was wearing a clean shirt, but did not look like a man who would walk into a bank with five hundred dollars. He was early, as Will knew he would be.

The draft was deposited, to the astonishment of the clerk, and Will wrote and signed a document attesting to the validity. 'Can you sign your name or is it to be a cross?' the clerk demanded of Michael.

'I can sign.' With painful concentration and awkwardness, Michael slowly scratched out the letters which stood for his signature on the deposit slip. As they stepped outside once more his face slowly broke into a smile and Will shook his hand. 'Have you thought what you will do with the money?'

'All night I've thought about nothing else.'

'I know about Patrick, but where are your other brothers?'

Michael shook his head sadly. 'One drowned just out in the bay. Two of them took themselves off to England looking for work. That was five years ago. We've never heard of them since. And one was hanged, for stealing.'

'I'm sorry.' Will could think of nothing else to say.

'You've seen the way we live. It's a good year when there's enough to eat. If we could buy a decent farm with good soil and grazing ...' Michael's face suddenly took on an excitement as he realised his dream could now come true.

'There's only one piece of advice I'll give you.' Will said. 'Learn to read and write properly as soon as you can. Seamus knew that was the only way. Otherwise there'll be too many people ready to cheat you.'

'You'll be right about that. But for now, I'm going to buy a mule. And I'll be loading him down with every luxury I can lay my hands on. We'll be having a feast tonight Mr. Bristowe, and we shall toast your health.'

The two men shook hands and went their separate ways. As Will looked back he was sure that Michael walked taller as he strode off to buy his mule. With his obligation to Seamus now fulfilled, Will boarded his ship. As he sailed away from Ireland his thoughts turned to the next task. He must find his son.

Chapter 17

Will's arrival at Twyford Manor was unexpected. From the ship he had taken the stagecoach and finally hired a cart to take him the last few miles down the flat valley of the Trent. From the cluster of farms and houses that made up the village, the church tower rose up proudly.

Retrieving his box from the cart, Will approached the front door of the Manor. The River Trent flowed just beyond the garden and the house stood tall and square. Elegant, it was not. Will had always felt that the building resembled Uncle Samuel's character – cold, imposing and dominant. He rapped on the brass knocker of the front door.

Uncle Samuel did not have a butler but he had employed the same housekeeper, Mrs. Draycott, for many years. She now stood in the doorway before Will. 'Yes?' was all she said.

Will could not believe that she did not recognize him, although ten years had probably passed since he had visited Twyford. 'It's Will Bristowe, Mrs. Draycott,' he said, expecting a smile of welcome or at least recognition. Her hard eyes were small in her bony face and her white cap flapped low down the side of her hollow cheeks. 'Your uncle is not here. We weren't expecting you.'

'I had to come over on business and thought I would call in to see him – and my son. Is he here?' She stared coldly at him, shook her head and reluctantly opened the door wider to allow him to enter. Will set his box down in the wide hall.

'You can wait in there,' Mrs. Draycott said, indicating the mahogany door leading into the vast drawing room. 'I'll send in a maid to light the fire.'

The forbidding exterior of the house belied the opulence of the rooms within. When it came to providing himself with the luxuries of life, Uncle Samuel always managed to overcome his reluctance to part with money. Will wandered around the room, examining the paintings and deciding which of the overstuffed chairs he would prefer to sit on. A young housemaid entered meekly and soon a fire was crackling in the hearth.

When a half-hour had passed and no refreshment or word had been forthcoming, Will rang the bell by the fireplace. Mrs.

Draycott appeared, displeasure written all over her face. 'When do you expect my uncle's return?'

'Any time now, Sir.'

'A cup of tea would be much appreciated, if you would be so kind.' Mrs. Draycott inclined her head very slightly and returned to the kitchen. Will was in no doubt about the coldness of his reception.

There was no view to speak of from the windows. The garden wall reared up just a few yards away, blocking out the light and giving a feeling of enclosure. Eventually, a carriage pulled up and Will could hear Uncle Samuel's voice. After Mrs. Draycott's harsh tones there was silence until the door opened. Will got to his feet. Uncle Samuel lumbered into the room.

'What are you doing here? I received no word.'

'I had business to attend to in Ireland. I decided to come over to see how everyone is.'

'What business in Ireland?'

One minute in Uncle Samuel's company and already he was having to explain himself. Things never changed. 'My business partner died last year and I delivered the money left in his estate to his family. They are just poor people, unable to read. I needed to explain to them.'

'How much did you give them?'

Will sighed. 'Five hundred dollars.'

'You gave Irish peasants five hundred dollars! They would have been just as content with one hundred. You'll never do well in business, boy.'

'I didn't give them the money. It was theirs by right. I just delivered it.'

Uncle Samuel slumped down in his high-backed chair by the fire. 'You're a fool, William.' He said dismissively. Will fought to control his annoyance.

'So, have you seen your father?'

'No. Not yet. I came straight here from Liverpool.' Uncle Samuel narrowed his eyes in puzzled questioning. 'To see my son,' Will continued.

'Your son?' Uncle Samuel's voice became harsh. 'I told you. In England, you have no son. I have your son.' Uncle and nephew stared at each other, like card players each looking for a sign of his opponent's weakness.

'All we ask is to hear news of him.' Will tried not to sound pleading. He raised his voice. 'His mother is beside herself with worry. Our letters have gone unanswered.'

'Your letters have been destroyed. It would do the child no good to be reading words from his natural parents, reminding him of his previous life. I thought you would have had his best interests at heart, William.'

Will took a deep breath. 'But you could reply to our letters. You could give us some indication as to how he is faring, how he is progressing. Just to help ease his mother's mind.'

'I told you to forget about your son. He's my responsibility now, not yours.'

'And where is he?'

'At school, of course. As we discussed, he is to have the finest education.'

'When will he be coming home? I should like to see him before I go.'

Uncle Samuel's patience snapped. 'That will not be possible.' He thundered. 'He will not be home for weeks and I have had enough of this conversation.'

Mrs. Draycott quietly entered the room and announced that luncheon was ready. As they ate at the long table, Will felt uncomfortable and miserable but Uncle Samuel appeared utterly unmoved. 'You may stay the night before going to your father's house tomorrow. My housekeeper will prepare a room for you. Now I have business to attend to.'

Will wandered outside through the front entrance gates and followed the track just a few yards until he came to the river. Deep in thought, he stood and watched the flow of water swirling past. The ferryman's boat was moored a little further upstream. From across the river there came a shout. A man wearing a parson's black hat and cloak walked to the edge of a small jetty and hailed across the water. 'Daniel, are you there?' From a thicket of low trees not far from Will, the ferryman emerged. He straightened his leather jerkin, patched and worn thin over the years, and slapped off the leaves clinging to his trousers.

'Yes, Reverend. I'll be over in two minutes,' he called. Rubbing the sleep from his eyes, he clambered into the boat and began to row across the water. It was a blustery autumn day and, although the current was quite sluggish, the wind whipped up little grey ripples on the surface. The ferryman made short work of his task and in no time at all the Reverend was stepping into the boat. He settled himself down to be rowed back to his parish of Twyford.

Will felt despondent. He would never have believed that his uncle could be so harsh, cruel and calculating. Kicking the loose stones idly as he went, he followed the track alongside the river. Ahead, where the bank fell away allowing them access to the water, a herd of brown and white cows had gathered. They stood in the river drinking copiously, and the water dripped from their noses as they lifted their heads to stare. Rather than disturb them, he cut up to the right and made his way across the field to the church.

The Bristowe ancestors were buried here, generations of them. Some in the churchyard in the family plot, and some in the church itself with marble plaques and Latin inscriptions. He hoped this would not be his resting place, despite it being a pretty enough church. Beesthorpe was where his heart was, where he belonged.

Brisk footsteps on the stone flagged path caused Will to turn. The Reverend was marching purposefully towards him, or rather towards the church door where Will stood. 'Good day to you.' He raised his hat without slowing his pace and was about to sidestep Will and enter his church when he suddenly stopped. Peering into Will's face, he said. 'I know you, don't I?'

'William Bristowe, nephew of Samuel Bristowe.' Will nodded in the direction of Twyford Manor.

'Of course. I remember you coming here to stay with your uncle when you were a boy.'

Will did his best to smile but his eyes must have remained sad because the Reverend said 'I hope it's not bad news that has brought you back to Twyford?'

'No. No. Not at all.' Confronted so unexpectedly, Will hurriedly excused himself and turned to go.

'Wait. Stay a while. Allow me two minutes to put these things away in the church. We'll sit over there in the sunshine and pass the time together. I'd like that.' The Reverend had put a kindly arm on Will's shoulder and, like some obedient servant, Will found himself sitting and waiting for his master.

'So, what brings you here?' The vicar settled himself down beside Will and began a gentle inquisition. With very little prompting, Will's story spilled out and he unburdened himself to the kindly parson.

'I know your son, Samuel. He comes to church with your uncle, when he is here.'

'How does he seem? Would you say he's happy?'

'Well, it's hard to make an exact judgement, but whenever I've seen him he hasn't looked unhappy. He is a most engaging child. I can quite understand his mother's anguish. And indeed, yours.' The Reverend looked at Will with kindness and concern. 'I wish there were something I could do to help.'

'Do you know where he is? Which school he is attending? My uncle refuses to tell me. He insists I shouldn't see him, but if I return to America without being able to offer my wife the comfort of having had at least one meeting with our son, it will break her heart.'

The Reverend clasped his hands together in front of him and tapped them thoughtfully against his lips. 'I do know where your son is.' he said cautiously.

Will's heart leapt. 'If you tell me, I'll be discreet and my uncle will never know.'

'It is the Thomas Burke School for Boys in Nottingham. Near the new courthouse.' Will shook the Reverend's hand and thanked him most profusely. 'I will pray for you all, William,' the vicar said as Will hurried away.

The next day Will bid a curt goodbye to Uncle Samuel and his disagreeable housekeeper, and set off for Nottingham. Weaving his way through the narrow streets he came to the High Pavement, on which the courthouse stood, and asked passers-by if they knew the location of the Thomas Burke School for Boys. Eventually, he was rewarded, and stood outside the establishment, his hand trembling slightly as he knocked on the door.

A servant opened it. 'I should like to speak with Mr. Thomas Burke, if you please.' He was shown into a small room and asked to wait. The smell inside the building was very distinctive, yet Will was hard put to say what it was. Thick dust had collected on the surfaces of everything he could see, but he felt convinced that the over-riding smell was that of old cabbage.

When Thomas Burke finally entered the room, he was plainly irritated by the intrusion into his teaching time. Dressed in a black academic gown, frayed and scruffy, with a grubby white stock at his throat, he carried a cane which he tapped constantly on the side of his boot. Will began his explanation, asking to see his son. He soon realised, however, that the man possessed a wildly wandering left eye, which was most disconcerting. Every time he sought to hold his attention and the eye set off on its own course, Will was forced to switch to the right eye which, alarmingly, he found to be staring at him intensely.

'Mr. Samuel Bristowe has been most explicit in his instructions. He pays me well to see that the child is educated and receives no visitors.'

Will dug deep into his pocket and jiggled a few coins around. He brought out a shiny guinea and placed it on the dusty books piled on the dusty desk.

'Well, perhaps one visit may be in order.'

Will pressed his advantage and rattled inside his pocket again. 'We shall of course, be writing to our son – from America, you understand. It is imperative that the letters reach him and that he be allowed to write back in return.' As Thomas Burke inclined his head slightly, Will produced two more glittering guineas and the left eye disappeared completely, leaving the right one fixed greedily on the coins.

'Very well. I'll fetch the boy.' In an instant he had scooped up the money and left the room, leaving a little cloud of dust hovering above the shelf.

When the door opened again, it was Samuel who stood there. From behind, Thomas Burke pushed him into the room. 'Five minutes only.' he barked. 'The child must not miss his lessons.'

Will stared down at his son. In fourteen months he had grown considerably. His arms and legs were longer and his baby curls had been cut off. His face was no longer chubby and round – in fact, Will thought it a little pinched. He dropped to his knees, smiled and opened his arms in welcome. Samuel walked slowly and solemnly towards him.

'Your Mama and I have been so worried about you.' Will took hold of Samuel's hand. 'Are you alright? How is it here at school?'

'I'm very well thank you, Papa.'

'Do you have friends here?' Samuel nodded. 'Is Uncle Samuel kind to you?'

'Yes.'

'Do you like living at Twyford? It's a very grand house, isn't it?'

'Have Mama and Mary Ann forgotten me?' The pathetic question took Will back.

'No they haven't, Samuel. They think about you every day and asked me to tell you how much they miss you. Mary Ann goes to a big school now, just like you.'

'Can I come home to America now?'

'No. Not yet. But now that we know where you are, we're going to write letters to you. And you can write back and tell us how you're getting on.' Will swallowed hard as he looked at the crestfallen face of his young son. 'It won't be long before we all come back to England, to live at Beesthorpe, and then we shall see you all the time.'

Just when Will thought that Samuel would come into his arms to be hugged, the child stepped back. A door closed between them. 'I'm glad you're doing well with your lessons.' Will carried on. 'Uncle Samuel is very proud of you.' He felt the need to keep talking, to keep him close for as long as possible. All too soon, Thomas Burke appeared in the doorway. 'Say goodbye to your father.' It was all Will could do not to sweep his son up in his arms and rush out into the street with him. Instead, he held out his hand and Samuel took it. Then Will knelt down and put his arms around him. 'No matter what happens' he whispered 'you must always remember that we love you and will never forget you. We will be together very soon, I promise. Now be sure to write back to us.'

As Samuel reached the door, he turned back to his father one more time. Will could see tears brimming up and sparkling in his eyes. 'I wish Mary Ann was here.'

'Come along, boy. No time for sentimentality.' Thomas Burke's harsh voice crushed Samuel's hopes and his arm propelled him roughly through the door. The child was gone.

Will stumbled out into the street, his heart thumping and his eyes stinging. How could he have done this thing? Naively, he had imagined that the meeting would leave him feeling better, and that it would have been a comfort to Samuel. But no, it was worse, much worse. There was no comparison between the lively, talkative child who had accompanied him to England, and the withdrawn, suspicious and now tearful young boy he had left behind. He bumped into people as he dashed along. Should he turn back? Tell Uncle Samuel that he was taking him home? No, that was not the answer. The only possible outcome of that course of action would be banishment from the family, and the estate, for ever. He couldn't risk it. He just wasn't brave enough, or strong enough. There was no other way. Please God, let the waiting be over soon.

At the inn he retrieved his travelling box and took the next coach to Newark, where he hired a cart to take him out to Caunton.

It was almost dark when he pulled up in front of Beesthorpe Hall. Will felt the gentle pull of home-coming as the soft, candle-lit glow greeted him. Thomas became quite overcome at the sudden appearance of the son he thought to be far overseas. One minute he was lost for words, his watery old eyes sparkling in the candlelight, and the next calling out in a crackling voice to give orders to servants and dogs. But he looked well enough. The house was a little shabby, with a great deal less attention paid to house-keeping than previously, but Thomas seemed to have everything he needed, including the constant company of his two large hounds. They padded by his side wherever he went, finally settling themselves either side of his chair, watching their master closely, and ever hopeful of titbits from his pocket.

'Chaff died in the spring.' Thomas said suddenly. 'He was blind, you know.'

'I know. I hated to see him like that.'

Will related to his father the events of the day. 'When Uncle Samuel first suggested that he educate little Samuel, it seemed such a generous gesture. I never realised he meant to steal him away from us so completely.'

'We have not seen the child either. Not since the day he left here,' Thomas said sadly. 'Samuel seems determined to keep him over there, either at school or Twyford.' Absently, he pulled at the nearest hound's ears. 'I'm sorry he's refusing to answer your letters or even report on his progress, but I suppose that's typical of your uncle. When he owns something, it is his completely.'

Father and son sat by the fireside in the candlelight, drinking port. Will recounted the details of his life, skimming over the 'accidental' death of Seamus and making no mention whatever of slavery, or the encounter with a highwayman of the Great North Road, thought to be dead. They talked late into the night, reluctant to break off the conversation. Just one more question, just one more piece of news. When finally Thomas stood up to go to bed, he turned a little awkwardly towards his son. 'I think I should say this to you now, in case I never get another chance. I have a long time to think these days, but with you so far away, you never know.' He paused, searching for words, undecided how to start. Will wondered and waited for what was coming. 'I know I've been hard on you at times, but I think you know the reason for it. But now, well, it's time I told you. I'm very proud of you, Will. Very proud.' Without hesitating for one moment to observe the effect his words had on his son, or to give him chance to reply, Thomas bent his head, turned and left the room, the hounds padding close behind.

Will stayed in his chair for a while, watching the glowing embers of the fire gradually die down. He poured himself another glass of port. How strange life seemed to be. For as long as he could remember, he thought his father had been hard on him. He couldn't ever remember words of affection passing between them, his mother being the only one to encourage and praise, and offer those craved-for signs of unconditional love. His father had kept his feelings hidden well.

With a sharp sting of regret, Will wanted the years back. He wanted his father as a younger, more vigorous man, to sit late into the night with him every night, discussing affairs as equals, with each of them offering their opinions and affording the other their right to hold them. But it was all too late now.

The warm rush of love he now felt towards his father turned his thoughts back to his own son. No matter that he had tried to explain to Samuel, the child did not understand. How could he? All he could see was rejection. As the fire embers crumbled to grey ash, Will knew that today he had seen for himself the makings of the resentment that his own son would hold for him. How many years would it take to undo the hurt? Probably more than his life would be allocated.

He felt tired and emotionally drained, and in a sudden pang of longing for Eliza, Will made a decision. He would pay a hasty call on Jane, for he could not bear for her to hear that he had visited and not called to see her, and then he would return to Liverpool and take the very next crossing. It was late October. He could be lucky and make it across the Atlantic before the winter storms. All he knew was that he wanted to get back to his wife, to his business and to his family. He would not make this journey again until they could all make it together.

Chapter 18

Despite the threatening skies and blustery winds, the severe autumn storms never materialised and Will made the voyage safely back to New York. Jane had shown her brother warmth and understanding, and he had been grateful. She had not condemned him, although his conscience had not been entirely clear, since he had – once more –omitted certain details. She promised to do all she could to glean news of Samuel and of course relate it to Will, but neither of them held much hope of this, in view of Uncle Samuel's stand. Will found himself envying Jane and her uncomplicated life of domesticity and Church. Marcus had welcomed him heartily despite the unseemly haste of the visit, and then withdrew to allow brother and sister time for quiet talk. Desperate not to miss the chance of a sailing, Will had stayed just an hour or so. He had tried to explain the many reasons for his hasty return, but Jane had silenced him. It was a comfort to know that there was someone for whom explanation was unnecessary. Jane had made a good job of assuming his mother's role in that she was now the one who understood him and showed compassion and unconditional love. The visit had done much to soothe him.

Eliza had worked hard to oversee the business, and on his return all seemed well at the warehouse. It was showing a decent if not huge profit. Will's account to Eliza of Samuel's appearance, state of health, education and happiness was exhaustive, if not wholly accurate. Night after night, they sat by the fireside whilst Will recalled every minute detail from the colour of his eyes to the length of his hair. His description of the school was positively glowing. Even so, the gulf that had opened up between them showed no real sign of diminishing. The happiness that some years earlier both would have expected to go hand in hand with financial security had not materialised. There were too many regrets. That winter, the New York snow covered the streets yet again and the dockyard activities ground down to a minimum. Despite a whirl of social engagements, Will felt that his life was flat and joyless and he grew bored.

It was a bitter February night when Will bid goodnight to Eliza and set off in the carriage to attend a gentlemen's dinner. The breath of the snorting horses hung in clouds and Will wrapped his cloak and the carriage furs tight around him. As he stepped from the snow-covered street and into the vestibule of the imposing building, the buzz of conversation and warmth welcomed him. He deposited his cloak and top hat with a servant and edged into the crowd.

By the fireplace a tall man was engaged in earnest conversation. He had his back to him but Will recognized immediately that it was Ned. Few men in the room still wore their hair long, the fashion now being for a more cropped style, but Ned's black hair still curled luxuriously under a black ribbon. His extravagantly styled jacket with the high collar and gilt buttons sat atop an embroidered waistcoat, and a pristine, white stock set off his handsome face. The charisma that he had always had was doubled now that he had the wealth to accompany it. Will felt just a small tinge of admiration for his style.

He threaded his way across the room, nodding and smiling to acquaintances as he went. Ned turned and noticed, immediately excusing himself. The two men faced each other once more. 'I had thought we might not meet again.' Will said as he accepted Ned's offered hand.

'Well indeed it would be strange if we were not to meet from time to time, as we are both here to pick off the profits to be made in this city.'

Will could not help the edge that crept into his voice. 'So tell me, Mr. Bailey, do you still run the slave market? Do you still pocket your percentage of human misery?'

Ned's eyes burned hard for a moment. 'Still taking the high moral road, then? Don't forget, respectability in this country comes with money. But the answer to your question, is no. I've moved on from the slave trading. As with yourself, it was a means to an end. There are more pleasant ways of making money.'

Will's eyebrows rose questioningly. 'Your plantation?'

'Not yet, no. Drinking and gambling houses.' Ned laughed at Will's surprised face.

'Does that include brothels as well?'

'Not as yet, but if the market leads in that direction, I shan't rule it out. Working men are flocking to this city and there's plenty of money to be made out of them. When they've a few dollars in their pocket they want instant pleasure – drink, gambling and women.'

Once inside the dining hall, Will found he was seated across the table from Ned and had plenty of time to observe the easy manner with which he conducted himself. As soon as was decently possible Ned rose from his seat and bowed graciously to his companions. Walking up behind Will, he bent down and whispered for him to join him. 'Come with me.' Ned steered Will towards the door. 'This is turning into a dull gathering for sure. I've a carriage waiting outside and I'll show you a bit of life.'

The coachman negotiated the icy streets with care and pulled up outside a new red-brick mansion. The atmosphere of the establishment hit Will as soon as he entered. It was pure decadence. Room after room, richly furnished and with discreet tables separated by concealing screens, filled with well dressed men and women. The aroma of French perfume mingled with that of expensive cigars. Beautiful ladies in the latest fashions and displaying exotically dressed hair, quietly slipped away from the gaming tables, seductive eyes half-hidden behind feathered fans, to flirt openly with Ned. There was none of the raucous and rowdy behaviour of the ladies of the taverns. No screaming laughter and bawdy innuendo here.

They wandered through the rooms with Ned acknowledging the occupants of each table and freely bestowing his beaming smile. He was totally at ease. 'Better than dealing in slaves don't you think?' They sat down at a table and a decanter was brought by a male servant in green and gold livery. Ned poured the wine into the crystal goblets and offered a toast. 'To success.'

Despite everything, Will could not help but admire the style and class of the man. He had come from highwayman to slave dealer to gambling salon proprietor. And everyone seemed to love him. The high life was his for the taking. He raised his glass to Ned and smiled.

'So, tell me about your life. Are you happy, Will?'

'I've made mistakes, but you know that. I miss Seamus, I really do, and the business misses him. It's not the same now.' Will sipped his wine. He would rather not confide in Ned but, as he considered the position, he remembered that he alone knew the truth of his companion's background. It gave him a certain hold, even if it was only a moral one.

'And what of your family? You have a wife and children?'

Will gave a wry smile. 'Oh yes. I do, indeed. And we should be happy – but I am afraid things are difficult at the moment. The warehouse was left to me, you know. The day after Seamus' death, I went to the lawyer to plead for an extension for the loan – and he read Mr. Bonham's will to me. He had left me the whole thing. So we needn't have done the slave deal after all.' Will's face contorted into a mirthless smile. He took a gulp of wine and then drained his glass. Ned filled it up.

'And I needn't have sold my son.'

'Sold your son?' Ned was incredulous.

'My uncle, who owns the estate in England, said that if I wanted to be sure of inheriting, I should let him adopt my eldest son. So – I agreed. I didn't want to, but it's done now.' Will spoke quickly in a matter-of-fact voice, to get the explanation over with as swiftly as possible. 'And it has come between us, as you might expect. My wife, Eliza, will never forgive me, I know it. We have other children, but she pines for Samuel. At times she hates me for it.' Will began to feel the effects of the wine. 'I can't expect her to understand. At the time, I thought my uncle wouldn't live much longer, that we would all be going back soon anyway. But it hasn't happened.'

Ned watched Will's face closely. 'I'm sorry. Perhaps, as you say, your uncle will not live to be a great age. Then all will be forgotten and you can resume the role to which you were born – a Squire and Lord of the Manor!'

A woman came to the table and playfully tapped Ned on the shoulder with her fan. The men rose to their feet and Ned kissed her hand. 'Rosette, may I introduce my friend, Will Bristowe.' The lady turned to Will and extended her hand. As he took it and bent low, his eyes came to rest for a moment on a voluptuous décolletage.

He felt a certain reluctant to force his eyes from the fullness of the breasts rising so provocatively above the tight, red bodice, and yet he was desperate to study closely the face above them.

When at last he managed to raise his gaze, he found himself staring into a beautiful face. Blue eyes danced with amusement and fair curls nestled into a graceful neck. To his astonishment, Will found himself quite speechless and could do nothing but stare. 'Will, may I introduce Rosette Barton,' Ned was saying.

'Delighted to make your acquaintance.' At last he found his voice.

'Have you come for the gaming tables, Mr. Bristowe?'

'No, Ma'am. I fear I have no luck for cards.' Will could feel his pulse racing and his cheeks beginning to flush.

'Will is an old friend of mine,' Ned continued. 'Rosette is married to Septimus Barton, the banker. You have heard of him, Will?'

'Yes, indeed.' A strange disappointment came over him.

With her heavenly eyes fixed steadily, and disconcertingly, on his face, Rosette smiled and extended her hand once more to Will. 'It has been a pleasure to meet you Mr. Bristowe. I'm afraid I must return to my husband's table and lend him all my support before his losses escalate even further.' With a swish of red satin and a flick of her fan, she turned and left the room and Will felt at once elated and dismayed as he watched her go. From the door, she turned and, finding Will still watching her, she threw him a coquettish smile, full of mischief. Her expensive perfume still lingered, as did her effect on him. He looked up to find Ned smiling at him.

'Her husband is old and rich. And she is very beguiling, don't you think?'

'Yes, indeed she is.'

'What you need, Will, is diversion. And I've had just the idea. What did you like doing most before you came to America?'

'Very little as far as I can remember.'

'You remember our flight from Newark? The excitement of the ride?'

'Of course.'

'We need to ride like that again. Go hunting. Gallop for miles and miles. We're too restrained now. What do you think?'

Will nodded wistfully at the thought. 'Well, old Septimus Barton has an estate just to the north and he keeps a pack of foxhounds. I have already been invited to visit. What do you say if I get you an invitation too? It won't be difficult judging by the way Rosette looked at you.'

'Whatever do you mean?'

'What I mean is, Will, a blind man could have seen the attraction! You need a bit of spice in your life and Rosette Barton could be the one to provide it. Leave it to me.'

The drive up to the Barton estate took most of the day. Initially, Will had felt guilty as he accepted the invitation, so effortlessly engineered by Ned, for a week's sport on the vast estate, but Eliza had seemed happy for him to go. Although he felt a little uncomfortable in his new-found trust in Ned, just as before, all those years ago, it was Ned who provided the excitement and the colour, and Will was happy to go along with it.

Of course, the real frisson of excitement was provided by none other than Rosette Barton herself. Will had met her quite a few times since the first introduction and on each occasion he had found her even more enticing. She exhibited sensuality and left him in no doubt about her interest in him. Her message was clear. Whether or not he was prepared to comply and fulfil their mutual attraction, he had yet to decide.

Ned's elbow digging into him woke Will from his reverie. 'The house is just up ahead.' At last the wooded area through which they had been travelling had given way to glorious open country. Rolling hills stretched away, green and endless, and on a hilltop stood a large house. The road snaked up towards it and the coachman urged the horses to keep up the pace. As they drew nearer, the house and stables grew larger until at last as they pulled up in the front court, the stately, columned porch and veranda loomed right over them.

By the time they had descended from the coach and begun to climb up the steps, Rosette was standing there, smiling a warm greeting. Will gave up all pretence of concealing his pleasure. He took her hand and kissed it lingeringly, only letting go when Septimus Barton ambled onto the veranda behind his wife.

'How do you do, Sir.' Will had seen the man before, but now – as he closely observed the alcohol-flushed cheeks and the slack mouth – he could not reconcile himself to this haggard old bear being the husband of the lovely Rosette.

'Glad you could make it.' Septimus Barton said once his wife had made the introductions. His manner was brusque and indifferent and he bestowed little of his time on his guests. 'Are there more or are these the last to arrive? How many are we expecting?'

'I think there are just two more and then our party is complete.' Rosette steered her husband back towards the door.

'Go to the stables when you're ready and choose your mounts,' he bellowed back over his shoulder, and with a grunt and a snort he wandered off, considering his duties as host to have been completed.

Rosette had different ideas concerning her duties as a hostess. From the stables Will returned to his room to prepare for dinner. As he lay on the bed he heard a soft knock but almost before he had swung his legs to the floor, she had entered the room and was standing before him, smiling. 'Do you have everything you need?'

'Yes, I think so. Thank you.' They looked at each other for a few moments and uncertainty hung in the air between them. The moment that they had desired had come about and they were alone together. Rosette came forward and took Will's hand. 'I'm glad you're here,' she said, pressing her body to his.

Unable to stop himself, Will leaned down and kissed her. She was as soft and as yielding as he had imagined, and he felt both dizzy and breathless when they eventually pulled away from one another. 'I'll come to you tonight,' she whispered, 'after the dinner. Septimus will drink too much as usual and will be asleep before he's even undressed.' Unwilling to let her go, Will caught her arm and caressed the length of it, savouring the touch of her soft skin. When she had gone, he lay inert and wondering, staring up at the canopy above him.

The grand and gracious dinner that night was a torment for Will. He had no appetite and was far too distracted to engage in any meaningful conversation. As expected, the company was a hand-picked selection from New York society, all relishing the prospect of a few days' hunting. The topic of conversation was of little beside the hunt the next day, but Will could think no further than the sport he would have that night – with his host's wife.

The chink of glass and silver competed with the enthusiastic banter of men who spent their lives making money and now had the chance to revert to the basic instinct of the chase. Bets were made and likely routes guessed at, times of departure and arrival home suggested.

'Best not try to keep up with old Septimus. He only knows one pace and that's flat out. Still riding that stallion, eh? Shan't be seeing much of you then. You'll be miles ahead of us.' The host showed great contentment as he accepted the praise for his horsemanship and Will vaguely wondered whether it was idle flattery. Septimus Barton did not look like the kind of man who could control a fiery stallion and ride hard all day.

The conversation droned on, most of it wafting over him as he sat, not daring to look in Rosette's direction, wishing the interminable meal to end so that he could make his escape. From his place further down the table, Ned kept a watchful eye, but the constant chattering of the lady beside him meant he could do nothing to help Will.

At last, the rich port and the fine cigars were finished and Ned and Will excused themselves. Out on the veranda, the gentle evening breeze was welcome.

'For one who is on the brink of adventure, you are exhibiting an air rather similar to that of a condemned man. I've been watching you.' Ned started down the steps and Will was forced to follow. He tried not to look furtive as he glanced back to make sure no-one else was around.

'To tell the truth, this is not a situation that I find very honourable. I shouldn't be treating my host in such a way, even if he is the most unlikely of husbands for such a beautiful woman.'

'Hah! He's a bumptious prig and you well know it. Anyway, honour and desire are rarely compatible, believe me. You do desire her, don't you?'

'Keep your voice down,' Will whispered. 'Yes of course I do. I'm not good at deceit, that's all. I haven't had your experience.'

Ned laughed. 'It's true, I am somewhat of a master of deceit – but then, so is the beautiful Rosette.'

'What do you mean by that?'

'She made a good marriage. Great wealth, as you can see. She gives him beauty and style but also deception on a fairly grand scale. Her ambiguity regarding her background was sufficiently misleading to promote the marriage, and now her conduct is, shall we say, of an independent nature. My friend, you will not be the first man to make a cuckold of Septimus Barton.'

Will stopped for a moment to consider. He had given no thought to this possibility at all. Ned laid an encouraging hand on his shoulder. 'There's no need to concern yourself for your host. When he chose such a young and curvaceous wife, he knew she would seek her pleasures elsewhere. Now, think of your duty to your hostess!' Ned slapped Will's back and in the twilight his white teeth flashed in a rakish grin.

Will went to his room and began to seriously think about how he had got himself into this situation. He had fallen for Rosette from the moment he first saw her, but now that he thought about it, she had definitely singled him out for her attentions. She had lavished her unspoken promise of sensuality on him, and it had awoken a delicious excitement. Was that because of Eliza's coldness and indifference to him lately? He pushed Eliza from his mind. He definitely didn't want to think of her at this particular time.

Will went to the open window and breathed in the coolness of the night air. The light breeze gently fanned his face, bringing a much needed calmness to his mind. He listened intently for a while, but no sound came back to him, no night callings whatever, no hootings or distant howlings, nothing to distract his mind. He searched the heavens but cloud obscured all but a handful of stars, nothing to give him an inspiration or indication of what he should do. He came back into the room and sat on the bed. Would she come to him, as she had said? Perhaps she couldn't get away. Disappointment crept up, or was it relief? He laid back and stared at the shifting patterns of the bed hangings as they rippled lightly in the draught from the window.

There was no knock at the door, just the gentle opening and closing as Rosette slipped quietly through. Will leapt to his feet. She stood before him, her silk robe shimmering in the candlelight.

'Rosette ...'

'Shh.' She put her finger to her lips. Slowly, she advanced towards him and with each step he became transfixed, mesmerised by the loveliness of her face, and the soft invitation she exuded. Her hair was down and the curls brushed through, the myriad of colours gleaming like gold in the flickering light. Her eyes were alight with anticipation as, with a slightly trembling hand, she placed the candlestick on the bedside table and reached up to caress his cheek. Her fingers gently travelled down to his open shirt and then, with sudden urgency, she began to undress him.

Desire drove all rational thought from his mind as their kisses became more urgent and demanding. Rosette entwined her graceful body around him and he delighted in the warmth of her softness as they fell back on the bed. Suddenly, unbidden, thoughts of Eliza came flashing into his head. They pulled apart.

'What is it?' She whispered.

The moment was lost. The spell under which they had lusted was broken and all sexual urgency gone. Rosette sighed and sat up. She waited in silence for a while but Will turned his head away from her and had no words to explain. He just wanted her to go.

'Is it your wife? I hear she is very beautiful.' Will was horrified that Rosette should mention Eliza, especially as she had, so inconveniently, entered his own thoughts just moments earlier.

'We have not been so close lately.' Will turned away.

'Do you love her?'

'Yes, of course I do,' Will answered sharply, acutely aware of the absurdity of the conversation and resentful of the inquiry into his private life. But Rosette just smiled. 'Oh, you'd be surprised how many men on the point of adultery discover that they love their wives after all. It happens all the time.'

'Does it? I'm sorry. I shouldn't have misled you.'

Rosette pulled her robe around her and made for the door. Her expression was petulant but she was resigned. 'I misjudged you too. It's a shame because we could have had a lot of fun, but don't worry, I'll find someone else. She must be a very special lady – and a very lucky one.' She sighed again and slipped quietly through the door. All things considered, despite the humiliation, Will felt quite relieved.

The morning dawned bright and clear. An enormous breakfast awaited the guests in the dining room and servants scurried about, ensuring that everyone had all they needed for the day ahead. Activity in the stables was even more frenzied, with every horse to be fed, groomed and tacked up ready for the day's sport. The foxhounds, from their pen, sensed the fervour and howled and whined in anticipation.

Will tried to avoid eye contact with both Rosette and Ned, but neither would let him. He had worried all night as to whether or not his hostess would be discreet about their unfulfilled assignation. Before long he was to find out.

'Your secret is safe with me.' Ned confided. 'And Rosette holds nothing against you.'

'What?'

'Don't look so horrified. Quite amusing really. I mean, what is a lady to do when her expectations are not fulfilled?'

'What are you saying?'

'Well, I couldn't leave the poor girl in a state. And I have no thoughts of a wife to distract me, do I?' Ned winked and looked mightily content with himself. Whistling jauntily, he sauntered over to the stables. Will shook his head in disbelief, and an embarrassed smile played on his lips.

Neighbours were to join them for the chase and soon began to arrive. Superbly conditioned horses, fit and rested, stamped their feet and tossed their heads whilst their riders attempted to avail themselves of their host's hospitality. Servants ducked and weaved between them, offering trays of titbits and drinks.

Septimus Barton, Master of Hounds, appeared on the veranda encased in a tight, red jacket. He raised his black top hat to the assembled horsemen and acknowledged their cheers and wishes of good morning. 'Time to mount up,' he growled to the last of his loitering house guests, and Will followed him across to the stables.

The horse he had chosen was a sturdy grey of sixteen hands. He had a noble head and he held it high as he whinnied his excitement. The grooms lined the horses up by the mounting block, and stirrup lengths and girths were checked. 'He's called Homer,' the groom informed Will as he gave him the nod that all was as it should be. 'He can be a bit headstrong, so watch him.'

'I shall.' Will joined the throng of riders and bent down to snatch a glass of brandy from a nearby tray. He tipped it back in one gulp and savoured the fiery comfort. Smiling, Ned came alongside on a rangy bay. 'Not as neat as my little chestnut. Do you remember her, Will? How she could fly!'

Will began to relax. 'I remember her. She could jump too.'

'That she could. And saved my life many a time.'

The foxhounds were released from the kennel and the sturdy dogs, in an excitable stream of brown and white, milled amongst the horses, sniffing and barking, anxious to be off. Seated on a prancing black stallion, Septimus Barton joined his guests. Will hoped that the reputation that his host enjoyed for his horsemanship was true. That horse would certainly be a challenge for anyone, for he was quivering with excitement and stamping with frustrated power, and the whites of his eyes flashed with meanness from under the long black forelock.

By now the charged atmosphere of anticipation was at a pitch, but as the master called for the off and lead away, the melee gradually subsided into an organized movement. From the veranda, Rosette stepped forward from the ladies grouped together to wave the riders farewell. Will glanced up and saw her smile, which was directed not to him, but to Ned.

The open countryside stretched enticingly away as far as the eye could see. If they had a decent run, the chase promised a vastly different experience from the hunting in Nottinghamshire, where hedges provided good jumping, but stock got in the way and slowed them down. Dotted around in the distance were patches of woodland, some no more than thickets, others extensively wooded areas. They headed for the nearest copse and the hounds rushed in. The huntsmen waited, keyed up and tense, anxious to be in prime position for when the break came. Will's horse, although under control, stamped and snorted, ready for action.

'You know, I've never hunted before,' Ned said.

'No. I don't imagine you have. Well, just ride as if the constables were behind us and you'll be fine.' They laughed. 'Remember not to overtake the master, although I doubt that will be a problem to you.'

The hounds crashed excitedly about in the undergrowth for some time before the cry went up and the hunting horn sounded. The action was instant. The din of the baying hounds in full cry, along with the insistent pitch of the horn, filled their ears as every rider surged forward to gain position and follow on. As the fox broke cover to make a run for it, the hounds leapt out from the trees in noisy pursuit. In no time at all the entire howling pack was streaking up the valley.

Homer could contain himself no longer. Keyed up and raring to go, he gave a mighty leap and took the bit between his teeth. At first Will tried to rein him back, but as this had no effect whatsoever, he quickly decided that a better ploy would be to ride him out and gain control gradually. His stride was huge and Will felt the enormous power of the horse pounding beneath him as they overtook the rest of the field. Ahead, he could see the red coat of

Septimus Barton above the haunches and streaming tail of the black stallion.

After a mile or so of hell-bent galloping, Will looked ahead to see the hounds disappear into a ditch in mid-valley and reappear on higher ground. He kept a close watch on the master to see what he would do. Not for a second did he check or slow his pace. The stallion took the ditch at full gallop, soaring into the air and reaching out for the far bank. The red coat swayed slightly to the side but recovered and horse and rider careered on.

Will looked back to see the rest of the field some distance behind. He made an effort to rein Homer back and was thankful to feel some response. By the time they reached the ditch, Will had control. He made sure the horse had time to see what was expected of him and in one clean leap the obstacle was behind them.

Exhilaration swept Will on. With every nerve in his body taut and alive, the thrill of the chase burned through him. His face stung and his arms and thighs ached with the effort of controlling the headstrong horse, but his spirits soared with unfettered joy. Mile after mile they hurtled, clearing fallen trees, ditches and streams with ease, until Will began to wish that the fox would go to ground. He had not ridden like this for a very long time and his muscles were trembling, painfully reminding him of the soft and inactive life he had become accustomed to leading. At last the horse responded and slowed to a canter. A few riders overtook him, and before long Ned was at his side. The trail of riders began to disappear into woodland.

'I need to take a rest.' Will said breathlessly, peeling off to the left down a slope. Ned followed and they eased the blowing and snorting horses down to a walk.

'Now that quite takes me back to old times.' Ned too was breathing hard and sweat streaked down his soil-spattered face. 'What a run!' he beamed. 'And what a distance we've come. Great sport, Will. I think I could be doing this on a regular basis from now on.'

The sun scorched down on them as both horses and men sweated freely. Gradually their breathing rates returned to normal and the baying of the hounds subsided into frustrated whines and yelps. 'What happens now?'

'It sounds as though this one's given us the slip and gone to earth. With a bit of luck we'll have a break before they put another one up.'

The slope on which they had come to rest fell away sharply beneath them, affording a spectacular view of meandering valleys and gentle, wooded hillsides. The trunk of an enormous, dead maple lay fallen some distance from them and ivy had begun to creep over it. Directly beneath, a landslide of some sort had swept away the soil, exposing a long drop of jagged rocks and stones.

Will gazed in awe at the beauty of the scenery before them. 'What spectacular countryside. I've missed this.' Silently he vowed to get out of the city more often, take Eliza and the children and enjoy the tranquillity. He must find the time somehow.

'Well, I think you've ruined your chances of being invited by Rosette again.' Ned could not hide his amusement in either his voice or his eyes. 'While I, on the other hand, may well become a regular visitor.'

Their attention became taken by a hullabaloo in the woodland. Riders patrolling the perimeters trotted anxiously to and fro, watchful for a sighting, while the hounds took up their baying, and shouts came from deep within the trees. A run was obviously imminent and they observed the action intently for an indication of the direction they should follow. It was only out of the corner of his eye that Will saw the flash of a deep red brush streaking past them, over the dead maple and on down the slope. The hounds took up the full cry of pursuit once more and came bursting out of the undergrowth. One by one, they leapt onto the fallen trunk before picking their way down the rocks and hurling themselves on in tireless pursuit of the scent.

Hard on their heels, hollering loudly, the master came crashing out from the wood. Seeing the open ground before him, he brought the whip down hard on the haunches of the stallion and set him galloping down towards the fallen tree.

Ned stood up in the saddle. 'He's crazy. The old fool will kill himself.'

'Oh dear God.' Will kicked in hard and the startled Homer lurched forward. Shouting and waving his arms, he rode as fast as he could towards the tree, desperate to get his attention and avert disaster. Will knew that Septimus Barton would have no idea that the ground fell away so sharply. From his angle, the danger was hidden – all that presented itself was an innocent tree trunk over which he knew he could easily jump.

Whether or not at the last moment he caught sight of Will frantically signalling, mattered little. The fearless stallion was set for the leap and without hesitation the massive hind legs launched and propelled them up and over, clearing the trunk in one easy bound.

Will pulled up and watched in horror as horse and rider took their last jump. Septimus Barton must have looked down into oblivion, for the landing he had expected never materialised. The horse kept falling, further and further down, thrashing its legs in desperation to gain solid ground, but with the cruel inevitability of a vicious end. The piercing equine scream of fear that echoed across the hillside made Will's blood run cold.

On impact with the rocks, the squealing intensified, filling the valley and Will's ears with an unbearable, relentless noise of pain and bewilderment. The red-coated body of Septimus Barton pitched clear and fell, dashed against the boulders like a doll. Will threw himself off his horse and scrambled over the rocks to where he lay, but even from a distance he knew that he was dead. The horse, though still alive, lay still, breathing low grunts of pain. Riders began to cluster near, quiet and shocked.

'I'll deal with the horse.' someone said. Within moments the hideous grunting had stopped. The sound of baying hounds in the far distance was all that could be heard.

Chapter 19

Will and Ned stayed with the body whilst a neighbour went to fetch a cart. They sat on the rocks in silence. Everyone else dispersed, some directly to their own homes, some, as Septimus Barton's guests, headed straight back to the house to break the news. Will felt relieved that at least Rosette would have been informed of the tragedy by the time they finally arrived back with the body.

The gruesome scene before them was no fitting way for such a thrilling day to end. In some ways the sequence of feelings reminded Will of the night they fled from the constables. Exhilaration and euphoria of the hard gallop, followed by a sudden ending, a place from which there was no turning back. He wondered if Ned felt the same. It didn't seem right to compare it though, so Will kept his thoughts to himself. The clouds began to bubble up from the west as they watched the tiny figure of a huntsman in the distance, calling and rounding up the foxhounds. The air grew heavy with sultry heat. Blowflies began to buzz around the carcass of the horse, such a magnificent creature, so full of energy and fire, and now so horribly silent, crushed and broken. Will adjusted the jacket that had been placed over Septimus Barton's face, anxious to foil the attempts of the flies to settle. He wondered about Rosette, and what this sudden death of her husband would really mean to her. If Ned had thoughts on the matter, he was not giving any hint, as he sat motionless and withdrawn, seemingly giving all his concentration to the vast panorama before them. By the time the cart arrived, the sky was overcast with deep shades of purple and magenta, casting a vibrant shade of russet over the ground, and angry cloud formations loomed large and threatening. The long journey back over the open country that had provided them with such great sport a few hours earlier now asked much of them to negotiate safely with a cart and very few tracks to follow. Thankfully, the storm seemed to veer off and away from them so the rain held off. Eventually, after many hours, the outline of the grand house finally loomed up in the twilight.

Rosette stood alone on the veranda to receive her husband's body. It seemed an eternity to Will since she had bid them welcome, warm and smiling, on that same spot. So much had happened. 'Please accept my condolences,' he murmured. She acknowledged him and turned away.

The first heavy raindrops began to fall as they lifted the body and carried it into the house. The rain beat hard on the veranda as Ned and Will sat together staring out at the blackness. Distant lightning flashed across the sky and thunder echoed around the valleys. There seemed to be nothing to say. The day had done its worst, bringing everything into murky shades of grey, so it was easier to sit in silence. Eventually servants called them for a meal and they roused themselves, stiff and sore, to go and wash. The sombre atmosphere amongst the remaining guests was a stark contrast from the excited party mood of the night before. Rosette did not appear again.

Will and Ned spoke little on the journey back to New York the next day. Curiously, far from being despondent after his near-seduction and the witnessing of the violent death, Will felt a strange sense of renewal. He had woken to the new day in a quite optimistic frame of mind, determined to return home to Eliza with a new appreciation of his life. The hunting, despite the tragedy, had stimulated him, and he felt strengthened by it. As the carriage bore him back to the city, memories of the early days of struggle crept into his mind. The ever-worrying scarcity of money hadn't diminished their love then, as this time of financial stability seemed to have done. Surely mistakes can be put right, resentments put behind them? He resolved there and then that one day, however long it took, Eliza would forgive him.

'I should like to meet your wife.' Ned seemed to have read Will's thoughts.

'Yes of course you must. You shall come to dinner very soon. You can count on it.'

As the weeks passed by and Ned became a regular visitor to the house, an improvement in Eliza and Will's relationship did occur. Details of the eventful hunting trip were kept to a minimum and Will never let slip any hint of Ned's previous life in England or his career as a slave trader. If Eliza knew, she would see his friendship with Ned as a great lack of respect to the memory of Seamus. The truth was that Will himself had spent a good deal of time wondering about the same thing, but he enjoyed Ned's company, and however furtive and secretive their friendship had been, not to mention criminal, Ned was a link to home, to his innocent youth, to England. But he couldn't expect Eliza to understand that, and he wasn't prepared to risk this new sense of closeness in their relationship.

No matter how many times he visited the gambling house, female charms had no effect whatever on him. He could thank Rosette for that. Delightful though she had been, he had no desire to find himself in an illicit situation again. Eliza was all that mattered.

'Your fidelity is highly commendable, Will,' Ned teased. 'Now let's think if there's some way you and I could go into business together. Perhaps we could consider that brothel after all.'

'I think I'll stay with cotton and furs, thanks all the same. Not very exciting, I'll grant you that, but it gives me a living. Slaves and women are commodities from which I intend to steer well clear.'

Their friendship re-kindled, the two had received further invitations to go hunting, and that season enjoyed many a good chase, thankfully less dramatic than their first experience. Eliza, whilst never giving up hope of hearing word of Samuel, spoke of him less and less, restricting herself to a wistful whispering of his name at poignant times, such as his birthday or Christmas. Will would squeeze her hand and they would exchange a comforting look with one another. Recriminations became a thing of the past. Family life settled into a comfortable routine. Sometimes Will even thought he really had been forgiven.

Some months after the hunting experience, Ned came to dinner. As always, he greeted Eliza warmly and bowed low as he graciously kissed her hand. Will had observed Ned's attention to women quite closely over the previous months. He treated them all with respect, even the whores and barmaids, but there was a tenderness in him with Eliza that warmed Will to see. Ned hid his past well, but Will sometimes wondered if that confident veneer with which he clothed himself was actually very thin indeed. Security and permanence had never presented themselves in Ned's life, and just occasionally, usually in Eliza's presence, the desire for a settled life of commitment and love showed itself. Countless times he had told Will how lucky he was, how he envied him.

'It's always a pleasure to welcome you here,' Eliza said warmly.

'The pleasure is all mine, dear Eliza, to eat your delicious dinners and enjoy the warmth of your domestic harmony.'

'Domestic harmony?' Will said. 'Be honest now, is that something you really want in your life?'

'Well, yes it is. And, in fact, I think it could be coming along quite soon, after all these years.' Ned gave a self-conscious laugh at the sight of Will's surprised face. 'A man needs to feel he has put down some roots and maybe the time really has come to settle down.'

Immediately, Eliza's interest was stirred. 'Are you saying that you have in mind to take a wife?'

Ned began to squirm. 'Let me say, I have no announcement to make as such, but before long perhaps.'

'But you can't evoke our curiosity and then not tell us the name of the lady! Can he Will?' Will enjoyed Ned's discomfort. 'Certainly not. Do we know her?' Ned held up his hand. 'All in good time. I shall tell you my plans as soon as I can. I'm sure you will agree it would be foolish to spoil things by hasty talk.'

The meal continued in good natured banter, but as Eliza left them alone and Ned took his leave, Will asked one more question. 'Is it the plantation? Have you made your decision?'

'Yes.' Ned admitted. 'I have one or two things to finalise but the purchase of a southern estate is now imminent. The time is right.'

Will shook his hand. 'I'm pleased for you Ned. I know how much it means to you to have your own place.' It was a poignant moment for two reasons and Will understood Ned's reluctance to impart his news. They both thought of Seamus and his dream, but also Will's enforced wait to claim his land hung between them.

'I know your heart is set on returning to England, Will, and I'm sure it will happen soon enough. And your son will be there to greet you.'

'Yes. Yes of course. Everything will turn out well in the end, I know.' Brightening up, Will said, 'Who would have thought it? The notorious highwayman of the Great North Road owning a plantation! But who is the lady, Ned? You can tell me now we are alone. Are you really to be married? Do I know her?'

'Oh yes, you know her quite well, actually.' At once Ned's eyes were both mischievous and secretive.

And in that moment Will knew. 'It's Rosette, isn't it.' The two men looked embarrassed for only a moment before laughing at the irony.

Just one month later, Will and Ned stood on the quayside together. 'If you should ever find yourself in Virginia …' Ned began. 'No. Of course you won't. You'll be back in England before long.'

Will forced a smile. 'I hope to be.' This has been a strange friendship, he thought to himself. We've been on different social levels, in different countries and with a totally opposite view of life, and yet – despite all of that – I'll miss Ned. I suppose I'll miss wondering where he'll turn up next.

'I suppose our paths just kept on crossing.' Ned looked out over the river and focused on a distant point.

'They did that alright. And usually at inopportune moments!' They both forced a laugh.

'I know how much this means to you and believe me, I'm glad for you. You and Rosette will be happy together, I know.'

'Oh we will! You could say we deserve each other, but you know, both of us have lived by our wits to make something of ourselves. Now we can just move on, be together and be proud of who we are. No more pretending.' Ned shook Will's hand, turned and walked briskly away. 'Of course, her money will help' He called back over his shoulder. 'Old Septimus left her plenty!'

'I'm sure he did.' Will said as he waved back. And this time he knew for certain that he would never see Ned again.

It was March in the year 1810 before Will felt that he could wait no longer, and the time was right to return to England. Five long years had passed. The family had grown in size with the arrival of a baby, Harry, who was now one year old. Simon was a rumbustious little boy of seven, and Mary Ann, still plain and given to scowling, was a plump fourteen year old. Samuel, of course, would be twelve by now.

It had been years before Eliza had finally given up all hope of ever hearing a word from her son. They had both written regularly to the school, each letter portraying a growing desperation for news of their son's welfare, and in return had received nothing – not a word from anyone.

Will's father had written from time to time, and Jane had kept up a regular correspondence, despite her busy life as the wife of Reverend Wilby of Muskham, and the mother of his four children. Yet neither had ever had a sight of Samuel since the day he left Beesthorpe at the age of five. Whenever Jane or her father had enquired of Uncle Samuel, he always replied that the boy was fine, and this scant information was the total sum of their knowledge of him.

Will despaired of Uncle Samuel ever diminishing in health and strength, let alone relinquishing his tenacious hold on life. But he was over eighty years old now. Surely it couldn't be much longer? In any event, Will decided that his time in America had come to an end and they should return. They would go to live at Beesthorpe, at long last.

Business had varied over the years, but overall it had provided Will with a good lifestyle and enough working capital. He was painfully aware, however, that although he had a sound grasp of trade and profitability, he lacked the flair and entrepreneurial spirit that Seamus had brought to the partnership. Lately, he had become somewhat bored by it all.

In allowing himself more free time in the last few years, Will had continued to indulge his passion for hunting. It had never failed to revive his spirits and seemed to give him the strength to carry on. Many of his friends and business associates owned estates and he was often invited to participate in the chase. Eliza never minded, for she considered his absence for a few days a small price to pay for the restoration of his peace of mind. Her family meant everything to her, so watching over her growing family was no hardship. They lived comfortably and she was content.

New York had steadily grown in size every year since Will's arrival, but now it seemed to be bursting at the seams. The great marbled City Hall, once on the northern limits of the city, and now nearing completion, had already been engulfed by building. The decision to use red sandstone for the north walls had caused much embarrassment to the city council, who had genuinely thought it would never be viewed from that side, but building in New York was like an epidemic. Will began to long for the tranquil, English countryside.

Arrangements began for the sale of the business. Interest was strong. It was still only the one warehouse that Will owned. He had never had the confidence to expand, to build a bigger enterprise or move into some other line of business. Seamus, he knew, would have owned half of New York by now – or lost everything. Will simply did not have that risk-taking attitude. Maybe he was too soft to be a really successful businessman. But if he was honest with himself, what he really did not want to become was an image of Uncle Samuel. If being successful necessitated an overriding self-interest and total disregard for others' welfare, then he just didn't have it in him. Nor wanted to. The ruthlessness of Uncle Samuel and the hard-hearted callousness of the New York City businessmen had been abhorrent to him. He simply could not conduct himself in that manner. He was not driven, like Seamus and Ned. As a result, deals often failed and losses were sometimes incurred. Also, it felt to Will that, having reached the age of thirty-four, he had run out of energy. He had made his way in the world, worked hard and enjoyed good fortune. All he wanted to do now was go home.

The passage was booked for the second week of April and Eliza worked frantically to prepare their departure and pack their belongings and everything the children would need for the voyage. They hired a maid, a skinny sixteen-year-old called Lizzie, to help with the children. Being without any family of her own, Lizzie was perfectly happy at the prospect of living in England, but confessed herself to be terrified of the sea voyage. Will was prepared to search for another suitable girl, one in possession of a braver attitude, but Eliza liked Lizzie. The girl was helpful and kind to the children, so Eliza set about the problem with characteristic charm.

'The truth is, Lizzie,' she had said, 'I am frightened too. But ships sail across the ocean all the time, and we shall be so busy keeping the children occupied that I'm sure the time will pass by quickly. We shall help one another to overcome our fears.' Lizzie was not convinced. 'Lizzie, I have no choice. I must accompany my husband and children. I would find it a great comfort if you could be with us.'

Lizzie had considered for a moment. Her life had been hard, with little love or respect, and a succession of tyrannical employers. Mrs. Bristowe seemed to be kindness itself. She could be happy with this family. Even so, the image of huge waves and deep, deep water filled her with terror. Eventually though, she managed to banish the fear long enough to inform Eliza that she would make the voyage.

So the organization for the journey continued. At times Eliza found it quite overwhelming, mostly because she too feared the sea and being aboard a ship in a cramped cabin for weeks on end. But for the sake of the children, and Lizzie, she did her best to hide her morbid thoughts. Many times Eliza blessed Mary Ann for her care of her younger brothers. She could always be relied upon to look out for them and indeed lavished a great deal of attention on them both. In return they adored her. It was to be hoped that Lizzie proved herself to be as reliable as Mary Ann.

Although the prospect of the voyage filled Eliza with trepidation, there was an added reason for her fears. Lately, the morning sickness had crept up on her, and she knew that she was pregnant once more. Will, as always, was delighted with the news.

Feeling daunted and emotional at the prospect of leaving her country, Eliza made a request. The week before the sailing, the family piled into the coach and set off for the Newark cemetery. They found the small, marble headstone for the two lost little girls and laid flowers. Eliza and Will sat down for a while. Simon raced around and Mary Ann entertained baby Harry. There was little to be said. Just their presence and a silent farewell. Eventually, their pilgrimage over, they left the cemetery for the last time and returned home.

The family stood on the deck watching New York grow ever smaller in the distance. As the city was reduced to tiny dots on the horizon, their gaze never wavered, clinging for the last few seconds to the security that it offered, and that they were now leaving. Even after the dots had disappeared their faces still turned in that direction, though now the only view before them was of water; choppy, cold, unforgiving and endless water. Will held his arm firmly and protectively around Eliza. Lizzie held tight to baby Harry, and Mary Ann clung to Simon. 'We're actually going to England,' she said in a soft voice full of awe. 'I can hardly believe it, Simon. At last, we are really on our way.'

Will escorted Eliza and Lizzie down to the cabins. Then he came back up on deck and put his arm around his step-daughter. Her excitement was a joy to him because, apart from an obvious love of her brothers, she rarely showed any emotion at all. Now she could barely contain herself.

'I'll see all the places you've told me about. All the fields and the flowers. The lake and the kingfishers. I know where everything will be. I remember every detail you've ever told me about Beesthorpe.'

'I know,' Will laughed, recalling all those endless bed-time stories, which he had found so cathartic and curiously Mary Ann had found so enrapturing. 'I just hope I've told you correctly. If I've made a mistake you'll be sure to notice.' After a while they grew silent. 'Beesthorpe is a special place for me, Mary Ann,' Will went on. 'I hope it will be for you too.'

Before entering the cabin Will could hear Harry's fractious cries. He lay squirming in Lizzie's arms, but she seemed oblivious, seemingly lost in her thoughts. Tears flowed freely down the young girl's face. 'What is it Lizzie? Are you sad to be leaving?'

Lizzie sniffed and hurriedly wiped her face with her sleeve. 'Not sad, Sir. As you know, I've no family, and I want to be with you, I really do. And to tell the truth Miss Mary Ann has told me so much about England that I truly want to go there.' She half-heartedly bounced baby Harry up and down, but still he cried and still Lizzie's tears flowed.

'Then what is the matter?' Will was puzzled.

'I've a terrible fear of the water. And it's all we can see. And they say the voyage will take four weeks or thereabouts. I can't swim, Sir and – I'm frightened.'

'I've crossed the Atlantic several times now, Lizzie,' Will said reassuringly. 'Sometimes the wind does blow strong and the seas grow rough. But this is a fine ship and we have plenty to do to keep the children occupied. Now dry your tears and go to see what you can do to help your mistress.'

The initial novelty of creating a routine out of the limited daily chores soon waned as the restricted space and tedium of the voyage began to wear them down. Eliza succumbed to a cruel seasickness and Will grew anxious for her condition. She mostly stayed in her cabin, only rousing herself when the need for air and a little exercise grew strong. Simon was laid low with nausea for a few days before bouncing back to his usual self. Mary Ann read books and spent much of her time on deck, gazing at the vastness of the ocean and watching for whales. Lizzie stayed below as much as possible, caring for Eliza and Harry.

They were making steady progress, the Captain informed them. The south-westerly wind had been fair and the voyage was progressing nicely. But at the beginning of the third week a dramatic change came about. The wind began to blow stronger, with alarming gusts suddenly and remorselessly battering the ship. Grey storm clouds scudded across the sky and sharp spray whipped across the sails, spattering loudly against the canvas. The ship creaked in protest under the strain, and the Captain shouted orders for trimming sails. The bows pitched deep into the wind-whipped sea and frothy water ran over the decks. The family huddled below, waiting for the heavy weather to pass.

Will did his best to calm their fears and the crew made light of the 'lively weather'. They had grown accustomed to the usual pitch and roll of the ship, even in a heavy swell, but now it heaved and plunged in a ferocious battle with the mountainous seas. In the galley, pots and pans crashed to the floor. As darkness descended, the storm raged stronger and louder. In intense discomfort and almost paralysed with fear, the family huddled closely together in one cabin, as the savage wind whistled and howled above them.

Will looked at the white, terror-stricken faces of his family. Eliza held Simon close to her as he cried quietly into her breast, his lips quivering and his eyes tightly shut. Lizzie shook uncontrollably and Mary Ann did her best to soothe baby Harry but his arms flailed wildly and he screamed as the ship pitched sideways time and again, hurling everyone into the panelling. Another crash came from above and distant shouts from the crew could just be heard over the raging din of the storm.

Will took the baby from Mary Ann as everyone righted themselves. Lizzie and Mary Ann now clung together, crying openly. 'I know we are all sending up our silent prayers to the Good Lord to save us,' Will said to them, looking around at the white, fear-stricken faces, 'but it might help us to pray together, out loud.' With faltering, shaky voices, punctuated with pauses whilst they held their breath for the ship to right itself, they embarked on the

Lord's Prayer together. The familiar words had never held such comfort. Will thought of all the times he had mumbled them, unthinkingly, or simply chanted along with the rest of the congregation. The words took him back to the safe, warm Sundays at Beesthorpe and the services at St. Andrew's Church. He pictured all the family riding down in the coach together and, as often as not, bringing the vicar back with them to partake in the Sunday lunch. Such a peaceful, tranquil memory to hold on to amidst the chaos of a doomed ship, as a kind of acceptance descended on them all.

Will and Eliza exchanged a love with their eyes, and held on tightly to the children. Even Lizzie stopped crying and sat meekly waiting for her fate. The night wore slowly on. The initial panic at the realisation of their imminent peril now turned slowly and grindingly into a stoicism that surprised them all. They could take no action to lessen the danger, but with each grim hour that passed, they could almost feel a shred of hope for their ultimate survival. But the storm showed no sign whatever of abating.

Will held Eliza's white hand so tightly that he felt they had welded together. Surely a ship of this size could only take so much when pitched against such terrible forces of wind and sea. The stomach-churning thud as the bow pitched down hard must be taking a toll of the timbers by now. Will could imagine the frame of the boat smashing into splintered shards of wood beneath them. They would be plunged into the icy cold depths. The entire family would perish. But then he remembered Samuel – all would be lost, except Samuel. Fate had dealt differently with him. He didn't know whether to thank God or his uncle, but he suddenly felt such an elation that he almost laughed out loud. Samuel was safe. When the little boat finally gave up the battle to survive, the blackness would engulf them and Will and his precious family would no longer exist. But not Samuel. He would still be there, safe at home in England, able to live a full and happy life, and to carry on the family name. Amidst such anguish, it was a very small comfort to which to cling.

Chapter 20

In the early hours of the morning a crash mightier than any other before came from the deck. Water cascaded down the companionway and swirled around in the cabins, causing full-blown hysteria in all of the passengers. Screams and wails competed with the clamour of the wind. It couldn't be much longer now, Will thought. We have endured this for hours and still it continues with its hellish intensity. How much later he could not tell, but some time after this crescendo of panic Will began to feel that the ship was not heaving to quite the same degree, nor the wind howling to the same pitch as before. Was it his imagination?

'I think the storm may be easing,' he finally dared to say. He looked at Eliza's white face and tried to smile reassuringly. 'I really think it is.'

Mary Ann and Lizzie looked at one another with blank expressions, as though unable to comprehend the meaning of the words, their tear-stained faces as white as chalk. It was almost too painful to dare to hope that their ordeal would soon be over.

When a crew member opened their door a little while later, to tell them that the Captain felt that the worst was over, the news was greeted with sobs of relief. Will realised that every muscle in his body was rigid with tension. He massaged Eliza's bloodless hand, and kissed each of his children. He even kissed Lizzie.

Exhausted, amazed and grateful, they snatched an hour or so of fitful sleep, propped up in each other's arms, and when morning came they began restoring some order into the wrecked cabins. Will made his way along the tiny gangway to venture up onto the deck. As he emerged into the new day that he had feared he would never see, he looked about him in astonishment. Broken rigging fluttered loose, cluttering the deck, and torn sails, shredded to mere scraps of canvas, flapped in the breeze. Where the main mast should have been there was empty sky, only a jagged, splintered stump remaining amidships. Exhausted sailors, their limbs moving with a concentration of slow motion, were attempting to clear the mess but the devastation was immense and the task daunting.

The Captain spoke to the passengers gathered in the dining salon that evening. The crew had spent the day putting right what they could and had fully assessed the damage. Sails were being mended as fast as possible but the loss of the main mast was serious and they would be limping home under less than half sail. Still, it was generally acknowledged that they had survived a very severe storm and everyone was grateful for their deliverance.

Three more tortuous weeks went by. Winds were light and progress slow. Strict rationing added extra misery to the burden of the passengers' ordeal. Having almost completed the crossing of the Atlantic, their entry into the Irish Sea was as unpleasant as it was unexpected. Once more, the ship was caught up in a fierce storm.

The family could not believe the ill-luck of it. Yet again, they crammed into the cabin to ride out the ordeal together, only too aware that the ship had been weakened by the earlier storm and proper repairs had not been carried out. Will knew the coast of North Wales was coming up soon and the prospect of a shipwreck could not be ruled out. Terror-stricken yet again, the family endured hours of stomach-churning torment in the tiny cabin as the furious storm raged and they were casually tossed about on the mountainous waves. Again the hatchways gave in under the torrent of water constantly washing over the ship. The cabin door burst open and water flooded in. Wet, freezing and terrified, the family could do nothing but pray and wait for the end to come. Such a cruel and callous fate. Will could not believe what was happening. Had they endured all that they had, just to be flung into a repetition of the same misery? It seemed to be so.

Will's thoughts turned again to his childhood Sundays. He could see the preacher leaning over the pulpit and wagging his finger over the heads of the congregation to make a point. Salvation and going to heaven was much promised. But had he done enough to get there? Would they all be re-united in some far-off, heavenly firmament, or was it just oblivion that awaited?

Yet once more, after hours of tossing the helpless ship about on the raging sea, having established its superiority over the stricken vessel, the storm abated. Once more they roused themselves from fear-induced stupor, stretched their aching limbs, and tried to relax their taut muscles. This time, the news that they had been blown off course greeted Will as he stepped on deck in the welcome calm. 'Way off course, we are. And down to barely a sail to raise,' the Captain said bluntly. 'We're making for the Isle of Man, Douglas if we can, for some proper repairs, but we may have to settle for Castletown. The truth is, I'll be pleased to see any harbour.'

'And so shall we all,' thought Will. In fact, he could add, dry land of any description would be a most wonderful sight.

The pumps were manned around the clock to keep the ship afloat and, two days later, perilously low in the water, they struggled pitifully into tiny Castletown harbour. All the passengers went ashore to arrange lodgings whilst the ship underwent repairs. Everyone was exhausted with worry and weak through inactivity and rationing, Will found rooms, cramped and inconvenient, but welcome nevertheless. He ordered food in abundance and never was a meal eaten with such gratitude. Each one of them, even down to little Harry, relished the taste of the meal and the feel of dry land beneath their feet. Eliza took straight to her bed and Lizzie and Mary Ann coped with the children.

Days passed by in peaceful recovery from their endurance of the terrifying voyage but, after a week or so, Will began to enquire as to when they would be able to complete their journey to England. The answer was at least a month, but arrangements could be made to transfer them to another ship for the crossing over to the mainland.

Unfortunately, Eliza's health had not been easily recovered. Her pregnancy was advancing, yet she remained weak. It seemed for the best when Will took the decision that they would wait for the ship to be repaired and her strength to be restored. He wrote to his father telling him of their misfortune, and sent the letter to Douglas to be despatched on any ship leaving for the mainland.

In the end it was five weeks before they were able to board the ship once more and set sail for Liverpool. The rest had done much to restore Eliza's health and her pregnancy was continuing well, but everyone had grown thoroughly bored with waiting and they were anxious to be on their way and be finished with the wretched journey. All except Lizzie.

'I just can't do it, Sir.' she wailed. I've been thinking I could perhaps stay here on the island. There must be some work I could find.'

Lizzie, this next part is not a long voyage. Just a short sail and we'll be there. The storms have done their worst for us and we have survived. I promise we shall be fine. No need to worry.'

Lizzie took no heed of Will's words. 'But I can't set a foot on that boat. Just to think about it sets me trembling. I've made my mind up, I'm staying.'

Mary Ann had been standing by the door. 'We can't leave you behind, Lizzie. Mama needs you, and I do too. Nothing bad will happen to us. You are part of the family and we are going together.' Spoken boldly and firmly, Mary Ann's words did not invite argument or contradiction. They were a plain statement of fact, reiterated by a forceful stare into Lizzie's eyes. As they stood, locked into one another's eyes, each reluctant to show weakness, Eliza called from her room.

'Best go to your mistress, now. Do your duty, Lizzie.' Will was relieved as Lizzie scuttled off, and quite amazed at Mary Ann's directness. Nevertheless, it still took a good dose of cajoling and reassuring to actually persuade Lizzie on board, although in some ways, having to do that actually helped Will and Mary Ann to suppress their own anxieties. No-one could quite believe it when at last the port of Liverpool finally came into view.

Will booked a post chaise but yet again Eliza became unwell. A doctor was summoned and he declared her unable to travel for at least a week. Even then the journey was to be restricted to no more than a few miles a day before an overnight stop. Eliza was distressed. 'I'm so sorry to be such a burden, Will. I am making the journey so slow.'

Will patted her hand and smiled, hiding well the frustration he felt. Yet more days and weeks sitting about passing endless, fruitless hours was the last thing in the world he wanted. The patience of them all, even the children and Lizzie, was being sorely tested. But he merely sighed. 'The journey has been quite the most hideous imaginable, for all of us. But not because of you, my love. We have survived and we shall arrive in Nottinghamshire in due course. Beesthorpe will wait for us. It has waited for years, so a few more weeks is nothing. Now you must rest. I've sent a letter ahead, so no-one will worry.'

In due course, their tortuous expedition to Nottinghamshire began, stopping at almost every coaching inn and hostelry along the way. One hot day followed another, with the family cooped up in the coach, dusty and sweltering in the heat of summer. Despite the frustration, Will was delighted to find himself drawing even closer to Mary Ann, who frequently joined him atop to enjoy the cool breeze and gaze in companionable appreciation over the English countryside. Countless numbers of times, they loaded and unloaded the baggage, arrived and departed yet another inn. It was at Chesterfield where the inn-keeper, hearing the name of Bristowe, came forward with a letter. 'This was delivered just yesterday, addressed to a Mr. William Bristowe, making his way to Nottinghamshire. Would that be you, Sir?'

'Yes, it would.' Will said, taking the letter and opening it. As he began to read, he frowned in puzzlement. Then a stillness came over him and he sat down on the nearest chair.

'What is it, Will? What's wrong? Tell me.' Eliza had been fanning herself by the window but when no answer came she crossed the room to see the letter for herself. Will snatched it away from her.

'No, my love. I will tell you. Just give me a moment to take in the news.'

Eliza bit her lip and waited. She knew from his face that it was bad news.

Will took a deep breath. 'The letter is from Uncle Samuel. My father has died. Over three months ago now, just before we set off on the voyage.' He delivered the news calmly.

'Oh, Will, I am so sorry. I should so have liked to meet him.'

'My letter was re-directed to Twyford. Hence this reply, telling us to proceed there rather than to Beesthorpe. It seems they thought us lost at sea, for the first letter from the Isle of Man has not been delivered.'

'But why must we go to Twyford?'

'I really don't know.' Will lied.

Chapter 21

The commotion of the arrival of the coach and the unloading of the baggage brought the housekeeper to the front door of Twyford Manor. She stood in the doorway, disapproving and unhelpful. Will took Eliza's arm to see her safely out of the coach and felt a huge relief that at last they had come to the end of their journey, even if it was to an unexpected destination.

'Mrs. Draycott, this is my wife, Eliza.'

The housekeeper inclined her head in icy acknowledgement. 'You'd better follow me. Your uncle is in the drawing room.'

Uncle Samuel did not rise as Will guided Eliza into the room but hailed them heartily from his chair. 'Glad to see you've arrived at last.'

'Uncle, may I present my wife, Eliza.' Eliza stepped forward.

'Forgive me for not rising. Leg not behaving today.' Uncle Samuel extended his hand in greeting and Eliza took it. 'I'm pleased to meet you, my dear. And sorry to hear about your ordeal at sea.'

Will felt a surge of relief at the civility his uncle was displaying. He beckoned to Mary Ann and Simon who stood uncertainly in the doorway. Mary Ann eyed Uncle Samuel distrustfully as she edged into the room, clinging tightly to Simon. Lizzie, holding baby Harry, hung back in the hallway. After Will had introduced them, Uncle Samuel scrutinized the family without uttering a word.

'Perhaps Eliza could be shown to her room to rest. The doctor has ordered that she must not be over-tired.'

'Of course. Mrs. Draycott!' At Uncle Samuel's call the housekeeper appeared in an instant and Eliza gathered the children and followed her out.

Will sat down opposite his uncle and waited. 'I'm sorry about your father. It was very sudden. His heart gave out.'

'Tell me, who is now living at Beesthorpe?' The question had been in the forefront of Will's mind ever since Uncle Samuel's letter had informed him so bluntly 'Due to the occupation of Beesthorpe Hall, please proceed to Twyford.'

'Now, you must understand that we thought the ship had gone down. Every communication from Liverpool suggested as much.' Uncle Samuel's tone was defensive.

'So who is living at Beesthorpe?'

'Tenants.'

'Tenants! You put up my home for rent?'

'I thought you had all perished. I was made an offer. No use leaving a good house empty.'

'But I have brought my family all the way from America to live there.' Will's exasperation boiled over and he began to pace the floor. 'What are we to do? Where are we to live?'

'You will live here. For one year. Until the tenancy has expired.'

The thought of living under the same roof as his uncle for a whole year filled Will with dismay. That was something he could not put his family through. 'No. We'll take a house somewhere. I have money.'

'I'm sure you do, but that is not the point. You will stay here. The house is big enough. If your children are properly behaved they need not trouble me.' Uncle Samuel shifted his weight in the chair and winced with pain. 'I should appreciate the chance to oversee their upbringing.'

So his need for control just went on and on, Will thought. He wants my family under his roof and his domination. 'No.' he said firmly.

A silence developed and it was in a surprisingly gentle voice that Uncle Samuel finally said 'You will do as I say, William. You know what is at stake. By the way, when is the baby due?'

'October,' Will heard himself saying. How could this be happening? Would he never be free of this man?

'Then it is perfectly clear that your wife must not travel further. She cannot undertake another long day's journey. I'm sure you wouldn't want any harm to come to her. Such a beautiful lady.'

'I must go to her,' Will mumbled and got up. He had reached the door before he turned. 'How is Samuel?'

'Doing well. He's a clever boy.'

'Where is he? Which school?'

Uncle Samuel hesitated for a moment. 'Repton. Don't go there – disrupting his education. He'll be back in a few weeks' time for the holidays. You can see him then.' Will left the room.

The family settled in. Will and Eliza's room was spacious, well furnished and overlooked the river. Mary Ann, Simon, Harry and Lizzie occupied the third floor, but Mrs. Draycott also had her room on this level, and they all lived in dread of bumping into her in the hallway or on the stairs, and thereby incurring her displeasure.

Will tried to allay everyone's misgivings about their unexpected stay at the Manor. Mary Ann took the news worst of all, and proved impervious to Will's attempts to placate her. She had set her heart on living at Beesthorpe, and although life at Twyford held interest and even intrigue, she was merely waiting, as patiently as she could, to proceed on to their proper home.

Eliza was disappointed but admitted that she felt quite unable to face any further travel. The task of setting up a household would have been too much for her and she was grateful for the sanctuary of her peaceful room. She sat by the window and watched the water swirling by, the shouts and tuneless singing of the ferryman crossing the river her only distraction. 'I can't believe that soon we shall see Samuel,' she said to Will. 'I wonder what he will look like.'

The enforced rest was beginning to have a beneficial effect and Eliza felt restored. Her cheeks regained their colour and her eyes were bright. Perhaps, Will thought, their stay at Twyford would not be so bad after all.

On Sundays they walked to the church for the service. The kindly old Reverend beamed down on his flock from the pulpit. Will was glad that after all these years, he was still here. He remembered Will too, and asked him to call for a chat as soon as he had the time.

Then Mary Ann began to give cause for concern. Will had frequently found her crying, something so unusual in her that he could not remember the last time he had seen her in tears, and her usual sullen expression had deteriorated into an alarming moroseness. However hard Will and Eliza tried to cheer her up, nothing would induce her to do so. Unfortunately, Uncle Samuel found her demeanour extremely annoying and decided he would not have it. He summoned Mary Ann to the drawing room.

'Sit down, girl, where I can see you.'

Mary Ann stared at the old man with hard, unfriendly eyes.

'What's the matter with you? Don't you like it here?'

'No. I don't.'

'What a dismal girl you are. Why aren't you happy?'

Mary Ann ignored him and turned her head away, pretending to look out of the window. Uncle Samuel picked up his stick and waved it across the room. 'Answer me, girl! You are under my roof. You will be civil.'

Mary Ann turned back with a sour expression. 'You stole my brother.'

After a few moments, Uncle Samuel gave a harsh laugh. 'Is that what they told you? Well, I'm telling you now, I've done more for that boy than his father ever would have. He'll do well in life with all I've taught him.'

'When can we see him?'

'When I decide. I shall speak to your father about your inso-lence. I'll not have that gloomy face in my house.'

'I don't want to be in your house. I want to go to Beesthorpe.'

The old man's eyes narrowed to a flinty coldness as he regarded Mary Ann. 'You're too forthright for your own good. But if you like plain speaking, I'll tell you straight. Samuel is not your brother. Not your real brother. None of them are. Think about it, girl. How could they be? You with your coarse, black hair and cold eyes.' Mary Ann jumped to her feet, visibly trembling. 'You may go now,' he said. 'And don't scowl, girl.'

Will took the track down to the river. He scanned the bank both ways, looking for a sign of Mary Ann. She had not been seen since the morning and now it was early evening. Lizzie had complained that she had not been there to help with the boys' tea and Will had been searching ever since.

Clouds of midges, illuminated in the orange light, danced in agitated circles above the ferryman's boat as the last of the sun's rays streaked out over the water. 'Are you there, Daniel?' Will called out. From his little hollow in the hawthorn thicket, the ferryman appeared.

'Are you crossing, Sir?'

'No. Daniel, have you seen Mary Ann this afternoon?'

'Why, then. Let me see.' With his limited intellect, the little man made a great show of thinking and scratching his head. Will waited. When Daniel's thought process could help him no further and he could think of nothing else, he sheepishly nodded towards the thicket.

Under the big hawthorn at the end, Mary Ann sat huddled, her head resting on her arms. As Will eased himself down beside her she didn't look up, but he could see that her cheeks were red and tear-stained. 'Mary Ann, I'm sorry we can't go to Beesthorpe just yet. Believe me, if we could go tomorrow, we would. By this time next year we will be there, I promise you.'

A sob escaped. 'It's not that.'

'Oh. Well, whatever else can it be that is making you so unhappy?'

'Uncle Samuel said that Simon and Harry and Samuel are not my real brothers.'

For a moment, Will didn't know what to do or say. Mary Ann looked up at him. 'Is that right?'

Will gently put his arm around her shoulders. 'Only in a way. He should not have put it quite like that. They are your brothers, but – only half-brothers. You remember how I've told you a thousand times how I left Beesthorpe and went to America. Well, when I met your mother, you had already been born. Your father had died. I fell in love with your mother and I've always loved you too. You know that, Mary Ann.'

'You're not my father?'

'I'm not your natural father. Your mother and I were going to tell you but we decided to wait until we were settled in our own home.' Silently, Will cursed Uncle Samuel for his callousness. He knew he had not taken a liking to Mary Ann, but had not reckoned with his confronting the child with this revelation.

'Can I still call you father?'

'Of course. It's what I will always be. Now we must go back. Your mother is beside herself with worry.'

Mary Ann stood up and brushed the twigs off her skirt. Will gently pulled some leaves from her hair. 'Do you think I've got coarse, black hair and cold eyes?'

'No. You have lovely hair and beautiful eyes.' Will didn't care if it was a lie. Mary Ann's charm was in her soul, but she was fourteen years old, and although she showed no promise of ever becoming a beauty, he knew that she really wanted to hear otherwise.

The weeks went by and still Samuel did not appear. Eliza fretted and Will confronted his uncle. 'If he's not allowed to leave the school, then I shall go to see him there.'

'That won't be necessary. I've agreed for him to return the day after tomorrow. He will stay for one week.'

Will felt his heart leap at the thought of the overdue, yet now imminent, meeting with his son.

On the appointed day, Eliza came down to the drawing room to await the arrival of her son. Her cheeks were flushed with excitement and although she was now well on into her pregnancy, she looked beautiful and serene. Uncle Samuel had retired to his room to nurse the pain in his leg. This was such an unusual occurrence that Will was convinced it was a rare show of humanity and he had deliberately left the family to the privacy of their reunion.

Mary Ann had hopped about between windows and doors for hours, gazing up the road for the first sighting of a coach. Even Simon rushed around excitedly at the prospect of seeing the brother he had never known. Finally, when it came, the long-awaited rattle of a coach took them by surprise and startled them into action. Will went out to stand at the door, Mary Ann and Simon hovering behind.

As the carriage crunched to a halt, the door opened, and a self-assured boy of twelve descended. He was tall for his age and slim, his light-brown hair was neatly cut and his clothes were expensive. He carried himself like a gentleman and had a cold, disdainful air about him.

Will stepped forward. 'Hello, Samuel.'

Samuel looked at his father. 'How do you do, Sir?' He extended his hand formally.

Will grasped the offered hand and moved closer to embrace his son but stopped short when Samuel stiffened and his haughty expression turned even colder. 'It's so good to see you, Samuel, after all this time.' Will smiled warmly and pumped his son's hand, all the while looking into Samuel's eyes, desperate to detect some sign of pleasure at their reunion. None came. Will became embarrassed and awkward and backed towards the door. 'Do you remember your sister, Mary Ann?' He said hastily, guiding her forward.

'Yes. I remember. How do you do?' Poor Mary Ann stared at the brother she had loved so dearly and played with so happily. In the face of his icy and aloof manner she remained speechless and looked as though she would burst into tears.

'And this is your brother, Simon.' Sudden shyness had overcome Simon and he took refuge behind Will. Samuel ignored him and started towards the door. 'Come inside, do. Your mother is over-joyed at the prospect of seeing you. She's in the drawing room, Samuel, waiting for you.' Will led the way. Once through the door, he stepped aside to allow Eliza full view of her son. Samuel stopped short, not wanting to cross the room. Will gently pushed him on.

'Samuel?' Eliza leaned forward in her chair and opened her arms wide but the boy did not approach her. From a distance he gave a short bow and then stood rigid. 'How do you do, Mama? I hope you are well.'

'Yes. Thank you, Samuel.' Will could see the disappointment in her eyes but he could also detect two spots of colour on his son's otherwise pale cheeks. It was the only visible sign of emotion.

'Come and sit down and tell us about your school. Your uncle says you are a very clever boy.'

'Where is my uncle?'

'I believe he is resting. He has a painful leg.'

Everyone sat down and the atmosphere was awkward. 'We had a difficult voyage coming over from America,' Will said, 'a terrible storm.'

'We nearly drowned!' Simon found his voice and Samuel looked at him for the first time.

'We were blown off course to the Isle of Man.' Eliza smiled and tried to relax, but Samuel remained stiff and disdainful. 'Mary Ann, why don't you go and ask Mrs. Draycott to bring us some tea?'

Mary Ann shot her brother a look of contempt and walked out of the room.

'Did you receive any of our letters?' Will asked.

'No. I received no letters.'

'We wrote to you.' Eliza said quickly. 'All the time. All these years, we wrote letters to you.' Eliza tried to press the point that they had not forgotten him but Samuel was unmoved.

From the hallway came the sound of a stick tapping on the tiles, and Uncle Samuel entered the room, painfully favouring his leg.

'Uncle Samuel! The boy rushed to him and guided him back to his chair, concerned yet obviously pleased to see him. The old man, although breathing hard with the exertion of walking, was delighted at the show of affection and the two engaged in an easy conversation for quite a few minutes. When the tea arrived it was as much as Eliza could do to pour it, and the cups rattled in the saucers. Simon grew bored and ran off and Mary Ann twisted the toe of her shoe back and forth over the patterned carpet and stared dolefully down at it.

Eventually, Uncle Samuel suggested that the boy should go and unpack his trunk and then Eliza excused herself. Mary Ann, clearly disappointed by the much longed-for meeting, stomped out of the room. Uncle Samuel's eyes narrowed at the show of graceless displeasure.

'He seems to resent us,' Will said bluntly.

'It's to be expected.' Uncle Samuel regarded Will coldly.

'Why?'

'He feels you abandoned him. That I'm the only one to care for him.'

'How can you say that? Is that what you've told him?'

Uncle Samuel's satisfied smile told Will all he wanted to know. 'We wrote to him, you know. All the time. I paid that headmaster two guineas to make sure he got our letters.'

'And I paid him more to make sure that he didn't. As I told you seven years ago, the boy is mine. Now perhaps you can see it clearly. Concern yourself with your own family and leave him to me.'

Will stared at the smug face of his uncle and in that moment he knew that he truly hated him. But there was no arguing. Samuel was his, and probably always would be.

Eliza and Will persevered for the whole week to try to establish some rapport with their son, and in the end were forced to acknowledge defeat. He remained distant and withdrawn from them all. When he returned to Repton School, Eliza was glad to see him go. The aura of resentment that he had created about himself only served to depress her spirits, yet even after his departure her mood remained melancholy.

Mary Ann did her best to be helpful and attempted to provide diversions for her mother but the effect that her estranged brother had made on the household had been most profound and everyone was in a low mood. One day she declared her forthright desire. 'I'd like to smack him on his snooty nose,' she said. 'Who does he think he is with his high and mighty manner and his pained expression?' Will and Eliza could not help but appreciate their loyal, down-to-earth daughter.

Serene September days passed by. A governess, Miss Handley, was appointed and Mary Ann's wanderings in the fields were severely curtailed. Still, she liked to learn and enjoyed helping Simon with his letters. In return he adored her. She made herself a calendar and began to tick off the days until they could finally go to Beesthorpe. She steered well clear of both Mrs. Draycott and Uncle Samuel and every evening, if she had succeeded in evading them both, she considered the day to have been a success.

One morning, as October drew to a close, Eliza went into labour. Will galloped off to fetch the doctor, leaving Mrs. Draycott in reluctant charge of the situation. She could think of nothing to do other than order Lizzie to sit with her mistress, and the governess to take the children out of the house.

Miss Handley handed Simon his coat and Mary Ann paused for a moment by her mother's bedroom door. She wrapped her cloak tight around her as Miss Handley beckoned her down the stairs and ushered her out of house. They wandered up and down the riverside a few times but the day was unfavourable for loitering, with a keen wind and an overcast sky. Mary Ann shivered and Simon began to cry. Eventually Miss Handley suggested that they go and shelter inside the church and it was there that the Reverend found them. He invited them back to the vicarage and fed them tea and cakes. Mary Ann always thought of that when she remembered the day her sister Caroline Augusta was born.

Will was delighted to have a daughter. The baby, the image of her mother, was no trouble at all and, most importantly, seemed to be perfectly healthy.

Chapter 22

Winter set in. Eliza preferred to keep to her room as much as possible, rather than risk annoying or inconveniencing Uncle Samuel. Soon she was back to her old self, and spent her time caring for her children. Mary Ann and Simon escaped from the governess whenever they could, preferring to wander the flat, wind-exposed valley and converse with the ferryman, rather than be cooped up in the big house.

Will tried to fill his time constructively, but mostly that consisted of travelling to and from Nottingham. He told himself that it was necessary to be on hand for any business opportunities that may present themselves, but none did. On a cold November day, quite on impulse, he told Eliza that he would be gone for two or three days, checking out a business proposition. In fact, he rode over to Beesthorpe to visit his father's grave at Caunton. As he stood in contemplation with his head bowed and his hat in his hands, he was glad that on his last visit his father had thought to tell him of his pride in his achievements. The discord that had dominated their relationship seemed to melt away. It had all worked out in the end. He could only hope that perhaps one day his relationship with his own son would reach a comfortable stage.

Will rode a short way down the drive to Beesthorpe and then stopped beneath an elm tree, surveying the Hall from a distance. He could make out a faint thread of smoke spiralling upwards from the main chimney. Someone was in the parlour. He felt a pang of sadness as he scanned the garden and front drive for a sign of life. There was none, which was something of a relief, as he had no desire to see strangers in his home. Reluctantly, he turned his horse, and headed down the road towards Muskham to pay a call on Jane.

'How absolutely dreadful!' Jane had listened to the account of the voyage and the enforced stay at Twyford, and Will was unsure which part had shocked her most. She sat in her vicarage parlour, domestic contentment and chaos reigning in equal measure. Children had been hustled hastily in to meet their uncle, but as yet Marcus had not returned from his duties within the parish. It was obvious to Will that Jane ran her household with both precision and love, for the servant was pleasant, the children happy, and the atmosphere was easy, just as he had expected it would be.

Will's previous letters lay scattered on her lap, as evidence of the scant information he had given her so far. 'We were so appalled when Uncle Samuel let the Hall to tenants, and so soon after Father's death. But worse was to come when he informed us that your ship was overdue and you were all feared lost. You cannot imagine how hard we prayed, Will, and God must have heard us, for here you are.'

Will smiled, silently wishing that God had seen fit to give him an easier journey, or at least a vacant house to come home to.

'But to be living at Twyford with Uncle Samuel; what a strain that must be for you all.'

'It isn't easy for Eliza or the children. In fact we're all just waiting to come home, as soon as the house is vacant.'

'And Samuel? How did you find him? Was he happy to see you?'

Will composed his face for a resigned smile. 'It is difficult. He is very unforgiving of us, although it is gratifying to see that he enjoys a closeness with Uncle Samuel. Strange, don't you think? He is so distant and remote from us, yet his great-uncle he clearly loves and respects.' Will shook his head in disbelief of it all. 'I'm afraid we have lost him forever.'

Jane's eyes brimmed with tears. She adored each and every one of her children, and could not bear to think of how she would cope in Will and Eliza's situation. But it was her duty to offer her brother comfort. 'The rift will heal before long, I'm sure of it. And as soon as the tenants have gone, you will all be back here, safe and well, and together at last.'

That was a prospect that had eluded Will for so long now, he could no longer believe that the day would ever come.

Uncle Samuel grew more irascible than ever. Walking and getting out became difficult, so a constant and steady stream of lawyers and businessmen came to see him at the house. But at least it meant that he stayed more and more in his room, allowing the family a breath of peace. Then, in the third week of January, the doctor was called. Obviously under Uncle Samuel's instruction, he evaded all enquiries regarding the state of health of his patient, but continued to call regularly. Mrs. Draycott showed him in and, after the consultation, walked him to the door. Neither allowed Will into their confidence or into Uncle Samuel's presence.

So it came as a shock when a carriage arrived at the Manor and young Samuel stepped down. Mrs. Draycott instructed him to follow her upstairs immediately. When, after some time, he emerged in the company of the doctor, he looked shaken and Will knew that at last his uncle was dying.

'It's hard to say how long it will take, but the power of speech has now gone and there are only rare moments of consciousness.' The doctor snapped shut his case.

'May I go up?' Will asked.

'If you wish to pay your respects, that will be in order but there will be no response,' he said briskly. 'I'll call again tomorrow.'

Will was stunned. It was true to say that he had been waiting for this day for years, but had almost come to believe that it would never happen. Mrs. Draycott moved quietly from room to room, pulling the drapes together, and filling the house with sombre respect. Will climbed the stairs and quietly entered his uncle's room. The oak four-poster stood in the very centre, and back on the pillows rested Uncle Samuel, his face chalk white. The dark green counterpane had been smoothed flat. He must have sunk low into the mattress, Will thought, for the mound of his body was very small considering the vast, weighty bulk of the man.

He looked insignificant as he lay there close to death. His eyes were closed, and even the jutting jaw and loose jowls seemed to have lost all their powers of intimidation. His breathing came in shallow bursts. Will stood motionless beside the bed, staring down at the man who had made his life so difficult, but who was no longer capable of torment and bullying. The fat, pudgy fingers clasped together on his chest would never again point accusingly, nor his deep voice bark out demands. Will looked down at his dying uncle and felt the most enormous relief.

Quite simply, all their lives would be so much easier without him. He had driven a deep wedge between himself and Eliza, alienated Samuel from them, callously destroyed Mary Ann's confidence and intimidated them all with his threats and bullying and veiled promises. Now the tyranny had come to an end. The family would start to heal and financial security would be theirs. At no time, as he stared down at the dying man, did Will feel the slightest compassion or regret. He had earned the inheritance that was coming to him. They had all paid for it, directly or indirectly.

With all these thoughts surging through his mind, Will had turned his head away from his uncle's comatose face. So as he glanced back he was shocked to see that his eyes were open. Will leaned forward in anticipation of a few words, but the only communication was in that last defiant stare. So many things Will read there, feelings even, that had gone unexpressed for an entire lifetime. He saw bewilderment at the loss of control, a willpower accustomed to dominance now forced into its own subservience to death. He saw fear, but of what? Death itself, or what lay beyond? At the very last, were Samuel Bristowe's thoughts concerned with the hereafter and his accountability for the life he had led? And there was remorse, hidden deep within him, but Will was certain that he saw it in his eyes. The old man was desperate not to let go. He was forcing his eyelids to stay open, knowing that when they closed it would be for the last time. And there, in that last gaze, that very final moment on earth, when all movement and speech were beyond him, Will clearly saw love. With intensity he reached out, with warmth he touched Will, and with love he asked for understanding.

Overwhelmed by the depth of the experience, Will stood at the bedside for many minutes after Uncle Samuel's eyes finally closed. He watched the shallow rise and fall of his chest and replayed in his mind what he had just witnessed, reluctant to let the image disappear. It was as though a different man had come to say farewell; a man whom Will could have liked, loved even. Was this the side that young Samuel had seen? So many questions, and no time left for answers.

Mrs. Draycott slipped silently through the door and stood waiting for Will to leave. 'I shall stay with him until the end.' she said.

In low tones and in the privacy of their room, Will attempted to explain to Eliza his feelings. 'I can't remember one occasion when he gave me any credit, or even acknowledgement of any sort of bond between us. And yet he has left me with a nagging doubt that I've misunderstood him, that he was really a better person than I gave him credit for.'

'Oh Will. Don't be so hard on yourself. The man had a lifetime to make himself understood. He chose to be heartless while you are kindness itself. I honestly feel that you have been set free. Your estate will come to you at last.'

'You're right. He has ruled our family with tyranny for as long as I can remember, and I'm glad it's over. And I shall never forgive him for taking Samuel from us.'

Eliza threw off the sadness she always felt at the mention of Samuel, forcing a lightness in her voice. 'Everything will change now, so perhaps he will come back to us. We must hope.'

Uncle Samuel clung tenaciously on to the thin thread of his life for another two agonizing days, while the passing bell tolled with mournful regularity from the church tower. The house filled with sombre-faced strangers, and young Samuel stayed mostly in his own room. He seemed contained and in control, and treated his parents with the same coldness and disdain as previously.

On the day of the funeral, black-coated men in tall hats gathered at the house. Distant cousins, mostly unknown to Will, arrived one after another, introducing themselves with a confident, hopeful air. Jane and Marcus were unable to attend, which was a disappointment, as Will felt in need of an ally, just someone who understood, someone he could confide in and know would give him sound advice. As it was, he felt alienated from his distant relatives and under scrutiny from the distinguished lawyers, magistrates and High Sheriffs, all men of influence in the cities of Nottingham and Derby, who came to pay their respects to the late Samuel Bristowe. The coffin was placed in the funeral carriage and the black-plumed horses carried the body on the last short journey to the church. Young Samuel and Will led the slow procession of mourners. They stared ahead silently, observing the formalities.

As they sat side by side in the Bristowe family pew, weak sunshine cast a faint shaft of light over father and son, the chief mourners. They pretended to listen attentively as the vicar spoke of duty and commitment, vision and dedication. Will noticed that the words humanity and love were never mentioned. The family vault beneath the side chapel had been opened. When the time came for the interment, they moved across and Will peered down but could see only blackness. Samuel stood beside the gaping hole and suddenly pulled back, swaying slightly off balance. Will put a hand out to steady him and felt him tremble beneath his touch.

Uncle Samuel's coffin was lowered and jolted to a halt with a dull thud as it came to rest above another.

Will barely heard the vicar's words but realised the prayers had been completed when two men began the task of levering the heavy cover back into position. The forbidding grating of stone on stone echoed painfully through the church until finally the granite slabs struck their niche with a deep reverberation. At last it was over.

Back at the Manor, sherry and brandy decanters clinked in the drawing room. Men with serious faces clustered, subdued at first as each pondered the prospect of their own mortality, but becoming more talkative as they shared their reminiscences. Eliza had joined the gathering and she and Will stood awkwardly together, accepting the condolences, yet ill at ease. These men were Uncle Samuel's contemporaries and had held him in high regard. They knew him to be a good businessman and citizen, who upheld and enforced the law and expected every man to know his place in society.

Eventually, the lawyer walked among them and discreetly invited the family to take their places in the dining room to hear the official reading of the will. They filed in and settled themselves around the long, mahogany table. A number stood by the walls, hopeful of a small bequest perhaps, or just eager to hear the will first-hand and witness any drama, should it unfold. An awkward silence developed during which the only sound was the scraping of the parchment scroll as the lawyer untied the black ribbon. He adjusted his spectacles and proceeded to read from the will.

'I have here the last will and testament of Samuel Bristowe, of Twyford Manor, dated the twenty-sixth day of September in the year of Our Lord eighteen hundred and ten.' The first prickle of apprehension stabbed Will when he heard the recent date. Surely Uncle Samuel had made his will long before last September? So had he changed it? Perhaps he had added a codicil. A bequest?

Will sat perfectly still on his chair, willing himself to appear outwardly calm, but suddenly his mouth went dry and his palms began to sweat. He tried to concentrate on the lawyer's voice, but it seemed to float away. He could hear perfectly well, and yet the words were meaningless. In panic he realised he must have missed a bit. This was the main section now. 'I thereby leave my entire estates and titles of Lord of the Manor of Twyford in the County of Derbyshire and Beesthorpe in the County of Nottinghamshire, all lands appurtenances and dwellings thereon to my great-nephew and namesake Samuel Ellis Bristowe.'

Will's peripheral vision began to darken. All he could see was the lawyer, opening and closing his mouth, and occasionally looking up. His voice sounded distant. '... to be held in trust for him until he reaches the age of twenty-one.

'And to my nephew, William Bristowe, I give permission to reside fully at the house known as Beesthorpe Hall in the County of Nottinghamshire and to receive two hundred pounds per year in recognition of his work in overseeing the improvements to be made to the said house and grounds in readiness for the said Samuel Ellis Bristowe to inhabit at his coming of age.'

The lawyer paused and looked up. 'I have here a full schedule of plans and improvements drawn up by Mr. Samuel Bristowe to bring the house of Beesthorpe Hall up to the standard required by landed gentry at the present time.' He briefly held up a thick sheaf of papers and put them down again on the table.

Will swallowed hard and, with his heart hammering loudly, he heard nothing further, although the lawyer continued to recount the minutiae of the document at great length. Eventually he stopped speaking and stood up. There was a scraping of chairs as others got to their feet. Will felt that his legs had turned to stone. In the chair beside him, Eliza sat perfectly still, although her eyes brimmed with tears and she reached out her hand to his. Everyone began to shuffle out, clearing their throats, checking their pocket watches and shooting sideways glances at Will. Samuel stood up and quietly left the room.

Storm clouds threatened, yet Will remained oblivious as he strode heedlessly along the bank of the River Trent. Underfoot, the ground was muddy and his boots soon became caked in layers of sticky clay soil. The hem of his long coat dipped to the ground from time to time, and he set his top hat firmly on as he bowed his head against the wind and marched on.

The inertia which had gripped him at the reading of the will had now gone. His veins pulsed with the flow of blood, his heart pumped and his legs demanded action. Only his mind remained closed. The events of the day, the greeting of mourners, the interment, the will-reading all seemed shrouded in a mist and he had no desire to clear it away. He knew that what lay beneath was the true hurt.

Will tramped on in the bleakness of the January afternoon. His cheeks grew red, burned by the wind, and his lips became dry and sore. Glowering clouds passed harmlessly over, but as he marched, mile on mile, the sky gradually changed. A chill greyness descended. He felt no wish to turn back. The distance he put between himself and Twyford Manor represented his need to separate himself from the pain of his uncle's ultimate rejection and deception.

Eventually, Will's path was blocked by an impenetrable thicket of brambles. The enforced halt cleared away a little of the fog from his mind and, breathing heavily, he looked about him, unsure just how far he had come. Dusk was falling rapidly as skeletal trees with stark branches presented black silhouettes against a heavy sky. He turned toward the river, now a winding ribbon of sluggish grey. There was no colour in anything, just varying shades of grey or black. Reluctantly, he began slowly to retrace his steps.

He knew he had to put his thoughts in order before he could face others. Everyone would know of his expectation to inherit, but no-one knew that it had been a promise given to him in return for his son. Even from the grave, Uncle Samuel had wielded his power and had won; just as he always had.

In a cloud of despair, tired of his clogged-up boots and the effort each step took, Will felt a great fatigue come over him. He cast about for a suitable place to sit down and found a log close by the river. The wind had eased and the only sound came from the gentle passage of water swirling through the rushes by his feet. The peace and solitude was calming, and even the rapidly descending darkness was welcome.

Suddenly he became aware of a pervading whiteness. Why was everything turning white? He forced himself to think. Puzzled, he looked up. He extended his hand in front of his face and white fell from the sleeve of his coat. He stared for a moment and then laughed aloud, for snow was falling silently. He brushed his coat and a flurry of white cascaded down. More snowflakes took their place, clustering together to cover and hide him.

Earlier, the wind and sky had been angry, and that had been exactly how he had felt. Now the falling snow created a peace in him, a serenity, and even an acceptance. He turned his face to the sky and the frozen crystals fell soft and gentle on his cheek, like a mother's caress. His feet had grown cold in his sodden boots and he stood up and stamped about. The snow was settling and, in the rapidly falling temperature, the ground felt hard beneath his feet. It was time to go back.

The very real possibility of losing his way on the snow covered bank and slipping into the water concentrated Will's mind. He cast around for an identifiable landmark, but beyond the swirling snowflakes he could recognize nothing. He had no idea how far he had come and no way of judging how long the difficult walk back would be. The snow continued to fall out of the blackness and there was no moon to guide him. He stumbled on, his senses alert for the barely audible sound of the river.

Every step could lead him into danger. He knew that in places the bank was steep and the swirling waters would be waiting to pull him down. The snow was rapidly obliterating the path and he forced himself on, anxious to gain as much distance as he could before the track disappeared completely and there was nothing left to guide him.

As the gravity of his predicament grew, Will's clarity of thought improved, and it was his family who came to the forefront of his mind. He began to feel a tinge of shame for his selfishness. This was no time for self-pity, he told himself harshly, he should be pleased for his son. The family needed him and he must not let them down. His stride grew more purposeful as his spirit strengthened. He needed to quicken his pace, for the cold was biting, clamping him tight in its grip.

Suddenly, without warning as he strode forward, the ground from beneath Will's feet gave way and he was catapulted out and down into the blackness. He cried out and flung out his arms, reaching wildly for something to hold on to. Tufts of sodden grass slid through his clawing fingers and thorns bit deep into his hands as he flailed about, grabbing indiscriminately, desperately trying to seize a hold of anything to break his fall. Thin branches crackled and snapped beneath his weight as he pitched down and down, until at last he hit the river. The shock of the freezing water took his breath away as he fought to surface. Momentarily, the cold immobilised his entire body, his blood seeming to freeze in his veins. He managed to gulp air into his lungs and thrashed his arms wildly, but his heavy coat dragged him down and the river closed in over him.

CHAPTER TWENTY-THREE

Eliza crossed the drawing room to sit in the padded armchair by the fireside. The skirt of her black silk mourning dress rustled as she settled herself.

'Sit down, Samuel.' She said.

How strange, she thought to herself. I can talk to my son for as long as I wish. No nervous glances towards the door, wondering when Uncle Samuel will come in. No subconscious listening for the tap tap of his stick in the hallway. She studied young Samuel for a moment, but as always his expression gave no hint of his feelings.

'This conversation is going to be hard for both of us, I think.' Eliza took a deep breath and straightened her back. She hardly knew where to begin. 'Honesty, I think is what we need. There are no other influences now. We must be truthful with each other and with ourselves. Can we agree to that, Samuel?'

The boy's expression remained inscrutable but he nodded, cautiously.

'Very well. I shall tell you how events came about. You were five years old when a letter was received telling us that your Grandmama was dying and it was her wish to see you. Your father took you to Nottinghamshire, where your Uncle Samuel met you and became fond of you. He asked your father if he could care for you and educate you. You must remember, Samuel, that at the time, your father was not a rich man and he was struggling to establish his business. It seemed to him, a wonderful opportunity to ensure that you had the best English education.'

Eliza noticed that Samuel had turned his head slightly away from her. She hoped he was listening. 'When the time came for your father to leave you, Uncle Samuel asked him to sign official adoption papers. When he refused, he was told that if he signed, he would inherit the estates on Uncle Samuel's death – and if he did not, then he would be disinherited forthwith.'

Samuel's eyes flicked back to his mother for a moment. She continued on with her story. 'It was a terrible decision to have to make – and one he has regretted every day since. I was heart-broken, as we all were. It took me a long time to forgive your father. He came back to find you. Do you remember him visiting you at your school?' Samuel nodded. 'He paid the headmaster two guineas to ensure that the letters we wrote to you were actually given to you. Apparently, Uncle Samuel paid him more to destroy them. You see, he wanted you for himself. He allowed us no contact with you. But we have thought about you every day, Samuel. We had hoped that on our return to England, you would be part of the family again. It has been a bitter disappointment to find you so distant and unforgiving of us.'

Eliza's voice trailed off and she gazed out of the tall windows into the bleak garden and the fading winter light. She let the silence develop, with just the clock rhythmically ticking off the moments, until finally her son shifted in his chair and spoke. 'When I was very small, in that first year, I thought I had done something wrong. Uncle Samuel was kind but I felt very lonely. After a while I hated you all for abandoning me. I imagined you in New York, being happy without me.'

'Did Uncle Samuel tell you that we had abandoned you?'

Samuel nodded. 'Yes. He always told me that he was the only one who cared about me.'

The door opened and Mary Ann came into the room. She looked at her mother and brother and sensed the tense atmosphere. 'I was looking for Papa, she said, and turned towards the door again.

'Wait. It's alright Mary Ann. Come in. We were having a frank discussion.' Samuel looked uncomfortable but did not display the look of total hostility that he normally would have to his sister. Mary Ann sat down. 'We were telling each other what it was like, being apart for all those years. Perhaps you could tell Samuel too.'

Mary Ann glowered from under her wiry, untamed hair. She hesitated for a moment and then plunged in. 'Papa is heartbroken that you could treat us all so coldly when we have lived all these years just waiting to be together again. I wrote dozens of letters to you, until even I realised that you were never going to write back. We thought of you all the time. I really missed you at first. Now I see Uncle Samuel has turned you against us all – and has left you his fortune. You must be very happy.'

Poor Samuel looked anything but happy. 'I … I really missed you Mary Ann. I often cried when I was small, because I thought you had forgotten me.'

The light in the drawing room was fading fast. Only the cheery, red coals in the fire grate gave a focus to the room and Samuel stared long and hard into them as he let the words of his mother and sister sink in. A knock sounded on the door and Mrs. Draycott appeared. 'Would you like me to light the lamp now, Ma'am?' she said, taper in hand.

'Thank you, Mrs. Draycott. I hadn't realised how dark it had become.' Eliza silently wondered how long the housekeeper had been listening by the door. With the lamps lit, the glow encompassed them all and the atmosphere improved. Samuel was the first to speak. 'I can see now that things were not quite as they seemed,' he said slowly, appearing to struggle to comprehend the situation from a different viewpoint. 'If Uncle Samuel really promised him the estates, after making him sign the adoption papers – Papa must be feeling quite wretched.'

At the mention of his name, Eliza suddenly realised that it was dark and Will had not returned. He had left the house hours before, pausing only to snatch up his coat. Eliza had seen the hard expression on his face and knew there was no consoling him. It was best he should be alone for a while.

At the window, Mary Ann pressed her face close to the cold panes and peered out. She turned back to her mother. 'It's snowing!'

Eliza became alarmed. 'Where can your father be? We should have searched for him before now. Something must have happened to him!'

'I'll go to look for him.' Samuel leapt to his feet.

'I'll fetch the lanterns and help you.' Mary Ann rushed through the door.

'Take care, children. Don't go near the river!' Eliza handed them their coats and was horrified to see the snow swirling and beginning to drift around the door as they set off into the night.

As the icy water closed in on him, Will hurtled into panic and fear. Fragmented thoughts raced around incoherently as he arched his back and thrashed helplessly in an attempt to break the surface. How bitterly ironic that his life should end like this. He had crossed the Atlantic Ocean many times, only now to find himself drowning in the River Trent. He fought with his arms and legs, kicking wildly, but his thick clothes tugged him down. His fingers reached to the ties of his long coat, desperate to release the weight from him. His lungs hurt, aching for air, and he knew his life was nearing its end. Suddenly his foot came into contact with the river bed and he could feel that there were boulders. The current was taking him on to where there seemed to be more rocks. He managed to gain a foothold and reached a higher level. With his last remaining strength he hurled himself upwards and his face broke out of the water. Greedily, he gulped the freezing air and, gasping constantly, unable to satisfy his starved lungs, he lurched towards what he hoped was shallower water.

On hands and knees, coughing painfully, Will emerged from the river. His legs were trembling as he pulled himself up and stumbled towards the bank. It must have given way because he soon found himself on hard ground. Grateful for not having to haul himself up a high bank, for there was no strength in him, and still breathing heavily, he looked around and tried to take stock. Water ran from his clothes and his teeth began to chatter but he felt sure there was something else out there. He peered into the darkness through the falling snow.

Shapes began to move before Will's eyes. Was he hallucinating? He distinctly heard a sound. Was it a cough? Then he realised that the shapes in front of him were the cows. The herd had huddled together with snow beginning to pile up on their backs, taking shelter as best they could under the lee of the bank. This was their drinking place and Will knew where he was. Though shivering violently, he laughed aloud with relief and lurched on towards the path.

With dogged determination, although chilled to the bone, he forced himself on and finally, in the distance, he caught the unmistakable sight of candlelight in the window of a Twyford cottage. Bowed low under the weight of his wet clothes, and squelching in his waterlogged boots, he staggered on. Before long he saw a lantern swinging and heard a call. He called back and stumbled on toward the light.

'Father!' the call came again.

Standing under his raised lantern, wrapped in a cloak and heavy muffler, stood young Samuel. His face was anxious. He stared as Will stumbled unsteadily out of the darkness, coughing and shivering, towards the glow of the lantern. He rushed to his father's side. 'Oh Father. We've been so worried. What has happened to you?'

Will forced himself to speak through chattering teeth and frozen lips. 'I'm sorry, Samuel,' he croaked. 'I lost track of the time. I'm sorry.'

Samuel peered closely at his father. 'You're wet through!'

Will began to shiver violently. Another lantern approached and Mary Ann appeared. Instantly taking charge, she led Will the short distance to the house. Eliza was waiting anxiously at the door.

Will turned to his son. 'You came to look for me. Thank you.'

'I'm so sorry. I didn't understand. Please forgive me.'

Will gave his son a puzzled look.

'Mama told me everything. And Mary Ann, too. I was angry with you, but now I think I know what really happened.'

Will laid his trembling hands on his son's shoulders. 'Samuel,' he gasped between painful breaths 'if you know what happened, then I think you must understand that it is you who must forgive me.'

The snow still swirled but, with an inextinguishable warmth of heart, father and son embraced.

In the comfort of dry clothes, Will sat by the fire in the drawing room, a brandy goblet in his hand. Eliza knelt beside him, massaging his feet. 'I'm sorry you were worried,' he said. 'It was stupid of me. I don't know why I went so far. And then it started to snow, and all I could think of was getting back to you.'

'I know. But Will, you could so easily have drowned.' He had deliberately played down the horror of his near-drowning, merely referring to it as a mishap, but even so Eliza was filled with anxiety, constantly placing her hand on his brow for sign of a temperature. 'However,' she relented at last, 'your absence did give me the opportunity to speak frankly to Samuel.'

'So I understand.' Will leaned forward and stroked Eliza's cheek. 'It was a wonderful welcome home. So unexpected that Samuel should come looking for me. You know, it's so hard to describe how I felt after the will was read. Betrayed, I suppose. How my very own uncle could totally disinherit me – it was beyond my comprehension. And after his monstrous deception, to know that he had poisoned Samuel's mind against us – it was too much to bear.'

'I know, my love.' Eliza's voice was tender. 'But I think I've begun to go some way towards resolving that this afternoon – with Mary Ann's help. Between us we told Samuel the story from our point of view. He was quite disbelieving at first, but then he began to understand. He knows everything now.'

Will was tired. He took a gulp of brandy and savoured the inner glow that it gave him. He gazed deep into the fire. 'I will try not to be selfish about this. Uncle Samuel has heaped great reward on our son. He has two estates, the titles and the houses. Better they should go to Samuel than someone else. It's just the disappointment. I'm sad – for you, my love.'

Eliza looked up sharply. 'Why me?'

'You haven't seen Beesthorpe yet, I know. But when you do you will fall in love with it. All these years I've imagined myself as the squire, but you as its rightful mistress.'

'Will, why are you talking this way? I shall still be the mistress. We're going to live there, remember? We'll look after it for Samuel.'

Will looked away. Yes, they would look after it, and enjoy it, but it would never be his. The deception would take a little longer yet to overcome.

Eliza rose to her feet and crossed the room. She picked up an envelope and handed it to her husband. 'The lawyer left this for you. You were to see it after the will had been read, but you had gone before he found it.'

The writing on the envelope was Uncle Samuel's and Will drew a deep breath before opening it.

My Dear William,

When you read this letter I shall be at rest within the church and you will know the content of my will. I am aware that your feelings will be of resentment towards me, and now you will think that I have wickedly deceived you.

Undoubtedly, I am guilty of deception but you must understand my motive. You will surely know that throughout my life my sole purpose has been the well-being of my estates. Bristowes have owned lands at Twyford and Beesthorpe for three hundred years, yet my very own cousin, through idleness and debt, brought Beesthorpe to the brink of ruin.

If an estate is to flourish, it must be managed efficiently. Land ownership denotes power and must represent continuity. It is true, you have made your way in the world, but even so, I feel you do not possess the qualities necessary to nurture and sustain the estate.

I have used my influence over young Samuel to instil in him a strength of purpose. He is clever and quick to learn, and will not shirk his responsibilities. You are a good man, William, and I am sure you will continue to discharge your family duties with honesty and compassion.

There is one more thing. Despite my success, I found in my later years that the absence of love was something I regretted. I was beguiled by Samuel and have genuinely loved him – a son I never thought I would have. He has been the shining light of my latter years and undoubtedly the most treasured person in my life. I thank you for that from the bottom of my heart. Try not to think hard of me, for like you, I have our beloved Beesthorpe at heart. May God bless you.

Your loving uncle, Samuel Bristowe.

Will put the letter down. Eliza searched his face anxiously. 'What does it say?' she whispered.

'He says it is for the good of the estate. That my character is somehow not strong enough. He didn't trust me.'

'Oh, Will.' Eliza took her husband's hand and pressed it to her cheek. 'How could he be so heartless? I am so sorry, my love.'

Will shook his head and tried to smile. 'It really doesn't matter. He loved Samuel. That is important.'

'There's something else we must talk about.' Eliza's tone was gentle but firm and Will wondered what it could be. His eyes were beginning to feel heavy and he was much too tired to think of any other issues.

'This afternoon, I gave Mary Ann something. We talked about her father. I told her about our life, before you came to America, and told her how much I had loved Eduardo.'

Will turned his face away and retracted his hand from Eliza's grasp. He couldn't bear to hear these words. Not today.

'Please, Will.' Eliza knelt before her husband and took both of his hands in hers. 'You remember the silver locket – with the lock of hair?'

Will felt his throat constrict and his eyes begin to sting. He was too vulnerable to cope with this. The self-pity that he had tried so hard to banish began to wash over him again. How could Eliza do this to him? He felt so utterly despondent just to think of the locket and all that it meant to her.

'I gave it to Mary Ann. I was going to throw it away, but then I thought she should have it as a keepsake. Nothing more. You are her father and she adores you – you know that. But ... I have to tell you something.'

How much more misery could this hateful day heap upon him?

'I love you, Will. With all my heart.' With a bewildered expression Will looked down on his wife's smiling eyes. 'I've never said that before, have I? And I am deeply ashamed of myself. In all these years, when life's trials have beset us and we've somehow battled through, I've never given you that small comfort. I married you because you are a good man and I knew you would care for us. But now, I can tell you that I truly love you. I love you for who you are – your kindness, your sincerity, your gentleness. It is who you are and I wouldn't change you in any way.'

Eliza's words took Will back. He stared down at her, so totally overcome with emotion that he could not speak. His heart soared and engulfed him, choking the words in his throat as his foolishness revealed itself with crystal clarity. This inheritance that had dangled and fluttered before him like a prize was nothing compared to the strength that Eliza had given him with her words. They had changed everything.

'I'm proud that your character is so unlike your uncle's. I don't care that you have no estates or titles. You are dearer to me than all the riches in the world.' Eliza's green eyes welled up and teardrops began to form as she reached up and kissed her husband.

Will tasted the salt tears, unsure whether they were his own or Eliza's, and in that moment he knew that he was richer by far than his Uncle Samuel had ever been.

Historical Note

The character I have called Will was in fact named Samuel Bristowe, as was his uncle and his son, but this would have been too confusing for the reader, so I have changed his name to Will.

Samuel Bristowe (Will) did indeed marry Eliza, a young widow with a daughter, Mary Ann. Her husband had been a captain who had gone down with his ship off the coast of Jamaica, but there is no evidence at all that this was a slave ship.

Seamus and Ned are both entirely fictional characters.

I discovered in the Nottingham archives Samuel's red leather diary, given to him prior to his departure for America. Disappointingly, it contained scarcely any information. However, there also existed a notebook written by Samuel's step-daughter, Mary Ann. Completed over a number of years, she was much more forthcoming and alluded to various family dramas. She wrote *"Due to domestic discomfort my father was forced to sail to America and arrived with only one guinea in his pocket."* She also wrote of her father having been *"wickedly disinherited"*

Uncle Samuel did educate his great-nephew, Samuel Ellis Bristowe, and leave his estates to him, thereby cutting out his nephew. Although there is evidence to suggest that Uncle Samuel was a strong and powerful character, he was probably not as heartless as I have portrayed him to be.

I am indebted to Mary Ann and her notebook, for giving me enticing glimpses of the lives of the Bristowe family of Beesthorpe Hall.